MW01017212

The Town of Watered-Down Whiskey

Jim Geiwitz

SOL BOOKS PROSE SERIES

The Town of Watered-Down Whiskey

Jim Geiwitz

SOL BOOKS

Minneapolis

Published by Sol Books,
an imprint of Skywater Publishing Company,
398 Goodrich Ave., St. Paul MN 55102.
www.solbooks.com

Copyright © 2012 Jim Geiwitz

All rights reserved. No part of this publication
may be reproduced in whole or in part
without written permission of the publisher.

Library of Congress Cataloging-in-Publication Data
Geiwitz, Jim.
    The town of watered-down whiskey / Jim Geiwitz.
    p. cm. -- (Sol Books Prose series)
    ISBN 978-0-9818279-6-4 (pbk. : alk. paper)
    1. Minnesota--Social life and customs--Fiction. 2. City and
town life--Fiction. I. Title.
PS3607.E379T69 2012
811'.6--dc23   2011036746

Photo Credits
Shutterstock, all

"Taking His Cue from Mao, the Boxelder Bug's Life Is a Long and
Persistent March", Copyright 1984 by Bill Holm. Reproduced by
permission of the Estate of Bill Holm, Marcella Brekken, executor.

To the memory of Bill Holm,
whose spirit pervades all stories
of Minneota.

Editorial—<u>The Minneota Messenger</u>, July 14, 1960

Too often, I say, we don't give proper credit to the town we live in—our community—and we just assume that all our happiness comes from ourselves alone, and not from our friends and neighbors, too. Minneota is a heck of a nice place to live, in the humble opinion of this writer, who has lived here all his life, as have most of you. I'm not talking about the physical town—the clean air, the good earth that nourishes the abundant crops of our farmer friends, the flat prairie land that allows you to see as far as your eye can take you. And I'm not talking about the town in terms of no crime, part of the great United States, and that sort of thing. I'm talking about people, our families and our friends. People we know and love. People who know and love us. People who are willing to listen to a new joke we're itching to unload. People who are willing to laugh out of respect and love even if the joke isn't all it's cracked up to be. People who are happy for us when good fortune comes our way. People who are sad when calamity strikes us. People to help in times of need. People to share in moments of joy.

I had a visit last week from David Sorenson, Pete and Teddy's boy, who just graduated from St. Olaf and is just back from California, where he is going to do some postgraduate sort of thing at UCLA, in Los Angeles. A lot of you remember David as basically a good kid but quick to argue a point, no matter what the point was. I remember one time David tried to convince me that the reason we were seeing fewer and fewer pheasants each year was because the season was too long, and he thought it should be eliminated altogether for a year or two, to let the pheasants get back to a good level. Darned if the next year, when our governor started saying the same thing, David didn't come in again, but this time he was on the other side, saying it didn't matter how long the season was. As long as you didn't shoot hens, it didn't matter because one rooster could handle 40 or 50 hens. I said to him then, weren't you just in here arguing the opposite last year? And David said, "Well, I learned something in a year." Glad to hear that! I said to him at the time. Well, this time David wanted to sing the praises of the big cities, like Los Angeles. He said that a big city is the place to be, not some sleepy little burg like Minneota. He said that life in the big city is a lot more exciting. It has good places to eat, better than the RoundUp, and lots of big time sports and cultural things like plays and operas, and it also has women dancing without any clothes on. I gave him that. But I said in reply, as we strolled along about 9:30 p.m. one pleasant evening last week, could you walk like this any time of night in any part of town, could you do that in your big city? Edna and Christian Flitter were sitting on their porch, and David and I gave them a big hello. Do you know everyone in your neighborhood, in fact everyone in town, in Los Angeles? David said, "Of course not, it'd be impossible." My point precisely, I said.

When we got back to the old abode, David and I made some popcorn and continued our great debate. I showed David the picture of Albert DeFlandre and his neighbors, the one that appeared in <u>The Messenger</u> last fall when Albert broke his leg falling off a ladder, and his neighbors came over to harvest his crop for him. That happen a lot in Los Angeles? That's what a small town is, I said. It's support. And as luck would have it, just that night in the Minneapolis paper there was a news item about some woman in Los Angeles who had been dead for a month until somebody found her in her apartment. That could never happen in Minneota. Never! And David

*had to admit it, too. The newspaper said that they asked
her neighbors who she was, but nobody knew. It made me
shiver. I know I could never live that kind of life. I don't
care how many operas and naked women you have for me.*

*I didn't even get to crime and prostitution, and stuff
like that, because as you can imagine, I pretty much had
David on the run by now. In a last-ditch effort to get
back on top, David tried the opera ploy again, "There's no
opera in Minneota (although there is an 'opera hall' in
the Big Store.)." Well, OK, so you can't have everything.
I admitted that I wouldn't mind seeing a real opera in
Minneota. But I wouldn't trade Mario Lanza for the
people of Minneota, I'll tell you that, and besides, I can
hear Mr. Lanza anytime I'm willing to crank up the
old phonograph. Plus, there's opera on the radio every
Saturday morning if you want to listen, and now there's
this newfangled thing, television, which just last week had
some famous songs from famous operas, so there's opera
around if you're interested. And some of our locals have
fine voices, too, though they prefer hymns and religious
songs, most of them, to the unintelligible Italian stuff that
opera singers lean toward. But I have nothing against
opera. Far from it. When Caruso hits a high note, I
tremble just like the next fellow. I don't understand why
they don't sing in English, though, and I don't think it's
because Italian is so hard to translate. I think the reason
is the words in English would make opera sound silly.
What would people think if this chubby woman walked
to the center of the stage, with all the lights in the place
on her, and sang something like "Out the door I go now"?
In Italian it sounds like philosophy or great romantic
stuff, but in English it sounds like a song that even Frank
Sinatra, who's not one of my favorites anyway, wouldn't*

take a second look at. Even though he, too, is Italian. But one thing Italians do appreciate, from what I hear, is family. They have deep feelings for their families, which have a lot of members to share deep feelings for. And that, I said to David, is what Minneota is like: one big Italian family. You all know what I mean.

Well, the big news in town this week, I've been told, is the sale of the Hooray Theater. Too bad Frosty couldn't make a go of it. I hear John and Burt are planning to use it as a funeral parlor. I hear the Swede doesn't think this is a very good idea. I hope he doesn't do anything stupid, like climb up a tree again.

1

The Hooray Theater

The Hooray Theater had just gone out of business. The business, rather, had just gone out of the Hooray Theater. Frosty De Coster, he ran the theater and was in competition with the movie theater in Marshall, the neighboring town and the county seat. It had almost first-run movies. Not Frosty. By the time Frosty got a movie, it was so old it would break three or four times during its showing. Old Frosty, he would act like the breaks were planned. Pop! The film breaks, and the screen goes all white. Frosty flips on the lights and runs—and I mean *runs*—he runs down to the stage in front of the screen, all the time yelling, "It's time for our drawing," and he'd draw half tickets from a fishbowl that matched half tickets of lucky customers. They got some little thing, usually a bowl advertising the local creamery, or . . . I remember one time the Big Store had some ties that had gone out of style, so Frosty gave those away. The creamery bowls were nice; I myself have several. I use them all the time. I won one of the ties, too, but I wouldn't use it to tie up a dog. Oh, it was ugly! It had a Hawaiian scene with palm trees and a pretty girl standing on a beach next to a cow. That's right. A cow! What in blazes was the cow doing on the beach in Hawaii, I'll never know, but as you can imagine, the Big Store didn't sell a lot of those ties, so Frosty got them free and passed them out during the breaks. But mostly it was creamery bowls. If it was a bad break, Frosty sometimes gave away six or seven bowls, and sometimes he didn't have six people in the audience. And sometimes the film broke three or four times. So sometimes you went to the show and came home with two bowls. Sometimes two bowls and a pitcher. If you were really unlucky, you came home with three neckties. My goodness! I mean, the movies were bad enough, and now you got stuck with these dreadful ties. Another reason not to go to the show.

One winter Frosty, he opened a Christmas tree lot across from the Big Store. He says he grossed more in three weeks than in a year at the Hooray Theater, so he decided to sell the Hooray Theater.

Well, you know who bought it? John Anderson and Burt Tostenrud. Can you believe that? They needed a funeral parlor, being undertakers and all, and the Hooray Theater, they perceived, was just the ticket. It was something, especially at first, before they did a little remodeling. They used to put the body and the coffin right up there on the stage, and the seats were still there, so the friends and family of the deceased would file down the aisle, walk up on stage, peer in on old Ebenezer or whoever, walk down the other side, and file out the other aisle. Sometimes the family would sit in the front row of seats, holding their vigil, watching who came to pay their respects. I remember this clearly. It always made me chuckle because they looked like they needed popcorn or something, or like they were watching a bad movie, all the family in a line stretched out across the first couple of rows.

Heck, the popcorn machine was still in the lobby. They coulda made some if they wanted to. The ticket booth, it was still there, too, and sometimes they had a little box in the ticket window for donations in memory of old Ebenezer. Funny thing, people used to drop in 75 cents, the price of a movie before Frosty sold out. Habit, I guess.

I'm making it sound grotesque, but it really wasn't so bad. It wasn't like there was this big white screen up there; the curtains were drawn, and these curtains, if you remember these old movie houses, were heavy and a dark, dark purple that looked almost like velvet. It felt almost religious.

It was the use of the marquee that got people all bent out of shape.

The Hooray Theater had this huge marquee, big and white—a great triangle that stuck out over the sidewalk like a slice of apple pie. At the top of each side, large red letters that looked plastic read "Hooray Theater." On one side, sculpted metal formed the words "Now Showing", gray and permanent over the white space where, once upon a time, the current movie had been spelled out. Well, John Anderson figured this was as good a place as any to tell people who was on display in the funeral parlor, so he put the name right up there in big black letters. In this story I'm telling you now, which was the first time he did it, it was Kenny Storvik. "Kenneth Storvik" was now showing at the Hooray Theater. On the other side of the marquee, the gray metal said "Coming Attraction," and the black letters read "Cora Ruysbroeck (Fri.)".

I'll tell you the truth. I thought it was funny. But a lot of people were mad as a wet cat, especially the Swede.

Well, now, since this is a story about the Swede, or one of the stories about the Swede, 'cause there's a bushel of

stories about that character—some of which I'll throw
in here, free of charge. Maybe I should tell you a little
about the Swede first. Now that I've said I was going to,
I find myself saying, "What do I know about the Swede?"
What does anyone know? Well, let's see. I think he was,
at the time of this story about 40 years old. But he could
have been 50. I don't know. He was kinda balding in front
and his nose followed a jagged line, like it had been broken
a couple times, maybe more. He was drunk. Maybe I
should say that right off; he was almost always drunk,
except when he was doing odd jobs to earn a little money
for more booze. He never drank anything but Jim Beam.
A high-class drunk. The thing that always amazed me
about the Swede was the way he walked. The way he
walked when he was three sheets to the wind. It was kind
of a skillful stumble, a mad scramble, and it looked like
he was just about to fall flat on his face. But he never did.
The Swede never, never fell down. He'd lurch. He'd teeter.
He'd throw his arms and legs out in this direction and then
that. You know, I always had the impression that he did
it deliberately, throw his arms and legs out like that, like
an outrigger on a canoe, and that made him stable, kept
him from falling down. Kids used to love to watch him. It
was a dance, the way he walked. It was a thing of beauty,
charming.

He had eyes, too, that made you sit up and take notice.
Most drunks have eyes that look like cesspools, but not the
Swede. I don't care how drunk he was. His eyes were always
bright. Always alert. Sure, they were bloodshot half the
time, and you could have packed all your belongings in the
bags under his eyes—he had two distinct rows of bags under
his eyes; labia minor and labia major, he called them—but
the eyes themselves, you knew he knew what was going on
all the time.

Some of you may not know about drunks in a small town like Minneota, Minnesota. For the most part, people like drunks, unless they get nasty, but it's not usually the drunks who get nasty. It's the guy who only gets drunk on Saturday night and likes to fight in the parking lot outside the dance hall. The drunks are useful. They have a "social function," as the big-city psychologists would say. Sure, they drink too much, but who gets hurt? Themselves alone. And to earn booze money, they are available to paint a house, lay some sewer, build a window planter, or clean up a backyard. They are darn good workers, so long as the job doesn't take up too much of their drinking time.

Our best alcoholic holds the position of "town drunk," which I think has more status than mayor. (Nobody wants to be mayor of a small town like Minneota. It's like jury duty or some equally repulsive civic duty; come to think of it, the town drunk is not infrequently elected mayor as well.) The Swede was not the town drunk, not at the time of this story. Wilson Howard held that honor. But it was clear that when Wilson died, the Swede would be "elected" to replace him.

Now, the town drunk is special, with a specific function in the community. The town drunk is a moral symbol. I don't mean in the sense of "Sinner! Sinner!" It's not that at all. It's more like unrealized potential. Wilson Howard, for example, was an M.D. He no longer practiced medicine, thank the Lord!, but he was a symbol of what might have been. Talent isn't enough. That's what parents told their children. Just look at Wilson Howard. Guts, that's what counts. You have to have guts, the courage to face life and grapple with all its horrors, without losing your spirit, without losing your balance. Maybe I'm not all I could have been, parents told their children, but at least I never gave up. Not like Wilson Howard. Not like the Swede.

The talents the Swede wasted were not as clear as those of Wilson Howard. He was intelligent, that's for sure—sharp as a whip. Maybe he was a schoolteacher. We didn't know where he came from. One day about ten years ago, he just appeared out of nowhere and moved into that old shack on the edge of town. He was good with his hands. Maybe he could have been a wood sculptor or a painter of wildlife scenes. I heard once he made a stained-glass window. I just don't know much about the Swede before he came to Minneota. I don't think anyone does. His best friends were probably David Sorenson, who thinks the Swede is some kind of god put on this earth to encourage and point him in the direction of the incredible fame and fortune for which he was destined (in David's opinion), and Sally Engstrom, but she's dead now. The Swede before Minneota is a big mystery, which, if you want my opinion, is just the way the Swede wanted it.

The Swede was an ace handyman, though—much better than Wilson Howard, who didn't do a lick of work anymore. As I said before, the townspeople like their drunks to be handy at odd jobs. It suited them. Wilson Howard was one of our best drunks in the area of tragic failings, but he was useless, living off some unknown stipend. (Some say he got a bundle from the will of a beautiful young woman who unexpectedly died under his knife during an appendectomy.)

Hey, but I'm getting away from my story. Not that that's so unusual. Not for me. Not for any of the storytellers in Minneota. You might as well get used to it. We are like cats. We don't like to go anyplace in a straight line. We like to meander—there's a good word for it. Big-city folks call it digression; we call it meandering. Why should you be in such a hurry? There's always interesting sideshows at the

County Fair, and there's always interesting sideshows in a good story.

Just so we've got that straight. I ain't agonna speed up my story just so you can find out what the Swede did. If you're so all-fired desperate to know the ending, I'll tell you now, and then we can get on with the interesting part, which is how we got there, to the end. But I know you. You don't want to hear the ending either. You think that spoils the story. So I won't tell you. And I won't hurry. And you'll get a better story this way. Just sit back and enjoy it.

So the names went up on the Marquee. Soon as he saw it, the Swede went charging into the Muni—that's the Municipal Liquor Store, which has the only bar in town. Curly Van Lerberghe, he's the manager there. He's the one who told me this part of the story. Wilson Howard was already there. Curly says that he and Wilson were expecting the Swede to come charging in, full of fire and brimstone, and sure enough, here he comes. Curly poured him an inch of Jim Beam and sat back to see what the Swede was going to do about the marquee. Knowing Curly, I imagine he was just sitting there on that stool he keeps behind the bar, wiping a shot glass like he does when he gets nervous about something, when maybe a fight's about to start, but now it's what's the Swede going to do.

Curly says that Wilson Howard was madder than a wet hen. The Swede doesn't say anything. Just sits there staring at his whiskey. Doesn't even take a sip. A concentrated look on his face. Finally, Wilson can't stand it any longer, and he starts shouting at the Swede, "Oh, for Pete's sake! Why are you so stirred up? Ain't no kin of yours. What the hell do you care? They're all dead anyway!"

Curly says the same thing. "Yeah," he says. "It ain't none of your business. Billy Storvik, maybe; it's his pa. Or Louie Ruysbroeck. What do you care?"

And the Swede says, "It's an insult to the community."

That's what the Swede always says. That's what we know about the Swede. That if he thinks something is bad for the town, he's going to do something about it. He always does.

So we knew he was going to say this. But, it doesn't matter. Wilson Howard nearly explodes anyway. "Oh, for Christ's sake! 'Insult to the community,' what kind of crap is that? Who's this 'community' you're talking about? Me? Am I included? I don't give a damn. Neither does Curly. Ken and Cora don't care. They're dead. Billy and Louie couldn't care less. Who's this community you're so all-fired interested in defending?"

The Swede, he doesn't say a word.

Wilson wouldn't let him be. "And you! You of all people! You don't even believe in heaven! You don't respect the dead. You think the body is garbage, once the life has gone out of it. Good for mulching roses. You told me that, your very same self!"

The Swede, he still says nothing.

Finally, Curly asked him straight out, "What're you gonna do, Swede?"

"I don't know. I'll think of something."

So the game was on, and Curly hurried around town telling everyone. We knew it already. Everyone in town knew the Swede would do something. The only question was "what?" This was the fun part, trying to guess the Swede's plot. John Anderson, who was going to have to bear the brunt of the Swede's dirty work, tried to guess the plot, so he could stop it. For the rest of us, it was just entertainment. This kinda thing is a main event in a small town.

Let me give you an example, as we meander toward the climax. About five years ago, Sorenson and Sons, they're the local John Deere dealer, they wanted to cut down this big elm tree so they could build a lot for used farm equipment. The Swede thought this was a horrible idea, to cut down a beautiful old tree, the only shade downtown, where families had a little picnic lunch on Saturdays, where the retired farmers sat on an old wooden bench and solved the political problems of the world. I have to say, I was on the Swede's side this time; it would have been terrible if we'd have lost that tree. But old man Sorenson was determined to have some place to park his used plows and combines, and the city council, which has never done anything about anything as long as we can remember, did nothing once again. So the Swede, what does he do but climb up the tree. He camped there. He stayed in the tree day and night, until finally Sorenson relented and said we could have our "damned tree." He was going to park his equipment on the lot next to the lumberyard. This gave us a bit of a start because on this lot was the old shack the Swede lived in. We thought old man Sorenson was going to tear down the Swede's home to get even, but he never did. He just parked his plows all around the shack, and the Swede didn't seem to mind. In fact, it was better this way because now someone cut the weeds back once in a while.

The tree, the one the Swede saved for us, still stands today. We call it Swede's Bedroom.

But what was the Swede going to do about the marquee? John Anderson was worried, and so was his younger brother, Dingus. I'll tell you the truth. Both the Andersons were mean SOBs; nobody liked them. But they were big and muscular, and they didn't care if people liked them or not. Still, they were worried about the Swede. They knew the townspeople, even if they didn't mind the marquee, were every last soul on the side of the Swede in this matter. The Swede would probably do something that would make them look foolish, and the Andersons would be tainted for life, remembered like Sorenson's tree in stories of the Swede's escapades.

I remember Dingus in those days. He was trying to protect his brother. He had a powerful, muscular face, but a child's face (though he was nearly 30). His face was red and weathered, with a white half moon just below the hairline, where the brim of his DeKalb seed corn cap shadowed his forehead from the all-day sun of the working farmer. One time I saw him, his forehead was screwed up in thought, running furrows through the white field, which gave me the impression that his forehead was rarely used in this way. That Dingus rarely gave much thought to anything, I think was an accurate impression. Dingus was a man of action, usually thoughtless.

I'm sure Dingus had the idea of beating the daylights out of the Swede, sending him to the hospital or the morgue. But even Dingus was smart enough to know that he couldn't do this. For one reason, the Swede was too popular. He had too many friends who would take revenge if Dingus beat him up. People knew what Dingus was thinking, of course, so they warned him in advance. Father O'Shea, the local priest, told me that he told Dingus to lay off. "If you touch one of the few remaining hairs on the Swede's head," he said to Dingus. "I'll cut off your balls meself." Several others made similar promises.

Another reason why Dingus couldn't use brute force was the Swede was a little guy. Measured in volume, the Swede was maybe half the size of Dingus, and less than a third the size of brother John. In a small town like Minneota, or it doesn't even have to be a small town, anyplace in the Midwest, maybe anywhere in America, people have a very strong sense of fair play. Little kids are protected by older kids and adults, who tell their attackers "pick on someone your own size!" The result is little guys are not vulnerable to physical beatings, and they can say just about anything, or do just about anything, and get away with it. You can't insult someone's mother. There are limits. I don't care how small or how popular you are. But the Swede would never insult someone's mother.

The Swede told me later that Dingus had actually come to him and threatened violence. He thought it was worth a try, even though they both knew he couldn't carry it through. Dingus came to him and said, "What are you going to do, Swede? Tell me, or I'll get rough. Rough tough."

The Swede tried to look afraid. "Don't hurt me. Please! I'll tell you!" Even Dingus must have recognized this as sarcastic, and I imagine that he also suddenly realized that he had made a terrible mistake. Now the Swede was going to describe fantastic and gruesome plots that he had no intention of doing, and Dingus was going to have to suffer through it. Who was doing violence to whom? Well, he should have realized what was coming. The Swede told him all kinds of stories, with decaying body parts, poisonous spiders, ringworm and leprosy, tar and feathers. Dingus, the Swede said, just sat there with his mouth open, sweating, trembling, but fascinated. The Swede described an electrical invention that can make a dead body rise and walk again. He was enjoying this. He took a long time and told Dingus many stories. Finally, he told me, Dingus started making gurgling noises, like he was going to throw up, so the Swede thought he'd better stop. He promised Dingus he wouldn't do any of the terrible things he just described. "And don't do anything else, either," Dingus had added.

"Well, Jesus, Dingus. I have to be doing something. It's impossible to do nothing."

"Well, OK, almost nothing, then. As close to nothing as you can get, OK?"

Dingus and the Swede had tangled once before. Just after the Swede had moved into the shack on the edge of town. Dingus, then in his teens, used that shack to smoke cigarettes, drink beer, bully young boys, and get fresh with girls. After the Swede moved in, Dingus took to shooting his slingshot at the shack late at night. Once a window had been broken, but usually the stones pinged loudly on the roof, which was made of corrugated aluminum.

The Swede didn't know for sure who was doing it, but he figured it was Dingus. He stopped Dingus on the street and asked him where he was "around midnight last night." Dingus, as you know by now, is dumb as a post, and dumb people make bad liars. "I was home in bed," Dingus answered. "Besides, I don't even have a slingshot!"

So about a week later the Swede again stopped Dingus on the street. This time with some bad news. "Debil DeBays is looking for you, Dingus. He says he's going to cut off your pecker and shove it up your ass."

Now Debil DeBays is always bad news. He's about the meanest, orneriest man in the county. The official town bully. Back then Debil was, what, maybe 26 or 27, but he was still hanging around high school dances, terrorizing the kids, or else he was leading a gang of ruffians into battle in a neighboring town. He'd just as soon break your arm as shake your hand. He once knocked out John Anderson with a single punch, and big John was no slouch in the kick-arse department. So Dingus didn't want to hear that Debil was wanting to look him up. No, sir! "Why?" he asked the Swede.

"It's because of the letter," the Swede told him.

"What letter?" asks Dingus.

"Debil got a letter signed with your name. It says you have this insane desire to get inside his sister's pants."

"Faith's pants?"

"Yes. It says you want his permission."

"It says what?! That's crazy. I never wrote such a letter. A guy'd have to be crazy as a loon!"

The Swede calmly told Dingus the truth. The Swede had written the letter and signed it "Dingus." In fact, he made two copies. One he sent to Debil, and one he kept, which he now gave to Dingus. It was written on a sheet of paper from one of those school tablets—my goodness, I remember them well—it had an Indian chief in a big feathered headdress on the cover, and the paper inside was so coarse you almost got slivers if you ran your fingers over it. Most of the kids stopped using these tablets after the fourth or fifth grade, but not Dingus. He thought they looked "rough tough," like something a real man would use for toilet paper. And another thing about Dingus, he always wrote his exercises in green pencil. He thought it looked classy, like having a big pair of dice hanging from your rear view mirror. Well, this letter was written in green pencil. And somehow the Swede had gotten a hold of something Dingus wrote, because when Dingus looked at the letter, he thought for a moment that he must have written it and forgotten about it. It was so much like his childish scrawl. It was in fact written on a page from Dingus's own tablet, which the Swede had stolen while Dingus slurped down a malted milk at the Korner Kafe after school one day.

"You see this?" asked the Swede, pointing to two lines wider apart than the others. "It proves it's from your tablet."

Dingus said, "well, I'll just burn my tablet."

"Too late. Debil's got your tablet."

"Debil's got my tablet?"

"I gave it to him," says the Swede.

The Swede told me that he never saw anyone so scared in his life. He said the look in Dingus's eyes reminded him of a rabbit he had surprised on a walk by the Yellow Medicine River. Dingus asked the Swede why he did it.

"Because you were shooting at me every night with your slingshot. Because you thought a malicious act was funny."

"Yeah, OK," Dingus had replied. "But this is serious business. Remember that kid from Lake Benton? All he did was date Faith, and Debil broke his jaw. Sent him to the hospital. Debil's gonna rip me to shreds!"

"You're right about that," said the Swede. "It's no laughing matter. Not anymore. If I were you, I'd hole out for a couple of days. Lay low until Debil cools down a bit. Sooner or later, Debil's gonna realize that somebody's trying to pull a fast one on you. Nobody in their right mind would write such a letter. Nobody would be that stupid. Not even you, Dingus."

So Dingus took off like a bat outta hell. That was the last anyone saw of him until almost two weeks later, when Jerry van Eyck, the game warden, found him camped by Dahlberg's Slough. He had been "living off the land," so Jerry fined him for hunting out of season. I don't know how many pheasants and ducks he shot. Probably not many because a lot of his food came off of old Dahlberg's farm, who was wondering why his vegetables and chickens were disappearing. Dahlberg thought he had a fox that liked tomatoes. But he never filed charges against Dingus. Not after Nels Anderson, the father of the Anderson boys, made good his debt. You can be certain that Nels made Dingus pay for his crimes, one way or another.

Of course, you know that the Swede never sent any letters to Debil DeBays, and sooner or later even Dingus figured this out. But Dingus never let on why he took off. Not the real reason. He told everybody that it was a test of "manhood," to see if he could survive by himself in the wilderness. "By stealing chickens?" his father would snort after each retelling. But it was the story of a dumb stunt, so people believed it of Dingus. And Dingus never again shot stones at the Swede's roof.

So let me get back to the main story, about the marquee at the Hooray Funeral Parlor. By now—I'm talking about later that first day, the day the names of the dearly departed went up in big black letters—by now, the whole town was buzzing. There was electricity in the air. Everyone knew that the Swede would react; he would do something. He always did. It's a kind of entertainment in a small town, this kind of event, a morality play in which even the audience gets to play a role. And the Swede was a polished entertainer. He had a sense of drama. He knew how to build suspense, how to paint the good guys white and the bad guys black, and he knew how to release the tensions he had generated. The Swede's dramas always had a climax. Once begun, the story always progressed until the final curtain. There was always a resolution; the Swede always delivered.

So the people wanted to know the outline of this story, since they were going to have to play their roles appropriately. Did he want the marquee to come down? Or did he only want them to stop putting up the names? What was his plan? Would they be privy to it, or was it to be a surprise?

It was to be a surprise they soon discovered. But if the Swede wouldn't tell them "what," they needed to know "when."

"When Cora opens at the Hooray Theater," the Swede announced. A fine decision they all agreed. Two days before Cora Ruysbroeck's body was to be placed on display at the theater—plenty of time for tension to build, plenty of time for people to call friends and relatives who had moved away, and most important of all, plenty of time to try to guess what the Swede was going to do. That was the real fun. And to do it on Cora's first day in the theater was also perfect. She was such a nice old lady. Everybody loved Cora. I don't ever remember Cora as a young woman, though, I'm certainly old enough; it seems to me she's always been old—maybe it's just my memory that's full of decay. I'll always think of her puttering in her flower garden, always with a kind word. A wonderful person. Cora brought food to the Swede when he was camped in Sorenson's tree. That's another thing that was right about Cora. "A tree's a kind of flower, too, you know," she said at the time. And it was Cora who finally convinced Carl Sorenson to let the tree live. She gave him the curse that only sweet old ladies can give, "Carl, you should be ashamed of yourself!"

The town felt a loss when Cora died. "Cora was a kind of flower, too, you know," said the Swede at the time.

So everything was set, and the townspeople began the contest of guessing the Swede's plan. Even the Swede was shocked by some of the ideas—everybody with an idea, you see, came and told it to the Swede, to see if they were right. Not that he would tell them, if they were right, but they hoped he would give it away with a look in his eyes—a look of disappointment that he had come up with a plan that someone else could guess. It was the big prize. Nobody ever won it, though. Never. Because, well, it stands to reason that if they did guess the plan, the Swede would have to change it. Especially since everyone brought their ideas to John and Dingus Anderson, too. And they would tell John and Dingus that they had guessed correctly. That the Swede's eyes had acknowledged their victory. I don't know why people talked to the victims, too, especially the Andersons; nobody liked the Andersons. Maybe they wanted to show the Andersons they were smarter than them. I don't know; I never played the game myself, although I nearly couldn't help myself. I had a few ideas. It's probably more likely that people wanted a better contest between the Swede and the Andersons, and they thought the Andersons were too dumb to come up with ideas. Or maybe—I'll bet this is it—maybe they wanted to make the Andersons suffer, because that's what happened. The Andersons had to listen to one gruesome idea after another. I'll bet that's it. It sure as hell didn't make the contest more even, because all the different ideas just confused those poor guys, and the details just made them sick.

The Swede liked this part of the game because people would buy him booze while they spun out their idea. He said to me then, "It's amazing what a good Christian mind can conjure up, given the problem of how to shame an undertaker." The Swede always complimented them on their ideas and said they might be right, which they knew meant they were wrong, but he needed a "foolproof" plan. So he told them, especially the ones with the ugliest ideas, to tell the Andersons, to see if they could come up with a way of stopping it. The Swede, I know for sure, did this to make them suffer. But it wasn't necessary, because, as I said, they all told the Andersons anyway.

Now, the Swede had one major problem here: What about Burt Tostenrud, John Anderson's partner in the Hooray Funeral Parlor? The Swede liked Burt; everybody liked Burt. He was a down-home simple man, friendly, and kind—who would not like Burt? He was weak, though. Weak in his dealings with John; John called the shots. Burt even went around telling people how much he hated the marquee, but as he told everyone, "What John says, goes. I just do the embalming. John runs the business."

Every couple hours or so, the Swede would get up from his seat at the Muni, which was half a block from the theater, and amble down to talk to Burt. He would say stuff to Burt, stuff like "Burt, my good buddy, listen to what I'm telling you. Just don't stand by the back door on Friday." Burt knew that none of these tips had any value at all. The Swede was making a gesture of affection, and Burt was grateful. He didn't want to be thrown in with John as one of the bad guys in the story. In exchange, he gave the Swede a spare key to the Hooray Theater.

Well, finally, it was Friday morning. Cora was now showing, or so it said on the marquee. It also said on the marquee, "The Swede not welcome," something that Dingus dreamed up, no doubt. Dingus, and John, too, were perched by the front door of the Hooray Theater, and by the looks of it, they were planning to stay there all day. They had themselves a big Coca Cola cooler out there, with beer in it and sandwiches, and they had a small table for playing cards. John and three other guys, cousins of his, were playing Buck Euchre—John was winning, as usual, because he could bluff the pants off any man in town. Dingus was standing by the door, standing at attention but with his massive arms folded across his chest, a stern look on his face. His 12 gauge shotgun was propped ominously by the front window.

You know, that front window wasn't a real window. I mean, you couldn't see through it, not to the inside. It was a display window, where Frosty used to put the moving-picture posters, with Clark Gable and Vivien Leigh and the South in flames. That kind of stuff. I said to John once, hell, you've already made the Swede about as mad as he gets. Why not go the whole nine yards? Put a little poster in there. Cora Ruysbroeck, *Gone with the Wind*, with a picture of flaming hell, or angels in heaven, depending on which way you think they went. Come on, John, whadda ya think?

John nearly split a gut. But it was too much, even for him. The only thing in the window was a small gray poster card with "Anderson and Tostenrud, Funeral Home."

I didn't really mean for him to do it, you understand. Just a little joke. I told you before, I thought the whole episode was pretty funny.

Anyway, the way the day started was Jerry van Eych—you remember him, he was the game warden, still is, for that matter—Jerry came by and saw the shotgun. He asked Dingus if it was loaded.

"You're damned right it is!" said Dingus.

"Well, that's 25 bucks you owe me, then. Now get it unloaded and into a case, or I'll confiscate the damn thing. Better yet, take the damn thing home. What the hell are you going to do with it anyway? Shoot the Swede?"

This cracked John up, and his cousins, and they started badgering Jerry. "Come on, Jerry, let him have his popgun! It ain't got nothing in it but a little rock salt. He's just gonna pepper the Swede's arse a little. Give him somethin' to remember. Dingus, he feels buck naked without his popgun." And then they laughed so hard, they were near falling off their chairs. Jerry, too, he laughed just as hard. But he said, no, Dingus had to put the gun away. "You're just lucky it was me that came along first," he said, "and not Roger." That'd be Roger Mohr, the local police force.

Dingus wasn't laughing with the others. He unloaded the shotgun and cased it, but he kept it near. He hid it behind the big red Coke cooler. It stuck out some, but that was the last we heard of the shotgun.

Well, I'll tell you, that Friday was a day to remember. People in a farm town get up at the crack of dawn anyway, and today they all came down to the Hooray Theater to see what was gonna happen. By 9 o'clock, there was already a big crowd. Around 11, Carl Sorenson and his parts manager, Flicker Eyjolfsson, set up a table on the sidewalk, where they served coffee and doughnuts and John Deere advertising brochures. Maybe an hour later, the Lutheran Ladies Aid set up another table and served Betty Eyjolfsson's ham sandwiches—she's Flicker's wife, so there was a little friendly competition between the John Deere table and God's table because the Ladies Aid was passing out advertising brochures, too, on how to get yourself a ticket to eternal life. I asked Betty how the Ladies Aid felt about the marquee, and she said she thought it was sinful. She didn't know about the other ladies. Pastor Bakken said he thought it was sinful, too. So I took a little poll, "sinful" or "funny." Most people I talked to said "sinful and funny." 'Course I don't talk to the really religious folks. They never think anything is funny. One thing that struck me, though, was what Louie Ruysbroeck said—he's Cora's brother. Louie said he felt terrible about it. He missed Cora so much—neither of them ever married, and they lived together in that big house over by the Icelandic church—and he wanted to—how can I say this?—he needed to have a time to feel really bad about losing Cora, and here everybody was laughing and having a good time, and he felt left out. He felt cheated. He asked John not to do it. Not to put Cora's name up there, but John said he had to, else it'd look like the Swede had made him back down. So I felt really sorry for poor old Louie.

David Sorenson turned up around noon, so I wanted to get his "theories" on the matter. David is one of the brightest kids to come out of Minneota High School; he's now out in California someplace, still going to school, even though he graduated from college already. Going to be a doctor, he tells me, but not a medical doctor. Doctor of Philosophy, whatever that means. Hell, I know what it means. It just means now he'll have the credentials to dream up the kind of crazy theories he was always concocting. Some college will pay him good money to teach his cockeyed theories to our kids. Well, that's all right. Keep our kids out of trouble. And I myself have a certain fondness for crazy theories.

"So what's your thinking about all of this?" I asked David. You have to understand that David, don't ask me why, has always been a good friend of the Swede's. The Swede is crazy, too, in that way that only smart people can be crazy, and he seemed to sense that David was the same. That they had something in common. Probably they sat around and talked about their theories of this and that. My goodness, what a thought! It'd put me to sleep in a minute, I'm sure. But anyway, you have to understand that David is for sure going to take the Swede's side in this, so what I was asking was, what's your theory about what the Swede is thinking, not do you think it's sinful or funny, like I asked the others.

"What do you mean, 'all of this'?" David asked in return. "You mean this circus here. These people out in the streets, having a good time, having a party? When something serious is going on? I don't know. I kinda like it. It's dramatic. It's better to not take things too seriously,

I think, especially serious things. It doesn't look to me like Louie is having a good time, though, and I wish he were. But you don't mean that at all, do you? You mean, what's my theory about the Swede? Why's he doing this? He's not a religious person, so why should he get so upset about some letters on an old movie marquee."

"That's it. What do you think?" I said.

"I think he's doing this for Louie. That's what I think. Louie and maybe a few others who get real sad when they see Cora's name up there. 'Now Showing, Cora Ruysbroeck.' That's pretty cruel fun, in my opinion. Even if only a few people are hurt. And to be honest, I think the Swede was hurt. He loved Cora, you know, and you don't have to be religious to be hurt by something like this. But John Anderson shouldn't be allowed to get away with this. He'll make Minneota the laughingstock of the county.

"I'll tell you a story about the Swede," David continued. "About five or ten years ago, when he first came to Minneota, the Swede had a cat. I think the cat had taken up residence in his shack before the Swede moved in—had squatter's rights, so to speak. The cat took a liking to the Swede. Kinda invited him to share. So they did. The Swede named the cat Hobo. He and the Swede were real close. Then, suddenly, the cat died. The Swede was real broken up about it, he told me. He felt so alone. His only friend gone. He left the cat lying there, right where it died, right by his davenport. He was hoping he'd get up, and stretch, and rub up against his legs. He was hoping he had dreamed it all in a drunken nightmare. Finally, he gave up hope and buried him. Put up a little cross. It's still there, the grave and the cross. He still puts flowers on the grave every once in a while. 'Why do you do this?' I once asked him. 'You're not the kind of person to bury the dead, much less put up a religious symbol.'

"'I wondered, myself,' he said. 'It seemed like a compulsion. Something I had to do. It hurt so bad. I had to do something to stop the hurt.'

"'Did it stop the hurt?' I asked him.

"'It helped. I don't know why, but it helped.'

"Then he made a memorial to Hobo, kind of a stained glass window—'Another god-damned religious symbol!' I pointed out to him. I always told him he was a very religious man, even if he didn't believe in any institutional religion. He denied it, of course. 'You think anything with strong feelings is religious,' he said back to me.

"I had to think about that for a while. I ended up thinking maybe he was right. But maybe strong feelings are religious. Whatever you worship, that's your god; that's what they taught us at St. Olaf.

"This stained-glass window, though, was something. He has a picture he took of it; it's real beautiful. Dingus Anderson, he says, shot it out one night with a slingshot. Made it from broken pieces of glass, beer bottles, coke bottles, all different colors and shapes, whiskey bottles, wine bottles. Made a little cat face out of green glass, with a brown background, with little pieces of orange and blue and red. Real beautiful. Fit it in his window on the east side, to catch the morning sun. He wanted to kill Dingus for that. Instead, he convinced Dingus that Debil DeBays was looking for him. Did you ever hear that story?

"Well, so that's my theory. The Swede doesn't believe in the hereafter, and he thinks cemeteries are taking up good farmland. But he has an understanding of the comfort of ritual, when you lose someone you love very much. And John Anderson is taking that away from the people who loved Kenny Storvik and Cora Ruysbroeck. And he'll keep doing it, too. When my father dies. When you die. Think of how your kids are going to feel. Your 'child bride' is going to feel like shit! Somebody's gotta stop him!"

David was getting a little worked up now. I figured I'd better calm him down before he went over and took a punch at John Anderson himself. That would have been the last of David's jaw line, at the best of it. So I said, "And the Swede's just the man to do it!"

"Yes, sir," said David, out of breath. "And it's Dingus again, to boot, Dingus messing with people's feelings again."

"So what's your theory on what the Swede's gonna do?" I asked, because if anyone knew anything, David was a candidate.

"I don't have one. I never could outguess the Swede."

"I think he's gonna blow the place up."

"Now, that's downright stupid! In the first place, a lot of people, innocent people, would get hurt. In the second place, Cora's body would be spread over Minneota like so many dandelion seeds."

"I heard the Swede has a device that can make dead bodies rise up and walk."

"I think that's what he wants you to think."

"So what's it gonna be, David? Don't you have any idea?"

"I truly do not. Maybe he's found a magic flute and is going around town, collecting all the cats, training them to scratch and bite anything that looks like a big tub of lard."

So David was no help. Neither was Fern Norum or Curtis Brown or anyone else I asked. I was getting bored, if you want the truth. The most exciting thing all day happened around three in the afternoon when Dingus all of a sudden fell down. I guess his legs buckled for lack of blood. He'd been standing "at attention" since nine in the morning, and it was a pretty hot day. And so it went, into the evening. The crowd was getting bigger and bigger. Buck Bleger—he's the local baker and tuba player—got his polka band out, the name of which, don't cha know, is the Whoopie Buck-and-Ears. Don't blame me. They roped off the street in front of the Hooray Theater and had themselves a street dance. Now, this street is a state highway, so Roger Mohn and a couple of brand-new deputies had to direct traffic around the block. Half of those stopped to join the fun, so pretty soon we had a crowd where maybe half didn't even know what they were celebrating. And of course, it wasn't a celebration at all. I don't know what the heck you'd call it. Curly Van Lerberghe rolled out a couple kegs of beer. It was a heck of a party, whatever else it was. Still pretty boring, if you ask me. I got a kick out of Shorty Peetroons. He was spinning around, doing a fast polka, when he hit the fire hydrant, right in the "groin area," as they say on football T.V. Oofta! That smarts!

Now, don't you get antsy. I'm coming to the end of the story. It was awfully close to midnight when the Swede finally showed up. It was funny how it happened, too, like one minute people were dancing and drinking and laughing, and the next minute it was quiet enough to hear a mourning dove. One minute no sign of the Swede. The next minute, there he was. He just stood there and waited as this ripple of quiet spread out around him like a rock thrown into the middle of Dead Coon Lake. Dead quiet, like a cemetery. The only sound was Buck Bleger and his damn tuba, and finally he stopped, too, although very much against his will. Then the crowd kind of surged like a bowl of Jell-O and reformed around the Swede.

The Swede was drunk. There was no doubt about that, and not just tipsy, either. The Swede was "see the little bugs" drunk, and his whole body wobbled, tipping to the right, then left, forward, backward, wobble, wobble, wobble. The motion was sorta hypnotic there in the dim light on the highway. He wasn't saying anything, and the crowd was dead silent. John and Dingus, I looked over at them, they were alert like squirrels trapped by an unexpected hound.

Then the Swede started to talk. And talk and talk and talk. You think I'm long-winded, man, you should hear the Swede. ". . . don't believe in heaven . . . blah, blah, blah . . . good for mulching roses . . . blah, blah, blah . . . funerals make the hurt less . . . blah, blah, blah . . . John Anderson is too damned cheap to tear it down. . . ." On and on. I was bored to begin with, and here I'm sitting through a philosophy class. "We know all this!" that's what I wanted to shout. "Get on with it!" Whatever *it* is. But no such luck. More talk.

Well, just as we were all about decided that the Swede's plan was to bore the Andersons to death, the Swede stopped talking. He walked over to the marquee and grabbed hold of a thin rope that was hanging down from it. Now, this is funny business, right off the top, because I'd been there since morning, one of the first, and I could have sworn there was no rope hanging from the marquee. Up to five minutes before, I would have bet my life on it. Now here it was, hanging down in plain view, and the Swede was tugging on it. Then there were some noises like tiny firecrackers—Pop! Pop! Pop! And about 15 or 20 big ropes dropped down, hanging all around the marquee.

So he's going to pull it down. Well, I don't know about that. This marquee must weigh a ton, at least. No way!

"No way," said the Swede, "there's no way I can do this by myself. I need your help."

Well, I don't know what the others thought, but I thought it was a nice touch. Get the community involved. If they wanted the marquee down, well, they'd just have to do it themselves. A damn good idea, but it didn't look like it was gonna work because nobody did anything. Nobody stepped forward; in fact, several people stepped back. I just said I didn't know what the others were thinking, but I did know. They were thinking, "OK, but why me?" "Someone else can do it." "I'm too weak." "I've been sick." "I just sprained my wrist." "I'm a woman." "Love to help, but I'm way back here at the edge of the crowd." Typical community response; they want action, but they don't want to act. I myself would have grabbed a rope, but I'm the editor of the town newspaper, and I've got to be taking pictures. (You see, I can talk a good game, but I'm just like all the rest. Except, of course, I've got a good reason. A news reporter should not get involved. You don't agree? Well, OK, so I'm a coward, too.)

It didn't help matters that the Anderson brothers finally got into action. Dingus made a bee-line for the Swede, murder in his eyes, but Debil DeBays planted his considerable self between Dingus and his target. John started shouting at the crowd. "You listen to me! The Swede is crazy drunk! You don't know what you're getting into! If you pull on those ropes, I'll have your arse in jail before the marquee hits the ground! You'll be six months in the jug, and you'll have to pay me for a new marquee! Do you know what one of these suckers cost? $10,000! $10,000, minimum! A thousand bucks for everyone who pulls a rope! Can you afford that?" He looked at David Sorenson. "Huh? How about it, David? You going to pull a rope, huh? You're still going to school. You can afford a thousand bucks? And six months in jail. Huh?"

I'm thinking about this speech of John's. More words than I ever heard out of him, and not a bad argument. He had David cowed. David was staring at his shoes like they were suddenly covered with boxelder bugs. I'm wondering, how does John know how much a marquee costs? I'm sure he's never priced one out. He's just making it up. Reasonable, though. Close enough to make us worry. And he's doing math! More like $500 a rope, I figure, but even so, I don't think John Anderson ever divided one number by another since the eighth grade when he dropped out to help Nels on the farm. People are thinking, he means business.

The Swede don't pay him no never mind. He just starts passing out ropes. He hands one to David Sorenson. "When I say pull, you pull." David nodded, but he was still looking at his shoes. The Swede gave a rope to Buck Bleger, and one to Fern Norum, who hesitated but finally accepted it. He gave one to Billy Storvik and one to Louie Ruysbroeck. He went around the edge of the crowd, until all the ropes were passed out.

"Pull!" said the Swede.

Nothing happened. Fern Norum looked terribly embarrassed, so did Billy Storvik. The rope holders looked at each other. A look of fear, I'd say. They wouldn't pull, or maybe they couldn't pull, but still they wouldn't let go of the ropes. Nobody moved; nobody did anything. There was no sound. Twenty people standing by a marquee with ropes in their hands. It was like a painting. My father used to tell me about the early cameras. They were so slow that people had to stand as still as possums for several minutes, or the picture would blur. That's what it was like.

Then one thing happened, and it led to the most spectacular event I ever saw in Minneota or any place else. It was Burt Tostenrud. Good ol' Burt. Everybody thought he had the courage of a rabbit. Burt came from outta nowhere, somewhere from outta the crowd, and he took the rope outta the hands of Shorty Peetroons. He started to pull on the rope with all his might. Pulling so hard his eyes started to bug out, and there was a sound. I figure now, thinking back on it, it was probably Burt, squealing under the strain. But then, it sounded like the marquee let out a creak. This little man. This huge marquee. And then Fern Norum said, "Oh, dear!" and started to pull. Debil Debays took David's rope and started to pull, and now there was no doubt, there was a lot of grunts and groans and squeals, and the marquee was creaking. The marquee was breaking! All of a sudden, there was a sharp crack, and the marquee tipped.

Debil said, "I'll be damned."

Then it cracked again, and tipped some more. The rope pullers doubled their efforts, and others joined in, three or four of us to a rope. (Yes, I'm sorry to say, I myself got a little caught up in the mob spirit and grabbed a rope.) The marquee began to wobble, and then firecrackers started. Yes, firecrackers! The Swede had planted them on top of the marquee—cherry bombs, Roman candles, sparklers, the works. It was like the Fourth of July. Little rockets flashing through the darkness. And the marquee was coming down. (The Swede told me later that he had loosened it a little.) It pulled slowly away from the wall, hung for a moment, and then collapsed onto the sidewalk below. Dust rose from the rubble and, with it, high billowing clouds of almost pure white smoke. I've never seen anything like it. It took one's breath away. The crowd cheered and cheered.

It took John and Dingus most of Saturday to clean up the mess. By Sunday, the debris was gone and a new sign had replaced the marquee, a rush job by Shorty Peetroons. It was flush against the front wall, like all the other signs on the block, and it said, "Anderson and Tostenrud Funeral Home." The Hooray Theater was no more.

To the editor of <u>The Minneapolis Star</u>, June 10, 1962

I am incensed about your feature story on the research of Daniel Schlicten (<u>Tribune</u>, June 9, 1962). Professor Schlicten is obviously trying to lay the blame for the Sioux Wars on the Dakota Indians, absolving the United States government. Twisting the facts into outrageous half-truths, Schlicten attributes fifteen years of conflict to a single impulsive act of a young brave named Brown Wing. Brown Wing shot and killed a white settler because he was angry about "an unintentional delay in government payments to the Indians," in Schlicten's words. Brown Wing was "a James Dean type," Schlicten claims, "a rebel without a cause." By extension, the Dakota Rebellion, too, was without a cause. Balderdash!

The truth (which is not in dispute) is that the US government bought most of Minnesota from the Dakota for a few cents an acre. The Dakota were forced to sell; it was "take our offer, or we will take the land for nothing." The payments were in installments, and using future payments to establish credit, the Indians bought feed and seed from the notorious trading posts along the Minnesota River. When the payments were made, the trading posts took it all, every penny. The traders made sure that the Indian's debt equaled the payment, even if they had to pad the bill a bit. Or a lot. At the time of which we are speaking—1862—the US government was unable to make the payment on their dastardly land grab (they were spending their money on the Civil War, killing their brothers in the South). Therefore, the default on the installment due was "unintentional"—they didn't mean to miss the payment. They just didn't have the money. The Indians didn't mind; they were to receive none of the payment anyway. What did matter to them was the traders' response, cutting off their credit. "Let them eat grass," said one prominent businessman.

So the Dakota were stripped of their land, and they were starving to death. The Sioux Wars were inevitable. Any little incident could have set it off. It just happened to be Brown Wing's misfortune to be the first to reach the level of frustration that erupts in violence. He shot a white settler without provocation. But he was neither a rebel nor without a cause.

The US government cheated the Indians out of their land and then starved them. The Dakota had a choice: to die without honor or to fight. How the blame can be laid on anyone but the US government is beyond me!

David Sorenson
Minneota, Minnesota

2

Rumpelstiltskin
Is Also Innocent

The Star didn't publish my letter, of course. They never do. It's a curse, to be interested in politics. It's like pounding your head with a hammer for no reason other than constant pain and frustration. Yet we soldier on. Why? We try to make a difference. We never succeed, but we must not give up trying.

I've done some research, so let me tell you about Brown Wing. He was maybe 18 or 19 years old, a man of the tribe, his rites of passage three or four years previous. He was a leader among the young braves and would have eventually become a chief if it had not been for his father. His father was a "shorthair," a traitor. The US government had been encouraging the Indians to become farmers. Brown Wing's father took the bait like a fat old Walleye. He cut his hair and wore trousers. He farmed a small plot of land that he called "my own." My own! What sacrilege. The Indian way was to hold all property "in community," owned by all, owned momentarily by the one who uses it.

Brown Wing did not live with his father. He lived in the Rice Creek village with the rebels of the tribe. It didn't help much that he left his father. His friends taunted him anyway. They said his hair was falling out. That he too would soon be a shorthair. They predicted his blanket would bind his legs as he slept. That he would awaken with trousers. He would become his father.

"Teasing" is too weak a word for it, which is why I said "taunting," with hatred inside of it. Hatred of the white man and hatred of the Indians who became like white men.

So, how did Brown Wing respond? How would we have responded? We'd become more Indian than anyone else, I suspect. That's what Brown Wing did. He became the best. The best at games and sports, and as he grew older, the best rider, the best hunter. He always knew it was not enough. He would have to prove himself. He would have to prove that he was a red man and not a white man. He would have to fight the white men. He would have to kill a white man.

And so it came about, on a hot and lazy Sunday afternoon, August 17, 1862. Brown Wing and three of his friends had been in the woods hunting. The hunt had gone poorly—a few rabbits and a quail—all the more frustrating because the people were starving. The four Indians entered a general store in the small village of Acton, west of St. Paul. They were hungry and hoped to trade the rabbits for some sandwiches. The storekeeper's wife, the sandwich-maker, was off visiting their son, but Robinson Jones told the Indians to follow as he went to join his wife. Brown Wing and his friends agreed to do so, which pleased Jones for a couple of reasons. One, he was going to leave two children alone at the store, a teenaged girl and her infant brother, children of a relative who had died of consumption; he didn't know these Indians and didn't want to leave them in the store with the children. And two, his son and his family were new to the area and were curious about Indians.

At the farm, the riders found Jones's wife, his son, his son's wife and two children, and Viranus Webster and his wife, also new arrivals to southwestern Minnesota. Jones knew a few words of the Sioux language, and Brown Wing knew a few words of English, so they carried on a brief conversation, speaking first in Sioux, then repeating themselves in English, to the amusement of the others. Mrs. Jones made sandwiches for all—a pleasant little picnic.

What I have said so far is a matter of record. It happened as I have said. But we don't know, of course, what Brown Wing was thinking at the time. I imagine he was seething. I imagine the white farmers knew his father. That they complimented him on having such a sensible father, such a good farmer. Someone who picked up the superior (white) way of life so quickly. No doubt Brown Wing's friends teased him mercilessly as the white people piled their fulsome praise at his feet.

And Brown Wing was tired from the hunt, hungry as usual, and frustrated by the lack of big game. I imagine he was in a very sour mood when he proposed a competition, to see who was the best marksman. Each man in turn fired at a piece of wood on a distant stump. Robinson Jones hit closest to the mark. The Indians reloaded their rifles. The white men did not.

Brown Wing raised his rifle and shot Viranus Webster in the forehead.

Thus began the Sioux Wars, some 30 years of slaughter and pursuit, wars in which the Dakota won not a single battle except for Little Big Horn (and that by accident, or rather, an incredible miscalculation by William Custer). Wars that did not end until the US Cavalry murdered several hundred unarmed Indians at Wounded Knee.

The four Dakota shot and killed Robinson Jones, his son, his wife, and, during their escape, the teenaged girl who had been left at the general store. The last victim,

Clara Wilson, waved to the braves as they thundered by. Apparently she was shot because one of the Indians, Wild Runner, had not yet killed anyone. He alone was without a trophy.

We know these events are true, or roughly so, because we have complete accounts from both the Indians and the survivors. I didn't make it up. I say this, because otherwise, you wouldn't believe what happened next. A man on horseback rode up at the farm and surveyed the carnage. Four lay dead on the ground, and four survivors huddled on the porch of the house. The horseman danced his horse among the bodies on the ground, dancing from body to body. Suddenly the man began to laugh, and the horse began to prance. "The horse prancing and dancing, his rider laughing," said the widow Webster later. "Then he said, 'The white man has the nose-bleed! It's good for them! The purification begins today!' He had a high, whiny voice. He slapped his thigh and cackled with laughter. He had a black hat and a big, thin nose. He looked like a witch on a broomstick. I thought at first he was the angel of death. He rode off, and we never saw him again."

Perhaps the rider was a prophet. Perhaps he was indeed the angel of death.

So then, how about Brown Wing? Is he a villain, or is he a hero? A villain, I suppose; I wouldn't call a murderer a hero, even in war. But to say that Brown Wing was responsible for the Sioux Wars is stretching the truth quite a bit, don't you think? It is true that the Dakota staged a preemptory attack on the trading post at Redwood Falls, . . . when? August 18, the following day. The Indians believed that reprisals for Brown Wing's action would be swift and vicious; they believed that war was now inevitable. And they were right.

But war was inevitable even if Brown Wing hadn't shot Viranus Webster.

Brown Wing was an excuse, not a cause.

Maybe I should be a lawyer. Lawyers and scientists are a lot alike, I think. They search for truth. I'm not so sure about lawyers, though. If I were a lawyer, I'd search for truth, and my client be damned! If that's where the truth led. . . .

Of course, I would prefer it if my client were innocent. Even better, if my client were innocent but had been convicted, in spite of the truth. Like Brown Wing. Except he wasn't innocent of crimes. Just undeserving of the claim that his impulsive killing had started a 30-year war.

I would like to be the attorney for the defense in the case of the People versus Rumpelstiltskin.

Have you ever read the story of Rumpelstiltskin? Let me give you an annotated version. An old man drags a young woman into the courtyard of the castle and offers her to the king. The king refuses to accept her. What would he want with a poor, dirty girl when he can have his pick of beautiful maidens? The desperate old man thinks fast; all he can come up with is the preposterous assertion that the girl can spin straw into gold!

Normally, the king would tell the peasant to bugger off. But stories have been circulating, stories of magic and riches from unexpected sources. He's heard of a goose that lays golden eggs, so he thinks perhaps he has found an alchemist who can convert common substances into gold. In any case, what would it cost him to give her a try?

The girl is locked in a room full of straw. If she fails to spin the straw into gold, she will be put to death. The old man is gone, having accomplished his purpose. He (probably her grandfather) must have known that she would die, but he can't afford to feed her; better she should die quickly. It's a blessing—a quick death. He's done his duty. And her death will be on the head of the king, not his.

The lies we tell ourselves to preserve our self respect!

Next: Rumpelstiltskin climbs in a window and spins the straw into gold. Rumpelstiltskin is described as old, short, and ugly—a gnome. I wonder what he really looked like. The canonical descriptions seem prejudicial, against the elderly, against short people, against those who are not good-looking enough to attract our sympathies. Perhaps he was young and tall and handsome.

Perhaps "spinning straw into gold" is a metaphor for incredible love making!

Am I fostering the prejudice against the old, the short, and the ugly with such wild revisionist speculations? Probably. Let's keep his countenance as portrayed. The principle we should defend is that his age, his height, and his looks should not assure his guilt.

He must have scared the daylights out of the maiden as she sat crying, bemoaning her fate. Imagine this old, short, ugly gnome crawling through your window. Probably she screamed or called the guards.

Come to think of it, he must have been short. If he had been tall and climbed through the window, she could have done the same and escaped.

Why didn't the guards come when she screamed?

How did Rumpelstiltskin convince her that he meant no harm. That he was there to help her, to save her?

"Don't be afraid. I'm a magician, and I've come to save you. I can spin the straw into gold."

How did it happen that Rumpelstiltskin had the very skill—turning straw into gold—that the situation required? It's not what you call "a common skill."

My guess is this: People had heard tales of someone who could spin straw into gold. The grandfather and the king had both heard these rumors. This explains how the grandfather gained an audience with the king, who ordinarily would have his soldiers protect him from such riffraff. When the grandfather made the claim to the king's guards, they were probably under instructions to relay any information about straw turning into gold. Thus, the king was willing to put the girl to the test. Thus, Rumpelstiltskin, who alone possessed the skill, could help her.

"Don't be afraid. I'm a magician, and I've come to save you. I can spin the straw into gold," says Rumpelstiltskin.

Perhaps the maiden was too tired, too desperate to resist. Perhaps she, too, had heard the rumors of such a magician. But she must have been skeptical: "Sure, sure, I've heard that line before! What do you want from me?" She assumes he wants sex. They all do. She prepares herself for an unpleasant duty.

"Nothing. I want nothing from you. Nothing at all."

Disbelieving, she offers him some bauble in payment for his services. He accepts.

All right, here is the first flaw in the prosecution's account. If Rumpelstiltskin were an evil magician, why would he accept a bauble for the performance of a skill worth millions of dollars? The only possible answer is he had sympathy for the girl. He wanted to help her. He saw the old man drag her in. He heard the exchange with the king—how else would he know of her needs? He wanted nothing in return—why would he accept a worthless bauble if not to relieve her of her feelings of being indebted to him? Rumpelstiltskin was a prince among men, I tell you. The evidence is incontrovertible.

But there's another problem for me. People can't change straw into gold; alchemy was a failure. I don't believe that Rumpelstiltskin had the ability; nobody does. So what does it mean to turn straw into gold?

There's only one possible answer. Rumpelstiltskin had to move the straw out of the room and replace it with gold from someplace else.

My guess is this: The only person with the amount of gold needed is the king himself. Somehow Rumpelstiltskin gained entry to the king's treasury and filled the maiden's room with the king's own gold. He probably gave the straw to the king's horses.

If so, he would have been popular with the horses. No mention of it in the story, but perhaps the author wasn't looking for it. No reason to do so.

I imagine the horses coming to Rumpelstiltskin's aid when the soldiers make fun of him—old, short, and ugly as he is. The soldiers start to beat him—why do we attack those who are different from us?—and the horses circle him and protect him.

Or perhaps Rumpelstiltskin had a reputation as a magician with evil powers. Perhaps the soldiers are afraid of him.

Probably Rumpelstiltskin cultivated the reputation for his own protection.

Twice more Rumpelstiltskin works all night to save the girl's life. Finally she is married to the king, who is no dummy. The third night is the charm, winning his devotion (or his greed, if you prefer). But she has no more baubles to give to Rumpelstiltskin. Rumpelstiltskin says he desires nothing in return. He just wanted to help. She cannot understand such altruism, so she offers him jewels, the jewels that she will own as the Queen. Rumpelstiltskin says he has no interest in jewels. Of course not, she thinks; why would he be interested in jewels when he can spin straw into gold? So she offers him her first-born child.

Rumpelstiltskin is stunned by this offer. He is speechless. How could a mother give up her child? He makes no response.

What do you make of this? How could a mother give up her child? I imagine she was desperate. Perhaps she thought the evil magician would demand her soul in return for her favors. Her problem is, clearly, that she cannot wrap her mind around the idea of someone helping her and asking nothing in return because that is exactly what Rumpelstiltskin was doing.

I mean, why does Rumpelstiltskin get the bad press, when the woman was the one to propose this dastardly deed? Why don't people get on her case?

A year or two later, Rumpelstiltskin reappears, and the Queen has had a baby. Thank God, she has also had a change of heart; she wants to keep her child. So once more she offers jewels instead of the child. Rumpelstiltskin's reply is, and I quote, "I would rather have some living thing than all the treasures of the world."

That's a funny thing for an evil magician to say, don't you think? And the next thing he says is even curiouser. He tells the Queen that she may keep her child if she can guess his name.

Why in the world would he do such a thing? If his evil is his desire for the Queen's child, why does he give her an out? One can only assume that he doesn't want the child. That he wants nothing in return for his favors.

You still don't believe me? Well, consider what Rumpelstiltskin does next. He builds a huge bonfire. One that can be seen for miles, and then he dances around the bonfire, screaming his name at the top of his lungs. "Rumpelstiltskin is my name!"

The next day the Queen's spies report their observations, and she guesses his name correctly.

Really, do I have to say more? Can you honestly say you believe the prosecution's story of an evil magician who was after the Queen's first-born child, and who was foiled by an inadvertent screaming of his name while he danced around a raging bonfire?

The puzzle to me is why Rumpelstiltskin is portrayed as evil? Why do children who hear the story do not see him as kind and caring? What is the moral? What is the message? Beware of strangers bearing gifts? Beware of ugly strangers, for evil has an ugly face? Is there some sort of hidden sexual message, as Freud suggests? He who spins the gold earns the young girl's baby? And how may this evil power be foiled? By knowing his name? By knowing who he is? Names are sacred. We all know that. The Jews cannot speak the name of their god.It is not for human knowledge. JAWVEH. Jehovah. Code words for the unspeakable god.

And Rumpelstiltskin's fire, what of that? Fire and sex, fire and passion. A man's downfall is always his lust, his uncontrollable passion. It betrays who he is, what he wants, and through it, the woman gains control of her children.

Nonsense! The truth is much better, don't you think?

* * *

One Christmas in Los Angeles, I made the rounds of Mexican bars, seeking to convince the bartenders that Santa Claus was a woman. In Spanish, Santa is the feminine form for "saint," as in Santa Maria or Santa Barbara. Male saints are Santo (Santo Domingo) or just plain San (San Diego, San Francisco). So "Santa Claus" identifies a female saint named "Claus." An unusual name for a woman, I agree, but of the sex there can be no question. The bartenders listened with a marked lack of interest, which slowly turned to disgust as I rattled on and on. "Have you ever seen Santa Claus?" I asked them. "Someone who claimed to be Santa Claus?"

"Yes, of course," they would answer.

"Was it a man or a woman?"

"A man."

"How do you know?"

"He had a beard."

"And tell me. As far as you could tell, was the beard real or fake?"

They did not respond. Most walked away at this point.

✱ ✱ ✱

Good grief! I was telling you about Brown Wing and the Sioux Wars. How far I've digressed. Around here, we call it "meandering"—it's considered a virtue.

So let me tell you what happened to Brown Wing and his friends. Sunday, August 17, 1862. Brown Wing lived in the Rice Creek village, a scruffy little settlement where the malcontents of the Dakota nation went to brood and plot. When Brown Wing and his buddies came racing in with their terrible news, they were treated as heroes. Now, the rebels thought the hoped-for war would surely begin.

Their first problem was a declaration of war. Their leader was Red Middle Voice, who had no status, wasn't even a minor chief; he couldn't do it. Red Middle Voice sent word to his nephew, Young Shakopee, a chief, in hopes that he would call the southern Dakota to war. But Young Shakopee told Red Middle Voice what he already knew, that only one chief had the status and authority. If there was to be war, they would have to convince Little Crow.

Thus, it came to pass, two hours before the dawn of Monday, August 18, a war council was convened at the home of Little Crow.

What a meeting that must have been. Nowadays, I suppose, they would have televised it. But we have several reports from men in attendance. Red Middle Voice and Young Shakopee spoke for the militants, recounting the numerous insults at the hands of the white man. In 1851, the Dakota gave up their tribal homelands—most of southern Minnesota, about 25 million acres—at a price of less than 15 cents an acre, to be paid in installments over 50 years. Each payment was disputed by the American traders, who claimed the Indians owed them money for food and equipment sold on credit. Many of these claims were exaggerated. Many were totally fictitious. The Indians received only a small portion of the funds due them.

The treaty of 1851 left the Sioux, as the white man called them, with a reservation on the upper Minnesota River, on a strip 150 miles long and extending 10 miles on each side of the river. In 1858, a second treaty gave the white man the entire top half of the reservation, the 10 miles north of the Minnesota, at 30 cents an acre. Most of this money went to traders. The upper Dakota received about $100,000. The southern Dakota, led by Little Crow, received nothing. Not a single penny.

This summer, the summer of 1862, had been one of particular hardships. Many Indians were starving. The land payment due them in June had not arrived and rumors spread that the United States government, engaged in a costly civil war with the Confederacy, was bankrupt. The Indians asked the traders at Redwood Falls for more credit. The traders refused. Andrew Myrick, one the major traders, said, "If they are hungry, let them eat grass." These words Young Shakopee now repeated in the war council, and even the Christian chiefs shook their heads.

Little Crow foresaw the future: the thunder of big guns, a "snowstorm" of white soldiers. "You will die like rabbits if you hunt the wolves," he said. He paused and then added, "Little Crow is no coward. He will die with you."

Brown Wing let out a whoop and ran to Rice Creek to spread the word.

The war was on.

By first light on the morning of August 18—a few hours before the Indian's land payment finally arrived—Andrew Myrick's store was surrounded. When his body was found two weeks later, it was full of bullet holes and arrows, too; a hay scythe was stuck in his back and his mouth was stuffed with grass.

The Dakota braves swept down the Minnesota River, killing white farmers and their families. But they could not take Fort Ridgely, the gateway to the valley that ran east to St. Paul. Nor could they break through the civilian defenses in New Ulm, the gateway to Mankato and the eastern half of the Minnesota River. These battles were decisive; although there were later skirmishes, Little Crow's war was effectively over on August 23, six days after it had begun.

The US Congress retaliated against the Minnesota Sioux by abrogating all treaties. Payments were stopped, and the last of the reservations along the Minnesota were opened to white settlers. Most of the Dakota warriors, those who were still alive, fled to the prairie west of Minnesota, and the others—women, children, old men, and braves of the upper villages, many of whom had refused to participate in Little Crow's war, and even the peaceful Winnebago Indians, who had not fired a shot—were herded to a tract of barren land in Dakota territory known as Crow Creek. The first winter, one of every four died of starvation and exposure.

A young Dakota of the western tribes visited Crow Creek and listened to the stories of his brothers and sisters; he was known to the white man as Sitting Bull. Later, in 1876, he would lead the Dakota nation at Little Bighorn. Among his warriors would be a Minnesota Sioux named Spotted Calf, to whom history accords the credit of killing General George A. Custer. "Spotted Calf" was the name Brown Wing took when he fled the killing fields of 1862.

To the Lipstick Smearers Union (LSU)

> *c/o David Sorenson*
>
> *From Sally Engstrom*
>
> *Re: The LSU Date Rate*

You guys are completely hopeless. Actually, I like your abbreviation, LSU, which will naturally be confused with the Lutheran Students Union. But your ratings of us girls after a date with one of us are really offensive, did you know that? The possible responses for figure (terrific, too tall, fatso, fried eggs for breasts, bazookas) are offensive even to me with my pair of bazookas. The "pork chop" kiss, the "weak, annoying, or disgusting" personality, and "wordy, moody, or prudish" morals . . . the "modern or dull" conversation abilities (or "shows signs of intelligence"), the looks rating for ugly ("good personality for a dog"). . . . The Date Rate stinks.

How would you like it if we girls did the same to you? (Are you sure we don't?) David has a "beanpole" figure, Curtis is a "spittoon" kisser, Jon has "gargoyle" looks. You all have weak, annoying, AND disgusting personalities, with no observable sense of humor. You all have the morals of a boar, which is a male pig with an intense sex drive, for those of you with no sign of intelligence.

So, how about a date? The Glenn Miller Story is playing in Marshall. We could sit in the back and neck.

3

The Incident
at Coleman's Farm

Well, all right, it's a nice enough day. Thank God! All
this rain gets me down. What can you do when it rains?
Sit and think. Sit and think. Sit and think. Sometimes
it seems my whole life is "sit and think." Some people, I
suppose . . . For some people, that would be a good life,
sure enough. The Swede, now, he likes it. He likes to sit
and think. For him, a rainy day is a blessing. A goddamned
blessing! Not for me, though. Not with my thoughts. Lord,
let me out into the sunshine.

But not like this, Lord! This is it, Lord? This is what
I get in the sunshine, the back seat in Trudy's Ford, a ride
around town, looking for boys? Spare me, Lord, have mercy!
Will you look at her? Next thing she'll be wearing nylons on
picnics or something. She's really strange.

Trudy Snorrasdottir. My friend, Trudy Snorrasdottir.
Let me introduce her . . . Of Icelandic ancestry. From a
country so backward they never did get around to naming
their children properly. Snorra has a daughter, so they call
her Snorrasdottir. Eyjolf has a son, they call him Eyjolfsson.
Like naming animals. What's that? Oh, that's Josephscow.
That's Petershorse. That's Jacksturtle.

Trudy is not very bright. She thinks everything is funny. She thinks everything is delicious. She giggles and eats. I sit and think. She giggles and eats. What a pair!

Trudy and I are best friends. I hate her. Why do I hang around with her? Beats me. Because we live in a small town. One of the worst things about a small town is that you're friends with the people you find disgusting. Don't have a choice in the matter.

And then there's Goose DeCoster, my other good friend. Goose likes to smoke cigarettes. Thinks it's daring. Her real name is Maud. She hates it. We call her Goose because she likes to jab her thumb between the buns of unsuspecting guys and gals. Especially guys. She is proud of her nickname.

Goose is a slob. She is popular with the fellows, though. She lets them handle her tits. I find Goose disgusting.

So here I am, driving around on a Saturday afternoon, in a car with two disgusting creatures—my best friends— looking for guys. Maybe that's why we're friends, Trudy and Goose and me. We're hunters three. The three musketeers. Out for love and adventure . . . preferably love. More like the three stooges if you want to hear the truth.

Why am I here?

It's the only game in town.

What would I be doing if I had a choice? I'd be living in Minneapolis. Or maybe in one of those rich suburbs. Edina. This afternoon I'd be going to a fashion show. Then in the evening . . . yes, yes, in the evening! Why is it "the night" in Minneota, but "the evening" in Minneapolis? In the evening, some tall blonde guy who's going to Harvard would pick me up in his Mercury convertible, and we'd go out to some fancy hotel for dinner and dancing. Oh my, they'd say, isn't that Sally Engstrom over there with . . .

with . . . Richard McDermott. Nah, Irish. Richard's OK. Richard . . . Richard Ford. Richard Dodge. Need something clearly European. That's the upper crust. Except for Ireland. Richard Hampton. That's nice. Richard Hampton. Nobody calls him Dick. Even his father calls him Richard.

Isn't that Sally Engstrom over there with the elegant Richard Hampton? How nice they look together! A beautiful couple, and, yes, they're so much in love. So much. He adores her. You can see that. Adores her. He just adores her. They're so much in love.

Back to reality, girl. There's trouble on the road ahead. Just what I need, a bunch of jerks from Marshall looking for the Minneota tramps. Well, here we are, Sweetie! Goose is a little antsy today. Oh, woe is me. I don't believe it. I'm a princess among the swine. Listen to them. A carload of filthy, vulgar creeps yelling obscenities at . . . another carload of filthy, vulgar creeps. Goose is their equal, that's for sure. She's got the foul mouth.

Am I . . . am I really a princess? Or am I just another filthy, vulgar creep? The Swede says that's life, trying to decide.

I need someone to turn my straw into gold. I need Rumpelstiltskin. I need a miracle, Lord.

Goose says if you put a sack over their heads, all guys look the same. Well, these guys need sacks, that's for sure. Look at them! Even their teeth are dirty. Can you imagine Richard Hampton with dirty teeth? Sacks wouldn't help the smell, I sadly fear.

But Goose won't have her way today. Two votes against these Marshall creeps, and only one for. Trudy votes with me. Trudy is in love, I think. What an idea! Trudy in love. Trudy in love is all gooey and sticky, a sucker on a hot day. Attractive and repulsive at the same time. Tommy

Lillehaugen is the object of her afflictions, methinks. Trudy said the other day she would like to be one of Tommy's socks, so she could be warm and sweaty from Tommy's foot. Tommy doesn't seem too interested, though. He gets the hots for her ripe, succulent body from time to time. Trudy told me that once he kissed her just after she vomited. Trudy thought this was a sign of true love.

Ooh. There's Tommy's car. One other guy with him. David, I devoutly pray. More likely it's Curtis. I think I saw his weasel eyes peering out. Can't wait to get his sweaty hands on Goose's tits.

OK, so we're going to change cars.

Now this is what life is all about. Sitting in the back seat of Tommy's car with two fat, sex-crazed girls, with two skinny, sex-crazed boys in the front seat. There's a kind of steamy smell in the air, and all the electricity of a boar approaching a sow in heat. What is there here for me? It's like falling into the pit where the outhouse used to be.

Am I so different? Really? I'd like to be David's underwear. Sally in love. Sally in love is single-minded and passionate, devoted . . . all those nice things. I could be good for David. He's too brainy. He needs passion. He lacks emotions. He doesn't have enough fun. He sits and thinks too much. He's too weak, he needs support. I could give him all this. All this and more. David, oh David! Why don't you accept my gift?

Nobody will accept my gift.

The Swede says my price is too high. Nobody could pay what I have in mind. What is that? He won't say. Intimacy, he says. Intimacy beyond what a person can give. What is that? He won't say.

Oh, David, we've come close. There've been times, oh, yes! I remember an afternoon we spent following a boxelder bug just to see what it would do. The time I went hunting with you, and you promised not to shoot anything. The spot in the high grass where the deer had lain, where we sat in the cool sunshine and talked scientifically about sex. Caressing your mind, that's what I was doing. Did you like that? I know you did. I could see it in your eyes. Don't you want some more?

Your eyes are always full of fear, did you know that, David? But that day the fear left your eyes. It's what you could be if you want it. If you let me in.

So close to a great love, David. So close. What does Sandy Kringen offer you? Can it be nearly as good?

A proper distance, says the Swede.

Well, we'll see. Sandy's in Granite Falls today. The sun is shining for the first time in a week, and I'm full of piss and vinegar. Sally full of P and V is hard to ignore. She's a force to be reckoned with. The battle for David is not over yet.

So where is David? Where is the bum? Where, oh where can my little boy be?

I know where I am. In a car with four creeps. I hate them all. God damn them, each and every one.

Why am I here? Where else would I be? This is the only place. The only place. The only place is a lonely place. The lonely place.

All right, there he is! Don't get too loud, now. Try to be ladylike.

Well, this is swell. Three guys in front and three girls in back. David makes an immediate hit by first asking where Sandy is and, second, staring at Goose's tits. Which I admit seem to be protruding a bit more than usual today. I wonder how she engineered that. Maybe if I shift around a little . . . there!

All his for the asking.

* * *

Five thirty already. I'm the only one hungry? Doubtful. Sally predicts: Tommy will turn left here and head out to Streuvel's Drive-In. Where else on a Saturday night? Where is Richard Hampton when I need him?

Oh, an added attraction: Krissy baby is going to wait on us. Fourteen years old and proud to be a woman. Look at those shorts, will ya' now! And the shirt! The poor lass, she can't afford a shirt all the way tuh her waist. Has to tie it in a little bow. How sweet! What's on the menu? Belly button surprise!

Curtis will speak first. He will ask her if she has a tender loin. She will blush, although she has no idea what a tenderloin is or even what Curtis is trying to make it sound like. It sounds funny. Sexually funny. So she will blush, and Curtis will smirk. Tommy and David will laugh. So will Trudy and Goose. I alone will remain silent. No one will notice, except maybe David, and he will disapprove.

I remember when I was 14. Ninth grade. Freshmen, all of us. I was in love. I guess he was my first love. Bob de Buisseret. Mom didn't like him. Too Belgian. Too Catholic. But I loved him. I loved him with passion.

I loved him more than anyone since, including David. Maybe it's all downhill from here.

His family moved away after the ninth grade.

We could have been sweethearts.

The story of my life. Good things disappear. But then, in the ninth grade, that sure was something. I fell in love in history class. He had dark wavy hair. He was slightly shy, with every reason instead to be self-centered. That's always been mighty appealing to me. It's sexy.

Mostly I talked and he listened. I jabbered on about everything, full up with high spirits spilling over. I argued with him. I said America was not the winner in the Revolutionary War. We looked at the major battles: defeat after defeat for our side. Then the French came, and something was happening in Europe, and suddenly it was over. Until 1812, when we damn near lost it all again. He liked it, all my jabber. All my crazy ideas. He got a big kick out of me. We had a good time in History.

I told him that Rumpelstiltskin was misunderstood. I made up the story on the spot. He did that sort of thing to me. He made me want to tell him ridiculous things.

And then he started writing me notes. I found this part of our romance very difficult. Open my mouth and out come the words; I got no problems there. But putting words down on paper, planning them, making a mark, leaving evidence of thoughts on paper—oh, that was hard. I had to be witty, I had to watch my spelling. I'd copy old poems from dusty old books. Some of them, geez!, I didn't have the foggiest notion of what they meant. "Love's not love, my love, which bends to move. Oh, no! Love's no thief of time, but speeds the error soon." It was the sound of love is why I liked it.

Bob liked it, too.

I sent him jokes sometimes.

Once I sent him a note that said, "Your fly is open." I don't remember if I knew what it meant. It was something I heard my brothers say, and laugh about. I thought it must mean something funny.

Bob blushed, but he didn't laugh.

Oh, I was deeply, deeply in love. Simply passing him in the hall made my l'il ol' heart go flutter, flutter, and my face! I felt like a goddamned traffic signal that just turned red. Well, so we'd pass by, look at each other, and smile. I'd kinda melt. And this one time he takes my hand and slips me a folded piece of paper. Our first note. I thought I was going to faint on the spot. I squeezed the piece of paper so hard, and my hand was sweaty, I had trouble unfolding it. It was glued together. I really thought I'd never get it open.

How would I have explained that?

But I got it open. You want to know something funny? I don't remember what it said. Not one word. But I remember the ending. Below the letter part, he crossed out the word "Sincerely" and wrote "too formal." Below that he "Love" was out, and he added "too soon." Below that he wrote "Hopefully."

I damn near wet my pants!

I remember I had to respond. I had to write him a note back. That was the next day. What did I write? Something half joking, I think. "I think your body is grand, but I don't care much for your personality." Or "If you wouldn't mind wearing a sack, we could make sweet music together."

It wasn't that exactly. I'd never heard about wearing sacks, and I don't think I could have said "grand body" or anything like that. But it was words to that effect.

Bob thought it was very funny, whatever it was. He said later that I always made it easy for him to love me. I put him at ease.

I remember passing my note to him. Geez, I nearly died!

I was nervous. I was very excited. Let's face it, I'm rather high-tension at the best of times, and here I'm desperately in love, and 14 years old. So damn young. I had no way to handle this tension, this love. No way to deal with it. I didn't know what it was, even. I felt like someone stuck a bicycle pump in my mouth and was pumping away. I was

filling up with air, getting lighter, taking off. I saw him in
the mass of kids coming toward me, and I was in the mass
of kids going toward him, like two great armies coming
together to do battle. I felt myself getting warmer, and I was
afraid beads of sweat were breaking out on my forehead. I
suddenly forgot how to walk. Oh, Jesus, it's all coming back
to me. I'd put one leg out, and it felt funny, as if the leg
were broken. I had to think about each step. I had to plan
each step. "Right leg forward, shift weight onto right leg.
Left leg forward . . ." A goddamned wooden soldier leading
a student army. I knew I was staring at him, but I couldn't
help it. My head was pounding, and—oh, yes! oh, yes!—my
ears began to ring. I remember. Louder and louder, like a
fire alarm, and I can remember thinking, it's a fire. It's a
goddamned fire! What a time for a fire. But I couldn't stop.
Later with the fire. My ears were ringing, and my eyes. My
eyes stopped working. It was like looking at him through
binoculars. Exactly like binoculars. He was split apart.
There were two of him, one each at the end of the two long
tunnels of my binoculars. Nothing outside the tunnels. A
haze. A haze of colors, mostly green. Sometimes a flash of
red or yellow. He was in clear focus, though. Both of him.

Time. Time just stopped, or almost. From beginning
to end, from start to finish, what are we talking about? Five
seconds? Ten? But it seemed just endless. As nervous as I
was, I remember thinking how peaceful it had become—like
death, only not so unpleasant. Everything in slow motion.

He was staring at me, too. I suppose he knew his
note was coming. I felt like I had this neon sign over my
head: "This girl is about to pass a secret love note to Bob
de Buisseret." I don't doubt I was pretty obvious. But his
eyes were what saved me; I remember that. They made it
peaceful. They gave me the guts. If he had looked away, I

don't know what would have happened. Probably I would have fainted dead away.

I think I just slipped him the note and passed by. That's a proper, objective description of the event; that's seen as a true scientist would see it, as David would say. But how dry. How . . .

We moved slowly together 'til we were close. Eyes locked. Faces smiling. Brows sweaty. My head felt like a jack-o'-lantern, burning inside. I raised my sweaty hand. He raised his. Was his sweaty? I don't remember. I turned my palm up and opened it, like a spring flower. He cupped his hand over mine. Our skin touched, hot, burning, wet. He let his hand lay there, skin on skin, melting together. Then he drew it away, stroking as he pulled away. Petting me really. Petting my hand, and he stopped when all we had left was fingertips to fingertips. He smiled, snatched the note, broke contact, and turned away. I tried to swallow, but there was nothing to swallow. Then I felt the waves of pleasure. Those warm shivers of delight. A climax! A climax, right there in the hallway of Minneota High School. Well, of course, I didn't know what it was, not then. I thought I had peed in my pants.

I remember not knowing what to do. I remember looking on the floor, expecting to see puddles of fluid. I was aware of my breathing, which seemed to me to be hurried and irregular and loud. I tried not to gasp or moan; I wonder if I succeeded. I had the feeling kids were circled around me, watching me, listening to me. "What's wrong with Sally?" "Why is she making noises?"

"She's peeing in her pants."

"Here?"

Sandy Kringen bumped into me and said, "Hi."

"It's the flu!" I remember saying.

* * *

What are we going to do tonight? Same old question, every weekend. Same old answers, too. Swimming? Too far to Dead Coon Lake. We're going tomorrow. The lake has got the itch in it. Movie? We've all seen it.

Oh, but it was good, that movie—*The Glenn Miller Story*. I can't imagine anything better than an hour and a half of June Allyson falling in love with Jimmy Stewart. Bob de Buisseret was like Jimmy Stewart. Was I like June Allyson? I like to think so. Jimmy was killed in a plane crash. Bob's family moved away. June cried. I cried. Was it so different?

So what are we going to do now? We'll drive around, I guess, drive around. Talk about other people, gossip. Pass other carloads. Talk about them while they talk about us.

"I'd like you to meet my friend, my very good friend, Richard Hampton. Richard doesn't talk about people, I should warn you. Only about ideas."

Well, now, things are picking up. There's a watermelon stand, and yes, we'll have one. A hot summer night, we'll drive to a secluded spot, get out of the car. Fresh watermelon, out of the back seat, standing next to David, brushing up against his hard, skinny body, laughing at his jokes. Maybe we'll wander off. Maybe we'll kiss.

Where to have the watermelon? I vote against Trudy's house. Too hot. (How can David and I kiss with Mrs. Snorrasdottir watching?) I vote against the park—might be people there.

This is better. The old Coleman farm, right? Whatever happened to the Colemans, anyway? Why did they leave?

Couldn't make a go of it, they said. Family troubles, they said. None of it made any sense to me. Tommy's father watches over it. Why? Who for? Are the Colemans ever coming back?

A deserted farm. How delightful. How spooky!

Oh, oh! What's this? Oh, Jesus! The goddamned road is under water. Should we proceed, or should we turn around? The boys want to go ahead. Fine for you guys, sure. What happens if there's no road underneath? Maybe it got washed away. It wouldn't be the first time. And then what? Bubble, bubble. Fine for you guys in front. Open door and jump out. Leave the girls in back to drown. No doors in back, and the rear windows in this goddamned Ford only roll down halfway. Maybe I could squeeze out, but how about the tub of lard next to me? Trudy'd get stuck in the window like a fat old bullhead in a pike net. Goose would get stuck in the other window, and I'd drown between two of the fattest asses in Lyon County.

To hell with that. I'll get out here while you drive across.

So, big deal. You'd think they just crossed the Pacific Ocean. Here we are in China. Risk your goddamned life, and you end up in Coleman's front yard.

Dark. Is it ever. Billowing black clouds, moving fast— probably more rain. The yard is nearly a swamp the way it is. Nice looking farmhouse, too. Count Dracula's summer home. Look at it. The place is starting to rot. Look at those cobwebs. Must be 5-pound spiders out here. Oops! Bats? Are those bats? ARE THOSE BATS?!

Paint peeling, fences down, yard full of weeds . . .

Oh, Jesus! Somebody's out there.

Somebody ran across the road there. Over there! That road, the little road running into that grove of trees.

I saw him. Goose saw him. Yes! We both saw him. He had on a hat. He was big. He wasn't a kid. He had on a coat.

Why are you asking these questions? Let's get the hell out of here!

They're going to investigate? Are they crazy? Tommy's father watches over Coleman's farm for them. Tommy, son of his father, has responsibilities. Tommy is not afraid.

Is this relevant?

Something bad is going to happen.

Why not get your father, Tommy? He'd know what to do. Why not call Roger Mohn, Tommy? Yes, let the police handle it.

It seems so quiet. Like death.

Stay in our headlights, Tommy. Stay in the light.

Oh, Jesus! He's been shot!

Am I going to faint? Easy, easy . . . head spinning, mustn't faint. Tommy's been shot. Blood on his face. Blood on his shirt. Is this a dream? It sure doesn't seem real.

Is Tommy dead? David is driving. Good. We'll find Roger Mohn. He'll arrest the killer. We'll be all right. Safe now. Everything's all right now.

The radio is reporting that a prisoner has escaped from Stillwater. Armed and considered dangerous. This can't be real. This must be a dream. Why would a dangerous prisoner come to Minneota? Why would an escaped murderer be lurking in our watermelon spot? It must be a dream.

But my armpits smell like real fear. I don't dream in this much detail.

What lousy luck.

Maybe it's me. I'm a jinx. I can spin gold into straw.

The killer made a big mistake. He made a mistake shooting Tommy. How far can he get out here? They'll catch him now, for sure. They'll put him behind bars. There's no danger to us now. He's the one in danger, now. Only Tommy shouldn't have . . .

I think I'm going to throw up.

Easy . . . easy . . .

Oh, my god! What now? Trudy is trying to climb out the back window. What is she doing? Grab her. Grab her! Where is she going? What does she want? It's safe here.

Save Tommy?

Save Tommy? Too late. It's too late for that. Save us. Save Sally, for Christ's sake!

Don't let Trudy out. She's hysterical.

There, see. She's stuck. I told you she wouldn't fit through those half-down windows.

Goose is good. Goose is talking sense to her. She's calming down. Still stuck in the window, but she's calming down. There, she's free. Lucky the glass didn't break. Lucky she wasn't cut in two.

Trudy cut in two. What a thought. Maybe each half would have grown a new Trudy like a worm. Which half would be better, the Trudy grown from her old ass or the Trudy grown from her old head? Most people would say they'd be damn near the same.

What now? Why are we stopping? David wants to go back? Trudy is right? We've got to try and save Tommy? Are they crazy?

Are you all crazy?! We can't go back. We're safe now. We're safe here. There is where the killer is. If we go back, he'll kill us all. What difference does five more murders make, after the first? He'll want to get rid of the witnesses. It makes more sense to get the police. It's better to get help. We can't help Tommy. Tommy's already dead. Tommy's dead, and we are safe.

Please. Please! Don't you understand?

Let me out here. I'll get out here and go for the police. I'll walk to town. It isn't so far. Please don't go back.

"Let Tommy die."

But we're back at the farmhouse. And, oh my god! There's Tommy. He's alive. He's covered with blood, but he's still alive. He can't seem to move.

Me drive? Are you crazy? You want me to drive? Well, sure, David and Curtis have to get Tommy, but why me? Why not Goose?

Oh, please, God, get me through this.

OK. Stay in control, girl. Just turn the goddamned car around. Easy does it. Oh Jesus, now I've done it. We're stuck in the mud. Don't yell at me, Goose. Rock the car. I know. I know. Rock the car. Back and forth. Back and forth. Killed the engine. Start, you bastard! Don't yell at me! Start, you good-for-nothing piece of junk. Start, you Ford son of a bitch!

Please. Please start. Please, God, make it start.

I'm stuck in the mud. The engine is dead, and a killer is out there, waiting for his chance. This can't be real. This must be a dream. Please, God, make this a dream. Why can't I wake up?

David will start the car. We'll be all right.

Tommy's alive.

Something's funny here. Tommy's alive, and Tommy's smiling.

It's a joke? The blood was really catsup?

But I saw . . .

Jon Coltvet was the "killer"?

A practical joke?

But the escaped prisoner on the radio . . . ?

Coincidence. Pure coincidence. Yes, David, very strange. Defies the laws of probability.

All a joke. All in fun.

Sally shit in her pants, yes. Wasn't that funny? Sally got stuck, yes. Sally killed the engine, yes. Sally was afraid. Sally said to let Tommy die. Yes, very funny.

Oh, no . . .

Damn!

Yesterday was not the best day of my baseball career. I made six errors on a single play, which I believe is a record that will stand for centuries. I was playing third base for the Minneota Midgets. Walnut Grove had a runner on first when the batter hit a soft ground ball to third base, that is, to me. I slapped at it, as was my custom, but I missed it, and it dribbled through my legs. That's one error. The ball came to a stop three or four feet in back of me, so I thought I might still catch the batter at first. I picked up the ball and threw it 20 feet over the first baseman's head. (Error #2) Jon Coltvet, who was playing right field, caught it on the fly. The runner, who had started the play on first base, was rounding second, headed for third, so Jon threw (perfectly) to third base. I dropped the ball. (#3) The runner took off for home. I picked up the ball and threw it in the dirt in front of Tommy Lillehaugen, the catcher. The runner scored. (#4) By this time, the batter had rounded second and was storming into third. Tommy threw (perfectly) to third—that is, low to the second-base side of third—and once more I dropped the ball. (#5) The batter was heading home. I picked up the ball and threw it over the catcher's head into the stands, where Albert Gulbrandson caught it on the fly. This was the sixth error.

Six errors on one play! Two guys scored on a dinky ground ball to third. "That's somethin', ain't it," said Albert later as he returned the ball to me. "You want to save this ball. It's one for the record books."

Today I threw the ball into the Yellow Medicine Creek. (I missed the creek, of course. The ball is still embedded in the mud on the far bank of the river. Some future archeologist will find it and wonder about the strange game played on river banks.)

Can you imagine my feelings after making a mistake of this magnitude? I can recall shards of pain shooting through my body as if a dentist had sunk his drill into a nerve. The stands were full: my family, my friends, the whole town. When it was over, after the two guys had scored and all, there was a kind of hush in the park. Really quiet. Tommy Lillehaugen told me later that he was frightened. He felt scared.

"Did you think the crowd was going to attack me?" I asked Tommy.

"No," he said. "It wasn't like that at all. It was . . . more primitive. Like a sudden fear that your father won't be able to protect you."

I know what he was talking about. I felt the same fear myself. Like the world had suddenly gone crazy. Like the world had become unpredictable.

And the shame was almost unbearable.

4

The Shame of a Viking

I became a "real athlete" in the seventh grade, when I tried out for a position on the Junior High basketball team. Like all young boys in the school, I was taught my values early: Team sports are good, clean fun. They teach you about life—what is fair and what is not; how to come back after a discouraging defeat; that no one player is responsible for the success or failure of the team; that "there's no I in TEAM"; and the most important lesson of all, that effort can beat ability. You can beat a superior player if you try harder than he does. Athletes are also taught "sportsmanship": play fair, be nice to your opponents, don't whine when you're beat, and don't crow when you win. But win! Whatever else you learn, learn how to win.

A player is more popular than a scholar. That's what I learned. Girls don't like "bookworms," which I always thought made my future prospects bleak, and I always thought unfairly so, because intelligent people contribute much more to society than fast, muscular dummies. But then I thought, well, I prefer cheerleaders to female bookworms, so I guess it's human nature. And blessing of blessings, I was one of the tallest kids in my class, so basketball might be a possibility. I was skinny as a rail, with thick glasses, so football was out, and besides, I got my appendix out during the epidemic of 1954, so I had an excuse not to play football, which I didn't like anyway. It hurt, especially with Nails DeBays roaming the field, looking for someone to drive his helmet into the stomach of.

Nails, the younger brother of Debil DeBays, the town bully, was an excellent athlete: strong, fast, coordinated. But he didn't care about football, so he never did much of note, except drive helmets into the bellies of the opposing team members. He just wanted to hurt people. He was mean, and he was dangerous. The teams that played us started using second-string backs to return kickoffs and punts (the only plays Nails was in on; he was too undisciplined to play at other times). And the second-string backs started running out of bounds as soon as Nails appeared before them; they're not stupid. Nails often hit them anyway—what did he care about lines and penalties? So the backs would run out of bounds and keep running to the safety of their own bench. Nails would chase them all the way over. It was quite funny, except for the times he caught up to them.

Bullies were a significant influence in my life, a topic to which I will return. Later. Right now, I'm supposed to be telling you what it means to be an athlete in a small town like Minneota. Well, it means a lot. As an athlete, you become a soldier in the town's armies—one army for each sport: baseball, basketball, and football. You carry the flag against Lake Benton, Ivanhoe, and Sleepy Eye. If you play for a good army, you might even beat Marshall or Tracy. Then you'd be a hero.

So, in the seventh grade, when I tried out for the Junior High basketball team, I had dreams of being a hero. Actually, most of my dreams were of dating a cheerleader. I thought being a hero would help.

But first I had to find an athletic supporter.

I remember the first day vividly. I and five of my friends reported to the coach, Mr. Conners. Mr. Conners started us off on the right note; he called us men! "Men," he said solemnly, "the first practice is Monday at three. Before then, I want you all to get a physical examination from Doc Klein, and pick up your equipment. You'll need a T-shirt, gym shorts, sweat socks, tennis shoes." Then he paused and looked at us funny, like he was sizing us up. "You'd better get an athletic supporter, too. OK, that's it for now. Any questions?"

In a chorus, we answered, "No, sir!" We were "men," we were soldiers.

We gathered outside the coach's office. Curtis Braun asked the question: "What's an athletic supporter?"

No one knew.

I suggested that Curtis ask Mr. Conners.

"You ask him," said Curtis.

No one dared.

On Saturday, we assembled in Doc Klein's office for physical examinations. We weren't sure what to expect, but we trusted Doc Klein and had no apprehension. Doc Klein was the wisest person I knew. Not only did he know all about medicine (not only could he save lives), but also he knew about people. He understood people, what they were after, what they were doing and thinking and why—often better than the people themselves. He seemed to know when to joke and when to be serious, when to threaten and when to plead, when to be angry and when to forgive. He seemed to be able to balance life in these ways, ways I feared (and still do) I would never learn.

I had just learned that Doc Klein was a Jew. This fact I found quite amazing not only because everyone else in town was either Lutheran or Catholic, but also because my only knowledge of Jews was from the Old Testament, men like Moses and Abraham. I began to think that Doc Klein was perhaps a reincarnation of King Solomon. Solomon, like Doc Klein, was good with people and with the balances of life.

Why God would choose to reincarnate Solomon in Minneota was a question that never entered my mind. I thought perhaps it was to guide David Sorenson to some brilliant destiny in the service of the Lord.

Doc began the examination by asking for a urine specimen. Well, of course, that was impossible. I had just peed, and so had all the other kids. I could never pee on demand anyway; something shut down so tightly that I couldn't have gotten fluid out of my body if my life had depended on it. But we were in luck. Jon Coltvet, bless his soul, had overslept, rushed over without peeing, with a full bladder that he was only too happy to unload on demand, as easily as he unloaded farts on demand. Jon managed to fill all six bottles, although the portion in the last, Tommy Lillehaugen's, was a bit skimpy.

We all giggled nervously when we presented our bottles to Miss Ryan, Doc's nurse, who, I noted as I blushed, was an unmarried woman. When Tommy presented his meager offering, Miss Ryan looked up with disapproval, a look that changed quickly to remorse; she was not the kind of person to disapprove of anyone's best effort, especially not a child's. Her disapproval was a reflex, something that occurred before she could stop it. The damage was done, however. Tommy blushed on top of his blush, looking rather like a ripe apple. The rest of us giggled again and looked at Jon. I'm sure Miss Ryan knew what was going on. She was probably praying that Jon didn't have diabetes, for then they would have to disqualify the entire seventh grade.

While Miss Ryan was performing mysterious tests on
the urine samples, we were called one-by-one into Doc's
office. I was first. Doc had me open my shirt and listened
to my heart with one of those medical hearing aids—a
stethoscope? I studied Doc's face, which was odd-looking.
That is, it didn't look at all like the Norwegian and Belgian
faces I was familiar with. It was handsome, not cute, with
a nose that didn't turn up at the end, as the Scandinavian
nose did. I thought he looked like Victor Mature. His hair
was black and curly, not blonde and straight. I began to
construct a theory of why there are variations in people's
bodies, but Doc interrupted my reverie with the first of his
questions, "How's your foot?"

I looked at my foot, which I had sliced up while
mowing the lawn that summer. Doc had warned me at
the time to be very careful with it, to watch for telltale red
streaks going from the cut toward the heart, a sure sign of
blood poisoning. "Wear only white socks," Doc said at the
time, "the dye in colored socks will kill you." I checked the
cut several times an hour, terrified. And Doc also gave me
a tetanus shot. "You know what happens if you don't get a
tetanus shot, don't you? Lockjaw." Doc said it slowly and
darkly. "Lahhhk . . . jahhhw!" In my nightmares, I confused
the two dangers, as red streaks ran quickly from foot to jaw,
causing my jaw to slam shut, never to reopen. Doc knocked
out a tooth and attached a rubber straw, with which I used
to eat cream of mushroom soup with for the rest of my life.
I knew that I would never experience the French kiss that I
had read about.

"Fine," I said. "All healed."

"And how's your father? Been cheating on his diet?"

"A little. Mostly rhubarb pie."

"We've got to watch his drinking, David. Not just for the ulcer. He drinks too much. Strange town, Minneota. Nice people, but they all drink too much. Dangerous stuff, alcohol. You'd do well to stay away from it, David. Rots your brain."

I tried to conjure up an image of a rotting brain. It looked suspiciously like lutefisk.

"I had a sip of beer once," I said, buttoning up my shirt. "It tasted terrible. I don't understand why people drink it." I thought I could interest Doc in an intellectual discussion, something he seemed to enjoy as much as me. "Why do you suppose people drink too much when it's not good for them? I mean, they drink too much and get sick and throw up. If they did that with food, they'd never touch the food again. But alcohol, they go right back to it. They want more. It's crazy, isn't it?"

Doc laughed. He was used to my crazy ideas. The last time I was in, for my foot, I pestered him with questions about the structure of the foot—why does it need so many bones? I drew a few alternative architectures. "I'm not trying to compete with God. I just want to understand the foot," I had insisted.

Since Doc didn't take my bait, I presented my own theory of alcoholism. "I think it's because alcohol lets them do things they wouldn't do when they're sober. If they do something bad, they can blame it on the liquor. But it's not all bad. It's not all fights and arguments. A lot of people can't be silly unless they're drunk. Lots can't have fun unless they're three sheets to the wind, as my father calls it." I imagined my mother's clothesline with three bedsheets billowing in the wind. I wondered why that's the visual metaphor for drunkenness. Drunks throw up. I thought that might be why. If you drink far too much and throw up three times during the night, you would have three sheets to wash in the morning.

"And my father never tells me he loves me unless he's drunk. I think he finds it embarrassing."

"Too bad we have to have an excuse for telling someone we love them," said Doc.

"Yeah," I said. "Why is it, do you suppose, we have to have an excuse for something like that? Why are we embarrassed by expressions of love?"

Doc laughed again but didn't reply. Instead he shuffled some papers and read a list of symptoms. I denied them one by one. "Anything wrong with you that you can think of?"

"No, sir."

"OK, that's it. You're a good kid, David. The town expects a lot from you." Doc wrote something on a piece of paper. "Just remember, you can't be an athlete unless you keep yourself in shape. Stay away from booze and cigarettes."

"Cigarettes! Now there's a question: Why do people smoke? I don't even have a theory!"

"And don't masturbate. You don't masturbate, do you, David?"

"Why?" I asked, warily.

"It's not good for you. Why do you think they call it self-abuse? No, you won't grow hair on your hand, but you know, that stuff about blindness, it's not all hokum. You can screw up your circulation by masturbating, and the blood doesn't get to where it should, to feed the tissues and prevent infection. Blindness, gangrene, you name it. I wouldn't take the chance. Would you?"

"I might risk one eye." An old joke, even for a seventh grader.

"Send in Tommy when you leave."

* * *

Jon Coltvet's urine turned out to be free of major detectable diseases, so we left Doc's office, clutching our medical forms, and walked the block and a half to the Big Store. August Deschepper—everyone called him Sugar—was the clerk in the men's department. Sugar was wildly obese, an enormous man who walked by throwing first one side of his immense body forward and then, when the first side had stopped reverberating, the other side. It was like watching a human made of Jell-O. People said Sugar had a glandular problem, which I always interpreted as "It's not his fault." Sugar was a nice man in any case; nobody disliked him except his wife, who claimed it was indeed his fault.

We turned over our list of needed apparel, and Sugar set about to fill our orders. Curtis had had the brilliant idea of simply adding "athletic supporter" to the list, in the hope that whatever it was could be gotten at the Big Store. It was a good idea since the Big Store carried nearly everything, including groceries and hardware in addition to clothing. In fact, if we couldn't get it at the Big Store, we were more or less out of luck; we'd have to go to Marshall.

But this time: Bingo! After we had been fitted with shirt, shorts, socks, and shoes, as we waited in fevered anticipation, Sugar returned to our list. "And supporters. OK. Right over here."

A sigh of relief. A tingle of excitement.

Short lived. Sugar stopped his Jell-O roll near the shelves on the far wall and turned to us with a question that renewed the panic in our hearts. "What size?"

Size? I looked at Curtis, and Curtis looked at me. I think Tommy moaned faintly. I realized that nobody was going to answer. We would stand there, looking at Sugar, saying nothing. He would stand there, waiting for an answer, and we would stand there, silent. We're going to look at each other until kingdom come. This is it, I thought. The rest of my life will be spent staring at Sugar Deschepper.

Sugar smiled softly. "Small, I'd guess."

It was the kind of divine intervention that convinced me there was, indeed, a God. Our luck was holding.

He turned again to the wall shelves and handed us an orange box with bicycle spokes on the cover. "Athletic supporter, small." That's all it said on the outside. No picture, other than the bicycle spokes, and no instructions. Each of us blushed in turn, as Sugar passed out the boxes. Sugar then put each boy's collection into a paper bag, noted the price for the family account, and sent us away with a cheery smile.

"Whoo-eee!" said Tommy Lillehaugen.

However intense our curiosity, we were not about to open our mystery packages in front of the Big Store on a Saturday afternoon. The band of men broke up into individual boys, and each of us went home. Each went to his bedroom, shut the door, and opened the orange box.

What I pulled from the box was obviously a garment of some sort. Something to be worn. It looked vaguely like underwear. It had a wide circular elastic band from which hung two straps on one side and a pouch of some sort on the other. I had never seen anything like it in my life.

I examined the supporter, looking for clues to its function and purpose. Aha! I found the label. I knew that labels are on the inside back of an article of clothing. I arranged the supporter thus and put it on. What I didn't know, of course, was that supporters—the reason, to this day, escapes me—have their labels on the outside front, so I had put my supporter on backwards and inside out.

I looked at myself in the mirror. My tiny penis dangled lifelessly between two broad straps. I turned around and looked over my shoulder at the white pouch that ballooned from my rear. I had a sinking feeling that I didn't have the knowledge I needed to cope effectively with life. It was a common feeling in my youth.

What could possibly be the purpose of such a contrivance? Why would an athlete want free access to his genitals? To pee in a hurry, in an emergency? I discarded that hypothesis quickly. Other athletic clothing seemed designed to discourage urination. The shorts, for example, had no zipper or buttons of fly.

I turned my attention to the pouch in back. I decided that the purpose of the supporter must be to protect the athlete from embarrassment if he should become too excited and get diarrhea, as had happened to me often enough. The pouch, I determined, must be a sort of pooper-scooper. *How disgusting*, I said to myself. But it's the price you pay for being a real athlete.

On Monday at 3:00, we found to our dismay that Coach Conners had asked us to report to practice early, so he could fill us in on the rules of the game and customs of the practice sessions. We had hoped to watch the older boys put on their supporters. No such luck, it appeared. We undressed slowly, in a race of losers, in hopes that someone else would put on his supporter first and perhaps comment on its purpose. Every one of us stepped into his supporter backwards. The practice lasted for about an hour and a half. Then the team began to strip for showers. The laughter of the older boys alerted Coach Conners. Solemnly he informed us that we had our supporters on backwards. He returned to the coaches' dressing room. The sound of muffled laughter drifted out.

This must happen every year, I thought. Why does he still find it funny?

Nothing was more important to the community than the relative standings of its athletic teams. Football was first, coming in the fall. Basketball was the winter pastime, the winter devotion. Baseball started in the spring, in the high school, and continued throughout the summer with recreational play. A true warrior of the community played on all these teams, and I was determined to be a true warrior.

One of the requirements for being an athlete was disdain for intellect. This was hard for me, since my goal in life was to be a scientist. I was a good student; I got good grades. I soon discovered that I would be OK—the other guys on the teams wouldn't make fun of me—if 1) I kept my intellectual curiosity to such questions as whether or not a fly in a moving boxcar would crash into the end of the boxcar as soon as it left the ground, and 2) I kept my name off the A honor roll. Even the B honor roll was suspect, but the football captain made it regularly, so it was reluctantly approved by the lettermen.

All I had to do to make the B roll was get one B grade every six weeks. Sounds easy, but in fact it was very difficult. I often failed, getting all A's, through no fault of my own. I plotted my strategy carefully, varying my B's from class to class because I didn't want college registrars to get the idea that I was particularly weak in one subject. I analyzed the grading systems of each teacher and so knew, by the end of the grading period the exact score I would have to achieve on the final examination to get a B for the period. I then deliberately answered questions incorrectly to achieve that score. As a sideshow diversion to go along with my masterful manipulation of the grading process, I exposed my answers to my classmates, who regularly tried to copy my answers anyway. I took care to make my answers plausible, an art I enjoyed, although it sometimes led to my downfall. Sometimes my answers were too plausible, and the gullible teacher perceived some sort of major insight and gave me an A+. At first, I would argue that my answer was not brilliant, simply wrong, but I had to abandon this tactic because it confused the teacher, angered my cheating classmates, and never accomplished its goal.

Once Miss Drabble, our English teacher that year, announced in class that three students had yet to hand in their book reports and that if they failed to do so, they would get an F for the period. I was one of the three. I rarely did an assignment before the last possible day. But I had never been afforded an opportunity like this! An F! I had never achieved a C, much less a failing grade. My God!, I would be a hero on the basketball team! And best of all, I didn't have to do anything to earn my F; it had been promised in a public forum. When the grades came out, however, the other two students got F's, but I got an "Incomplete." Furious, I went to Miss Drabble and demanded my F. "It's unfair to give F's to the others and not to me."

I liked Miss Drabble a lot. She was a good teacher, interested in her students, full of praise and reluctant to criticize; she honored ideas, which—always puzzling to me—few of my teachers did. She was also an attractive young woman, so there was kind of a sexual buzz that permeated our discussions, from my end at least. She usually wore sweaters, which proclaimed her ample bosom.

And she had a nervous habit I enjoyed, which was to pull at her sweater at the nipples—I don't know why; perhaps the sweater would bind and catch on these mammoth structures. Since her hands were usually covered with chalk, her nipples, by the end of the day, were outlined in brilliant white. As far as I know, she was completely unaware of the targets she had painted on her chest. For a young boy, however, it was exhilarating. At times, I would nearly swoon.

"I know it's unfair," she said in response to my complaint. "But, David, I can't give you an F." She paused, searching for the right words. "It wouldn't reflect on you, it would reflect on me. This is my first year of teaching. How would it look if I gave David Sorenson an F? I'd be the laughingstock of the faculty." She began to cry, and I felt like an ass. I wrote a hurried essay and ended up on the A honor roll. Since my position on the honor roll was established after an incomplete, it was announced a week after the other students were listed. A special announcement, just for me! Broadcast it to the world, why don't you?! "David Sorenson has smarts coming out of his ears!" The other guys on the basketball team refused to practice one-on-one with me. "Brains make me nervous," said Jon Coltvet. And Jon was one of my best friends!

As much as I wanted to be an athlete, a warrior for the Minneota Vikings, I was never very good at it. My athletic skills were not bad, about average, and except for Nails DeBays, I was the fastest kid in our class. But I was thin (how I hated being called a "beanpole"), and my brains made me nervous. In baseball, for example, I would consider every possible way a play might go wrong, rendering me useless if the ball were hit to me. Basketball was my best sport, but I lacked self confidence; I would pass to a teammate rather than shoot. The ball rarely came back to me. If it did, I would stumble authoritatively and give up the ball on a traveling call.

I do owe to basketball, however, my first experience with . . . well, I don't know what you call it. Athletes today call it the "zone," something like that. It's when you start playing so well that everything seems to go right; you lose all sense of your self. It's the strangest damn experience! You'd do anything to repeat it but, for me at least, it was far from common.

In the ninth grade, when I was starting on the junior-high basketball team, in a tournament game at Tyler, I was having an average game. I think I had four points, with a minute left to play, our team behind, 38-32. I drained a jump shot from the corner. I stole the inbound pass from the opposing team and laid it in. 38–36, with 15 seconds left. Tyler brought the ball up court; I knocked the ball out of the hands of their star player—I still remember his name! Larry Peters—and into the hands of Curtis Braun. Curtis was fouled immediately. He was given one free throw, the rules at the time, so he had to intentionally miss to give us a chance to tie the game. He did so, and the rebound flew into—of course!—my hands. I turned, I shot: nothing but net. In the overtime, I scored 8 points to Tyler's 2. My teammates hugged me, Coach Conners hugged me, and Sandy Kringen hugged me. I was in heaven!

In later years (including now), I have often thought of that experience. It's bigger than a "hot streak," smaller than a good life. It's a moment when everything clicks, everything feeds off of everything else, you're doing everything right. Your emotions, your intellect, and your body are all synchronized; you're being the best you can possibly be. You are totally un-selfconscious. If you are conscious of anything, it's being one with the universe. It's just wonderful. I decided that the purpose of life was to experience such moments. I still believe it.

I was much too thin and fragile and cowardly to play football well. With guys like Nails roaming the field, looking for someone to hit, I would fumble to avoid being tackled, often fumbling the ball directly to the tackler with a pitiful look on my face. But luckily, in tenth grade, when boys were expected to try out for the team, I had my appendix removed, so I couldn't play. I couldn't be expected to play. Thank goodness!

I got appendicitis the same time as about three quarters of my classmates. In fact, about half the high school had their appendix removed in one summer. Doc Klein was at a loss to explain the epidemic; we blamed it on the popcorn at the Hooray Theatre. Why popcorn, I wondered? I think people thought the large, scratchy kernels passed through the appendix and injured it, inflamed it. Stupid theory, but the epidemic was very real. It wasn't some kind of mass hysteria, either; I'm not capable of imagining that kind of pain!

Doc Klein told me he once took out 11 appendixes in one day, 10 from his own patients and one from a patient of an Ivanhoe doctor, by mistake. "I just got on a roll," Doc said, laughing. "Thank God they were all appendectomies."

So football was out, and basketball was infrequently successful. It was clear that, as much as I hated baseball, it was my only hope.

I played more baseball than any other sport. Baseball went on endlessly, it seemed to me, through the year, through my life. In high school, baseball was the spring sport, but we also played all summer long. We started as the Peanuts, graduated to the Peewees, moved up to the Midgets—summer teams for little tykes. Then we played on the high-school team, then we played on the Junior Legion team. We completed our 25-year career on church softball teams, until our knees gave out. We called softball "kittenball"; the name was the only thing about the sport I liked.

My biggest problem with baseball was my deep-seated fear of the ball itself. A baseball, after all, is like a large rock that is constantly being thrown or hit in your direction. Many of my teammates, hard and muscular from work on the farm, were capable of propelling a baseball at speeds near a hundred miles an hour. Typically, these farm boy pitchers were also uncontrollably wild, so stepping to the plate was a justifiably terrifying experience. I imagined my skull as a coconut: hard, but with few mushy spots. The most prominent mushy spot was the temple, which, I assumed, provided direct access to the brain. A fastball on the temple was certain death, or worse: permanent paralysis. Stories filled the sports sections of newspapers of promising young shortstops whose careers were brought to a halt by beanballs. Don Zimmer, who played for St. Paul, had been one of my favorites, a certain major leaguer, the heir apparent to Peewee Reese of the Brooklyn Dodgers, when a beanball . . . well, he played again, but he was never the same.

And what if the fastball hit the groin? I was tormented by images of a young man with a permanent crouch, with a hesitant limp, forever gone the possibility of fatherhood or even sex.

But I had a surprisingly fluid swing, and I usually hit the ball, which gave me an advantage over the hard, muscular farm boys who could hit the ball a mile but usually struck out. I punched the ball, usually on the ground toward the pitcher, but sometimes the ball would encounter a pebble and dart to the left, or the pitcher would slip, or something would happen, and I would beat it out for a base hit. With a moving ball, there's always a chance. (I began developing this theory into a philosophy of life; you could do worse!) Once I hit a ground ball to left field that disappeared into a gopher hole. I was awarded a homerun, although nobody knew for sure what the proper ruling was. There was nothing in the rule book about gopher holes. It was the only homerun of my career. But my batting average, thanks to numerous pebbles, slips, bloops, and twisters, was usually over .300, and often I had the highest average on the team.

My fielding average was often under .300. I don't know if you know baseball statistics, but a batting average (percentage of hits per at-bats) over .300 is very good. A fielding average (percentage of achieved outs per chances) should be close to .900, so a fielding average under .300 is dreadful. What it means, in other words, is that in some years I was more likely to hit safely in a given turn at bat than I was to catch a ball thrown or hit to me in the field.

I thought too much to be good at baseball, a game that moved slowly even in its hurried parts. I analyzed each situation and worried about the potential plays to be made. For example, one year I played shortstop (they kept moving me around, trying to find my "best" position). Here's the way I thought: There's a runner on first, so I have to remember to cover second base on a bunt. The batter is left-handed, so I (and not the second baseman) have to cover second on a steal. I should follow a hit to left field, that is, run out into left field to relay throws from the left fielder (this is especially important in Peewee play, because none of us could throw more than ten yards or so). I should cover second on a hit to right field. On and on and on. By the time a ball was hit in my direction, I was so nervous I would jump straight up in the air, swat at the passing grounder with my glove, and sprawl on top of the ball if I managed to knock it down at all. My nervous analyses of potential plays were compounded by my fear of the ball, which led me to assume fielding postures (usually several feet from the path of the ball) that protected my groin from possible injury. To this day, I am remembered as the worst fielder in the history of Minneota baseball. I still hold several fielding records: lowest fielding average for a shortstop, most errors by a first baseman, etc.

I told you about the six errors on one play. In another game, an opposing player ripped my pants off. This game was the District finals, so there was a big crowd, really big, including most of the girls I was trying to impress at the time. About the fourth inning, I hit a single. The next guy up hits it hard to right field, another single. A man on first base should make third on a single to right, so I round second base without breaking stride. Their right fielder makes a good throw, but I slide into third ahead of the tag. Safe!

When their third baseman leans over to make the tag, he steps into my back pocket. You know those baseball uniforms? Cheap flannel, with one huge pocket in the back. I don't know what the pocket was for. Your glove? I don't know. Anyhow, this guy's foot is in it now.

I'm feeling good about making it to third, a good slide, a great photo for the Messenger. Their third baseman is not feeling as good, since he didn't get me out. So I move quickly, and he doesn't move at all. I jump up, but my pants stay down. There I am, Mr. Hero, buck naked at third base.

Actually, I wasn't completely naked. I was wearing my athletic supporter. Thank God, I had the pouch in front!

The Swede? Heck, yes, I knew the Swede. He was livin' in that old shack there, up there by, well, it was Harvey Muylaert lived there then, across the street from Harvey, up near the edge of town. The Swede, yes sir, he was somethin', that guy, why he pulls down the marquee on the Hooray Theater, you heard that, didn't you? Goldarnit, the Swede was always doin' somethin' like that, some kind of blamed mess all the time. Oh, sure, he drank a bit here and there, and it kill him, I think he died from it. But he was a pretty nice guy.

I remember one time, the Swede got all upset over this here tree that Old Man Sorenson was agonna cut down. He was, the Swede was, tryin' to get the city to stop it. This was before it didn't work and he climbed up in the tree to roost and save it that way. But the city council was havin' a big meeting to discuss the tree, and the Swede, of course he was wantin' to be there, to put in his two cents. He was doin' some work for me that day, well, he was a darned good worker for a day or two. So I asks him to take a look at this old Ford I got sittin' out by the barn. I just got it a new battery, but it's got a lotta things wrong, ignition, needs plugs, and the Swede, he was pretty good with cars, so he says sure, he'll take a look at it. Well, the old battery, it's pretty corroded and everything around it, too, eaten up like it does, and the Swede had to clean out all that blamed stuff and put in a couple of new cables and things, too, it was pretty messy in there. He sets in this new battery and of course it drops clean through the platform it's supposed to sit on. Well, darned if the danged battery don't start leaking! We was doin' Spring work, and

I was busy plantin' over on the north eighty, and I says, well, darn it all! it'll just have to wait. But the Swede somehow got the blamed battery out, the new one, which was wedged down there with the tie rods and junk, and he gets in the truck and gets me a new one. A NEW new one.

Finally the Swede gets the old car runnin', nice as you could ask, but it's gettin' pretty late there and, well, we was both thinkin' about the council meeting, so we all piled into the pickup for to get there on time. The council, well, they don't do nothin', as usual, but we was sittin' there, and the Swede was gettin' this funny look to him, so I says, you sick or somethin'?, and he don't say nothin', just looks down in his lap. I looks too. Man alive! I couldn't believe it! There wasn't nothing there! The goshdarned battery acid ate clean through his overalls, and there he sits in his BVDs. Well, I starts to laugh. When I get to laughin', I go at it pretty good, and it ain't no easy thing for me to shut it off. The council and the others, they was wonderin' what the heck I'm laughin' at, 'cause the council sure ain't sayin' anythin' funny. And I can't say. Well, pretty soon the Swede starts laughin', too, and the two of us was sittin' there in the back, yuckin' it up somethin' fierce! I gives the Swede my cap to put over the biggest hole, which was in the central section, but there was little holes all over, and more come every minute, it seems to me. But nobody said nothin'. Maybe they thought me and the Swede was samplin' the dandelion wine or somethin'. Anyhow, we just sat there 'til everybody went home, and then we walked out, the Swede, well, he was walkin' pretty close behind me, like a couple of dancers in vaudeville, and even I was thinkin' this looks kinda funny, but, geez, I just laughed and laughed.

Beginning of the End

I was the architect of the incident at Coleman's farm.
I was, therefore, a perpetrator of Sally's pain, although
certainly I did no more than provide the opportunity for
her to express the traits that were the ultimate basis of her
embarrassment. She needn't have responded as she did.
Goose didn't. Nor did Trudy for that matter, and Trudy,
most would have said, possessed far less character than Sally.
Even after the event, someone different from Sally might
have laughed it off—a practical joke is all it was.

No, it does no good to blame David Sorenson. After
all, I was merely carrying on an honored tradition of
the practical joke. Mine was not the most elaborate the
community had ever seen, nor was it by any means the most
embarrassing. Consider, for example, the fake letter from
the Internal Revenue Service that led Ben Dorsey to confess
a felony fraud, or the one-way see-through glass Ray de
Grunne installed in Ellen Korchak's shower, allowing us to
watch from outside. The people of Minneota were forever
thinking up grand schemes to involve their best friends
in manufactured environments, hoping to elicit amusing
behavior. Candid Camera, live. Every young mechanic
was sent out looking for a left-handed monkey wrench,

and at each place he asked they replied that they had them last week; try someone else. It took days, sometimes, for the joke to run its course. Someone like Cora Ruysbroeck would take pity, and spill the beans.

The practical joke! Why, the community itself had begun as a practical joke, at least the naming of it. And the community was proud of its practical-joke history, retelling the story at 25-year intervals, at celebrations of the town's birth.

The story of how Minneota got its name, strangely enough, is related to the story of Brown Wing and the Sioux Wars. What Brown Wing had begun was not to end for many years, not until Sitting Bull was shot in 1890, 28 years later. The Indian battles were to bring many colorful characters to the Midwest, certainly not the least of these George Armstrong Custer, the handsome and egotistical General of the U.S. Army who led his troops to total destruction at Little Bighorn. When Custer first came west, after the Civil War, his troops had traveling with them an Army surgeon, an old-looking young man by the name of Thomas Seals. Everyone called him Doc. Shortly after Custer arrived in Dakota territory, Doc Seals made the fortunate decision to quit the cavalry.

In the beginning, Doc Seals operated a general store in Flandreau, South Dakota, trading mostly with the Indians. After that, he drifted slowly eastward, until he reached a small group of settlers who had organized a community around a spot where the trains of the Winona and St. Peter Railroad stopped to take on water for their boilers. The settlement was later to be known as Minneota, but now, in

1874, it was called Pumpa, the Norwegian word for water tank. Minneota was one of the original tank towns.

Doc Seals opened another general store in Pumpa, where he found himself in competition with the store owned by Nils Jaeger, a settlement pioneer. Doc of course could offer more than Jaeger: doctoring, tooth pulling, and drugs of all varieties, including a popular cure-all tonic known as Doc's Bitters. The formula was secret, but the bite of the bitters was legend. "Spun me around and kicked me out the back door," said one farmer. The Indians around Flandreau had been fond of Doc's Bitters, too. Doc was a new kind of "medicine man," and his magic was powerful indeed. Their visions were big and bountiful, always in color, with Doc's Bitters—better than the holy tobacco, better than the vision quest. Doc's guarantee, however, included only colds and the flu, measles, epilepsy, and constitutional inertia.

One day Doc found his supply of bitters running low and thought to extend the supply by dilution. A young Dakota brave purchased a bottle. Some hours later he returned and demanded to see the medicine man. Fiercely he waved the nearly empty bottle of bitters in Doc's face, all the while shouting, "Minneota! Minneota! Minneota!" Doc hadn't the slightest notion of what the Indian was complaining about, and finally the young brave left his store.

But the word, the word stuck with him. A nice sound, like Minnesota, like a singular form of Minnesota. Minneota. He let it roll on his tongue as he said it over and over, and he put the two together: Minneota, Minnesota. It was a pleasure.

It meant "too much water in the whiskey."

But all Doc Seals knew was that it sounded nice. Or so he said. Doc's word can be doubted in this matter, for had he known the meaning, it would have added to his pleasure, and he would have been more likely, not less likely, to name the community with his Indian word. It does seem a bit unlikely that Doc had no idea what the bottle-waving brave was complaining about.

In the late 1870's, the growing community of Pumpa began agitating for a better name, a real name, an official name, something permanent for a settled settlement. The post office had been named Nordland, but nobody seemed to want to continue with that, least of all the U.S. Postal Service, which had Nordlands and Norselands peppered throughout the Scandinavian Midwest. Some liked the idea of using the name of the ford by which the railroad crossed the river nearby—Upper Yellow Medicine Crossing. Doc Seals suggested the name "Minneota," but he had few supporters. Norwegian nationalists championed Oslo and Eidsvold. A small group wanted Horten. A large group wanted Jaegersville, after Nils Jaeger, the settlement pioneer. Doc's rival. An election was called for February, in 1878, to choose a name by democratic vote. Horten and Jaegersville were the clear favorites.

On the day of the election, on the very day and before the polls closed, John Swanson rode into the village on his mule with a sack of mail. In the mail was a letter from Washington, D.C., informing "local authorities" that the town had been officially designated Minneota. The townspeople were aghast, then furious. It was obvious Doc Seals had something to do with this, but what? How?

Doc and his friends, on the other hand, broke out the bitters: a celebration! Doc surrounded himself with poetic frontiersmen, the sort that live aggressively to generate a good story they can later tell their friends. And this! This was a beauty! What incredible fortune, that the word from Washington would come on the very day of the election.

Lewis Anderson, one of Doc's less intelligent friends, heard that they were counting the ballots, even though the town's name had been decided. He stomped out of Doc's store and marched over to the train depot. He seized the cigar box full of ballots and threw them into the potbellied stove. The outcome of the election was never known.

Feelings ran high for some time afterwards. Many townspeople were particularly hostile toward Doc Seals. They wanted to arrest him—"For what?" asked Nils Jaeger, his competitor and friend. They wanted to have the name of the town changed legally to Jaegersville—"What for?" asked Nils Jaeger, who had never been comfortable with the idea of a town named after him. So gradually the tumult subsided, and "Minneota" stuck. Its literal meaning, "much water," was acceptable, though there was not much water around Minneota, and its meaning-in-context, "too much water in the whiskey," inspired a certain pride, suggesting a rough, frontier town like Tombstone or Deadwood. So Minneota it was, Minneota forever.

A new beginning.

I was attracted to Sally, mightily so at times, and we did date for a while. I suspect I broke up with her because my parents approved of our relationship, one of the few girls in Minneota on which they deigned to bestow their blessing—at least until she had the affair with Mr. Swenson, the history teacher. Sally was acceptable to my parents because—get this!—her parents drove a Ford! That's the way Minneota was. There were "warnings" about "mixing the faiths," i.e., Lutherans dating Catholics, but it was cars that incurred the wrath of parents.

The people of Minneota took their cars seriously. In the late fall, the new models arrived, covered, shielded from view, with huge question marks on the cover: **The New Chevrolet! ???? See it November 7 at your dealer's showroom!** The unveiling was a major event in the community, with coffee and doughnuts and brochures that compared the new model with its competitors. The Ford, the Chevrolet, and the Plymouth. There were other car companies—one saw a Studebaker now and then—but these companies were not represented in the village of Minneota. Chevy was the best seller, but Ford was moving up, thanks to the incredible design breakthrough they had engineered with the 1949 Ford. That design held, as most of them did, for three years, until they stretched it out in 1952.

I developed several theories about why the community accepted or rejected relationships based on automotive compatibility. My first theory was that people were competitive about their cars, that they were like players on a sports team: they didn't like members of their team to fraternize with members of the other team. Ford owners wanted to ridicule Chevy owners, beat them away from stop signs, yell "Get a horse!" at them as they changed a flat tire along Highway 68. They didn't want to share punch at a wedding reception with them. In addition, by this time, the deep divisions in the community based on automobile ownership had been institutionalized by their control of previous relationships, so that all the Chevy owners were related to one another, by blood or marriage, and all the Ford owners were related in the same fashion. But there were no links from camp to camp. "They're not our people," my mother said one night, as I was leaving to take Goose DeCoster, the daughter of the local Chevrolet dealer, to the Hooray Theater for a movie. "You can't marry her, so why date her?"

My sister Jeannie married Doug DeCoster, the son of the Chevy dealer. My father Pete was the Ford dealer.

This was sacrilege of the highest order! This was mixing automotive bloodlines at the level of royalty! Nobody went to their wedding (except for a few close, rebellious friends). I wanted to attend, but my parents forbade it. A week or so after the wedding, I asked Albert Gulbrandson, a local farmer, what he thought was going on. Albert replied, "Well, you know, it ain't just cars. All the Ford owners, they's all Lutheran. And all the Chevy owners, they's Catholic. And it's tractors, too. If you's Lutheran and drive a Ford, you buy a John Deere. Catholics drive Chevys and buy Farmall tractors. I don't know a single Lutheran with a Farmall or a Chevrolet, not a single one. Gosh darn strange when think about it."

The Swede's theory was that the Lutheran/Catholic dimension was basic. But people didn't like to admit to religious prejudice, so they chose a correlated dimension—car preferences—on which to base their approval decisions. Tractors would have worked, except that not everyone had a tractor. Everyone had a car.

Oops, I'm meandering again. I was telling you about my relationship with Sally. I want to tell you about my first kiss.

It was 1952 when I first kissed Sally, which was my first kiss ever. I had taken Sally to the skating rink twice now. "Taken her," that is, as in asking her to go, being with her at the rink, skating together once or twice, sitting by the wood stove together in the warming shack, sharing a blanket. I had read somewhere that a kiss was inappropriate until at least the third date, and the movie coming up this Saturday, I figured, was Date No. 3. Time for action. I planned the kiss in intricate detail, practicing on a pillow for weeks beforehand. The arms were my first problem: Where do the arms go? Both on top of hers? Both below hers? Some alternating pattern? Which alternating pattern, her right up with her left down, or the reverse? (Must remember that her right is my left, I wrote in my notebook.) Then it was noses, where do they go? How long should the kiss last? Most importantly, how do I lead up to this event? How do I communicate my intentions, and how do I gauge her willingness? At times it seemed hopelessly complicated, and I despaired. I thought of the priests and the nuns, who didn't have to think about such things, and I formed the belief that their motivation to such callings was a desire to avoid the torment I was going through.

Maybe I should just stick to science, I thought, bury myself in my lab and make great discoveries to benefit the human race. I have no time for women. With a mind like mine, it's a gift, I shouldn't spend it on frivolous problems like kissing. I looked at the array of test tubes on my desk, each corked and labeled. Each contained one of Curtis Braun's farts. I was opening one per day, tracking scientifically the decay curve of fart aroma. So far, the stimulus had lost none of its potency, although I was beginning to doubt my measuring instrument—my nose. I thought perhaps I was hallucinating the smell, from expecting it, knowing it. Perhaps I should have Sally over. She could smell the test tubes with no preconceptions. And she would have to get used to sharing my life as a scientist, if she were to be my wife. Would she be my wife? Probably, I thought. I couldn't imagine anyone else, and this kiss, well, that's a commitment of sorts.

The movie at the Hooray Theater was an old Ma and Pa Kettle, and I bought two bags of popcorn, as planned, in spite of the fact that Frosty DeCoster's popcorn was being blamed for the recent epidemic of appendicitis in town. Sally refused to let me pay for her ticket, though it was only 25 cents, and also bought her own bag of popcorn, leaving me looking rather silly with my two bags. We picked a pair of seats on the left side of the theater, about midway down to the screen; the total audience was maybe 10 or 12, and the others preferred the right side. Jon Coltvet was there with his brother, whispering, pointing, and giggling from time to time. I felt proud. One bag of popcorn spilled a bit, when I bent over to park my gum under the seat. I munched my popcorn furiously, finishing both bags well before Sally finished hers. The feature had not even begun yet, the cartoon was still running, but I had plans that required a free arm.

As soon as I slipped my arm around Sally's back, it went to sleep. The pain was unbearable, and I pulled it back. I hadn't counted on this, nothing like this happened with the pillow and the two chairs. I tried it again with the same result. The arm around Sally was a key element in my plan to perpetrate a kiss—it was to be a clear signal of my intention, so this development set me thinking of alternative cues. I was not following the movie, and didn't laugh when I should have, so Sally looked at me as if I had just sneezed in church. Nothing is going right, I thought. It's a disaster.

Sally took my hand in hers. A warm flush swept over me, and I thought for sure I was going to pass out. My hand was greasy from the buttered popcorn. I pulled my hand away from hers, to wipe it on my trousers, but when I returned my hand for more holding, hers was gone. I rubbed the side of her coat in the darkness, hoping to find the missing hand. She asked me what I wanted, and when I didn't reply, pushed my hand away. She slapped it gently. I tried to slip my arm around her shoulders again, but the pain was immediate and intense.

After the movie, we trudged silently homeward through a light snow. The sound of our boots on the fallen snow was a peculiar crunch, crunch, crunch, a sound like no other on earth, I thought, except possibly the sound the dentist makes when he packs filling into a cleaned-out cavity. The street lights made an eerie cavern of light in the falling snow, like a cocoon, and in the cocoon there were no sounds at all, a deep silence except for the crunch, crunch, crunch of our boots, packing the snow. I was quite overwhelmed by the lights, and the snow, and the silence, it seemed to me quite mystical, a time of great events, when Jesus would reveal Himself to two ordinary children in Minneota, things of that nature. Perhaps it was an omen, portending a sexual epiphany. I was encouraged.

When we reached Sally's doorstep, the two ordinary children turned to face each other. I began my prepared speech about how custom suggested kissing on the third date. Like an anthropologist, I lectured Sally on the reasons for avoiding intimacies on the first two dates and for initiating intimacies on the third. I tried to make it sound as if we had no choice in the matter: We had come to the third date, so like it or not we had to kiss, we had to keep tradition alive. Sally said nothing, but her eyes were darting; she was thinking something. Was she smiling? It was dark on her face, and I couldn't tell. At least she hadn't moved away. She hadn't reached for the door, at least.

I finished my speech with an affirmation of some interest on my part to honor the third-date custom. I looked at Sally's face for some sign of go-ahead, but her back was to the light over the Engstrom's back door, and all I saw was a black circle, with an occasional reflection from her darting eyes. Finally I could stand it no longer. "Is it all right with you?" I asked directly.

"We have to honor custom," said Sally.

Waves of unusual excitement swept through my forehead and through the front part of my brain. My ears started ringing, and I felt I was sweating, although it was quite cold. I slid my left hand under Sally's right arm, and

placed my right arm on Sally's left shoulder, the pattern
of arms I had decided was the most efficient. I pulled her
abruptly closer, so our bodies were touching at waist level,
touching through several layers of winter clothing. I closed
my eyes, as I had seen movie stars do as they kissed. I moved
my head toward Sally's and wondered, where are her lips?
I can't see a thing with my eyes closed. It didn't matter on
the practice pillow, which had no definable lips. It didn't
occur to me to open my eyes, or if it did, I dismissed it as
unromantic. I prayed that my initial positioning would guide
our lips together. I moved my head closer and closer to hers.
I tried to sense her breathing, I tried to locate, in my mind's
picture, her nostrils. I felt my lips brush against her nose
and moved them downward toward her lips. I came to rest
slightly off to one side, basically on her lips but with a good
deal of upper lip included; about a third of our lips were
on target. I pressed down with intensity, trying to focus on
the third of my lips attached to hers. She moved her head
in a kind of circular fashion, a response of some sort, and
her breathing began to sound irregular and labored. So does
mine, I thought. I pushed harder on her lips.

Finally, after a few seconds that seemed to us both as
several minutes, we broke apart. I opened my eyes and
thought I saw Sally smiling. I said, "I like traditions."

"So do I," said Sally, and then we said good night, and
Sally went inside. I had several blocks to walk to my own
home, but I ran them, hollering joyous whoops, sliding on
ice patches, alone in my snowy white cocoon. I rubbed my
lips to remove the lipstick. The more I rubbed, the warmer
the spot on my lips felt, the spot where our lips had met. The
warmer the spot got, the more I rubbed, until it felt like fire.

I was consumed by passion.

✳ ✳ ✳

About two years before the incident of the Hooray Theater, Sally Engstrom was found dead in a tool shed in back of her parent's house. Her parents claimed it was an accident, but most people believed that she had committed suicide. Word spread that she had stuck a shotgun in her mouth.

"Did you know that Sally was part Indian?," I asked David.

"Yeah, I knew that. One eighth Sioux is what I heard."

"Don't say Sioux. Dakota. Sioux is what their enemies called them. Means snake or something. Call them Dakota."

"Tell me something, Swede. You think it was suicide? I mean, there's no chance that Sally's death was an accident?"

"No chance; it was suicide."

"No doubt whatsoever?"

"No doubt whatsoever."

"How can you be so sure?"

"I was there."

✳ ✳ ✳

David and I were sitting in my shack, having what David called an "intellectual discussion." I gave him my theory on Minneota suicides. "Four of them," I said. "Four suicides in the past few years, all by shotgun. Never once inside the home. Always outside someplace."

I felt David warming to the topic. Not only was he having an intellectual discussion, he was talking with a drunkard, a bum. But, as David kept insisting, I was a man with ideas. A thinker. One of the few in a burg like Minneota. Me and Doc Klein, David said, that was about it. David asked me if I had been a scholar before I took to drink and diatribes. I just smiled. I don't talk about my past.

About Minneota suicides, David said, "Yes, it's very strange. Makes no sense to me. Shotguns must be very messy. I'd prefer sleeping pills. In movies, it's always slit wrists." David was nattering, uncontrollably, a sign of nervousness. What was he nervous about? Sally's suicide? It knocked him for a loop when it happened, I have to say; had it retained its power? "I don't understand it, that's for sure," David continued. "I read that freezing is one of the most pleasant ways to commit suicide.

"What does it mean?" David asked. His favorite question. "It's the only question worth asking," he once announced to me.

"What does your life mean?" I asked in return.

"Well, geez, I don't know. Yet. I hope to find out." Then David said something important, and I told him so. "I hope to make my life meaningful," he said. "It's up to me."

"Have I made my life meaningful?," I asked. "What does my life mean?" I knew this question would give David trouble, because he thought of me as a failure in life.

"Well, geez, I don't know," he replied nervously. "It could have meant something." He winced as if he wished he hadn't said that.

"And Sally's life?"

"Well, geez, . . ."

David was not going to offer an explanation of the Minneota suicides, so I issued my own theory: "They weren't suicides. They were executions." I paused, to let my major premise sink in. "That's why they used guns. Guns are for executions. Sleeping pills are for suicides."

I think I saw in David my younger self, myself in innocence—before I took the wrong turn. Whatever that was. My instincts, therefore, were protective. I wanted to strengthen David, strengthen his mind by argument and contradiction, by dialectical reasoning and debate. Get him to examine his views carefully. Be prepared for the "mind vultures" who attacked "free thinkers," picked out their brains and left them for dead. As they did with me.

The trouble was, if I was to protect David, I would have to strengthen his soul. But I didn't believe in the soul. So I had absolutely no idea how to proceed: How is a soul strengthened? Isn't that an intensely personal sort of thing? Isn't it "up to him," as he says?

Intellectual discussions strengthen David's mind, I thought. Perhaps moral discussions strengthen the soul. Worth a try.

David responded enthusiastically to my theory of suicides. "Executions? What a brilliant idea! You mean the town. The town shot Sally. Isn't that what you mean?"

"That's how we punish the sinners. We line them up and shoot them dead."

"And we even get them to pull the trigger!"

"Hell of a system! Well? What do you think of my theory?"

"Interesting," he said. "But what's your theory say about why she did it? Why the town wanted her dead." Not a brilliant response, but strong. Answer a question with a question. A pure intellectual tactic . . .

"She cut herself off," I replied. "She offended the community, and the people turned against her. She was all alone. She looked ahead to a life of more of the same, and she couldn't face it. So she ended the life."

"I used to date her, did you know that?," David said. "I was . . . we were 14, maybe 15. I was a couple of years older than she was. It broke up gradually. She was a nice girl then. She was the first girl I ever kissed. I loved her, even. I think."

"Why?" I asked. "Why did you love Sally?"

"Why?! What a question! I don't know. She had a kind of spirit, or something. Even after we broke up, even at the end, when she came back and tried to get in the church. She was very aggressive toward life, almost as if life were some sort of toy that would yield more pleasure if she played with it more vigorously." David smiled his little smile. He was proud of the last line. He had no doubt read it somewhere and saw (correctly) that it fit the present discussion.

"Don't you think that was her problem? She enjoyed life too much?"

"Enjoyed?" I responded. "You mean sex?"

"No, no! Not sex. Not sex exactly. Although sex is a good way to enjoy life." As if David were an authority on the subject.

"Tell me this," I said. "Why do you think she got involved with Danny Swenson?"

"Hell, that's easy. She just plain fell in love with him."

The strengthening of mind and soul would have to wait. David wanted to read his novel to me. I wanted to be encouraging, but the novel was stupefying. Okay, so the booze didn't help. The combination was deadly. I couldn't keep my eyes open.

I didn't fall asleep, but my mind began to wander. I started to daydream about Rumpelstiltskin, one of Sally's favorite stories. David and I had discussed it many times. Sally thought Rumpelstiltskin was a hero, not a villain. She convinced David, and she convinced me.

My daydream, however, made me smile and chuckle, so David knew I wasn't listening to his dreary novel, which had no humor at all. Finally, peeved, he asked, "Are you dreaming a better story than mine?"

"Not like that's so difficult," I said, teasing. "But you're right, and I'm sorry. I was having a fantasy about Rumpelstiltskin."

"Rumpelstiltskin? Again? Sally's version? Why? I thought we had that sorted out. Rumpelstiltskin was innocent of all charges against him."

"Yes, but we lack detail," I replied. "In my daydream, Sally plays the queen, and you play the king."

"I get it," said David. "You play Rumpelstiltskin! I'm the evil king and you get to play the magician! I want to play the magician!"

"It's my damn fantasy!" I said, feigning anger.

"OK, OK," David said, submissively. "What's happening?"

"The old man is trying to dump his daughter on the king. He tells you that Sally has sinned beyond redemption, that nobody wants her around. But maybe you do, he says, because she can turn straw into gold.

"Dingus Anderson is standing next to you, holding a shotgun. He's wearing a chamber pot. On him, it looks strangely attractive. Dingus tells the old man to go away, nobody believes his stupid story. Take the tramp with you, he says, and he pokes them both with his gun butt."

David interrupted peevishly. "Listen, Swede, if you want to continue this drivel, at least let me play myself."

I was eager to share, so we both closed our eyes and continued the daydream out loud, creating a mutual fantasy.

King David was now on stage. "I say to the old man, 'What's this? She can turn straw into gold? Is that possible?'

"Dingus glares at me and says, 'Don't be such a fool! Can't you see, the old man is just trying to get rid of her.'

"And I reply, 'But what if the old man is telling the truth? It would be a scientific miracle! Think of it! Alchemy proved! I'd be famous! Not to mention rich beyond dreams. Is it not worth a test? What would one test cost us?'"

I added a few lines: "Dingus has been chewing on a piece of straw. He throws it at Sally. 'Here, wench. Make us some gold.'

"Sally kicks him in the shin."

Back to David: "'No, no, Sir Dingus,' says the king. 'We must have a proper scientific test. We'll lock this girl in the Hooray Theater tonight, with a couple of bales of straw. Will hay do as well? No, he said straw, better stick with straw. Make sure she's alone. Make sure she has no gold on her. Better put her in there naked. It won't matter to her, she's already disgraced. Put a couple of guards by each door, make sure no one enters.'"

"Naked?" I imagine Dingus asking the same question, drooling.

David ignores me and presses on. "'Do you think this will be a proper test, young lady?' I ask Sally."

My turn: "Sally picks up the piece of straw and waves it. 'Stick it up your royal ass, Sire!'"

"'Well, I'm sorry you feel that way, fair maiden,' the king continues. 'Whether you like it or not, you are going to be part of a great scientific experiment. I want you to try your best. If you fail, you will be put to death. I'm sorry about that, but that's the way it is in fairy-tale daydreams. You'll die a horrible death, unless Sir Dingus wants you for a wife. In that case, thou shalt be spared!'"

Me: "'I choose death,' says Sally.

"I wait until dark, then enter the theater by a side window. Sally is crying. She doesn't recognize me. 'Who are you, you little runt?' I ignore her and concentrate on transferring gold from the king's treasury (Minneota's Farmers and Merchants State Bank) into his dungeon (the Hooray Theater)."

David: "Dawn breaks, and King David is very excited. Alchemy has worked. A scientific breakthrough. But he's wary, as all good scientists are. He suspects a trick. He designs a replication of the experiment, with even tighter controls. So that night, he locks Sally in the theater again, fills it with straw, and doubles the guards at the doors. 'If she fills the room with gold once more,' says King David, 'I will marry her. If she fails, I will drown her in Dead Coon Lake.'"

I describe another night of work, transferring gold, replacing straw. "Sally has offered me her first-born child as a reward. 'How can you suggest such a thing?' I ask her angrily.

"'Well, I figured that, since you can make gold out of straw, what good would it do to offer you money, or jewels, or whatever. But you can't make a child out of straw! Smart, huh?'

"'Smart?! Dumb! D-U-M-B!'" I was so upset by this offer, I could hardly speak. Even though it was a fantasy. "I don't know if I can continue. It's too ridiculous."

"You don't have to accept her offer", said David. "You can help her out and then refuse the baby. If she ever has one."

I reluctantly changed the straw into gold. I decided to forget about her promise; I would never claim her child.

David: "Well, of course, King David is very pleased with the results of his second experiment. He marries Sally. About a year later, King David and Queen Sally become the parents of a lovely baby girl, whom they name Lilith."

"Lilith?" I exclaimed.

"Yes," replied David. "I like the name. According to Jewish folklore, Lilith was Adam's first wife, before Eve. But Lilith was uppity and refused to submit to Adam's authority, so he kicked her out of the Garden of Eden. God made Eve out of Adam's rib to replace Lilith, I think because He thought a woman made out of a man's body parts would be less rebellious. Bad mistake, as it turned out. Adam didn't have much luck with women. He was a lot like me, I think."

"Like you?"

"Yeah, you know—bad choices in girlfriends, an insatiable desire for knowledge that leads to my demise."

"So, what happened to the real Lilith?"

"Oh, very interesting! She became the mother of demons! She became a witch, the goddess of night! She flew around at night and swooped down to kill the infant children of Adam and his progeny. She was greatly feared. The Jews would sing to their babies, 'Lilith, abi,' which means 'Lilith, go away.' It's said that these songs were called Lilith-abi's, which eventually, through mispronunciation, became 'lullabies.'"

I had no reply to this stunning revelation, so I picked up the story: "Not long after that, I have to go to the market in the courtyard of the castle. I need chickens. Mine have been killed by town kids. Again. They think it's funny to kill the livestock of the little runt who lives outside of town, by the creek. In the courtyard, I encounter Sir Dingus, who, out of pure malice, decides to pick on me. Calls me a funny-looking little creep and starts pushing me toward the gate. Tells me to go away, they don't want anything so ugly around the King. Picks up a big stick and starts pummeling me around the head and shoulders. I fall down, bleeding profusely. A crowd gathers and cheers Sir Dingus on. Dingus starts kicking me.

"Just then, one of the King's horses looks over and recognizes me as the little man who had fed them those nights when the guards had taken their hay for Sally to make gold out of. The horse's name is Balaam."

"Balaam?," David asked, perceiving revenge for naming his daughter Lilith. "What kind of name is that? That's your mother's name?"

"It's a name from the Bible," I said. "It's a good choice."

"Okay. But I have another problem," David said. "Sally made the gold out of straw, not out of hay. Horses don't eat straw. Maybe they sleep on it, but they don't eat it. They eat hay."

"Most people don't know the difference between straw and hay," I countered.

"This is not the fantasy of 'most people,' it's ours. And we know the difference. We have to be true to ourselves." (David issued the last statement sermon-like, with obvious pride. It's his one characteristic that I find disgusting.)

"Let's change the straw to hay, then, right from the beginning. It makes for a much better story, with the horse coming to my rescue," I said, ignoring the moral implications that David had asserted.

"Well, I don't know," replied David with a dejected air. "Okay. We can call it hay for a while, to see how the story develops. We can change back if it doesn't work."

"Deal," I said, and continued. "Balaam recognized me. He bolted from his stall and charged into Dingus, knocking him down. Balaam stood close to me, threatening anyone who might do me harm."

"Okay, good. I like it," David said. "But Dingus will probably shoot the horse."

"Well, I thought of that," I said. "Let me show you how I save Balaam. The commotion attracts your attention, that is, the King's attention. And Sally's, too. You look down on the courtyard and see nothing but a bunch of peasants making noise. But Sally looks down and recognizes me. She's suppressed the memory of her promise to me, but now it comes flooding back. She's terrified. She's certain that I have come for Lilith. What can she do?, she worries.

"She sends a soldier to the courtyard. As Dingus raises his shotgun to kill the horse, the soldier tells him to stop. 'The little man is a magician. He can communicate with the animals. If you shoot the horse, you will surely die yourself.' Dingus, a superstitious man, trembles and lowers his gun.

"The soldier asks me to come with him. He takes me to the Queen.

"'I know why you've come. But I made a terrible mistake when I offered you my baby. I love her, and I can't part with her. Please, will you not take jewels and gold instead?'

"'I want nothing, my Queen,' I reply.

"'Oh, I know you want nothing! You're a magician, you can turn straw . . . I mean, hay into gold.'

"'I mean, I don't want your child. I want nothing at all. I was glad to help in your hour of need.'

"'What's the catch?' asked Sally, skeptically. 'What are you really after? If not money, then what? Power? You want me to kill the King, don't you? You want to be King! My God! It's worse than I thought!'

"This woman is mad, I think. Incapable of understanding or even accepting human kindness. I will teach her a lesson. 'Tell you what. If you can guess my name,' I said, 'you can keep your child. You won't have to kill the King. I'll leave town. I'll move to Sleepy Eye, and I'll never come back. I'll never trouble you again.'"

"Okay, stop there. Nobody could be as dumb as the Queen," David asserted. "You offered her an out, said you wanted nothing, and she ends up jeopardizing both her child and her husband. Nobody's that dumb."

"You think not? That's not my experience. My experience is that everybody's that dumb. People always think there're strings attached if you do something kind for them. People think there's no free lunch. Even if Sally accepted the fact that I didn't want her child or the King's power, she'd live in constant fear that, sooner or later, I'd be back for what I really wanted. Not knowing what that was would drive her crazy."

"I read a book about organized crime," David said in agreement. "They would do you a favor, but then you owed them. Sooner or later, they'd come back, wanting some favor in return. It was rarely a favor you wanted to do. Like kill someone."

"'John, William, Charles, James,' Sally guessed. 'Harry. Buckshot. Halvor. Stumpy.' A hour of names, every one rejected. Sally was sobbing. I told her she could rest. I would return tomorrow, and she could guess some more."

"You know, I was just thinking," David said. "Sally had an abortion. She really did give up her firstborn."

"Geez! That's pretty gruesome. Why did you bring that up?"

"I was just thinking that Sally really was like the Queen, in some ways. And you're like Rumpelstiltskin, in a lot of ways. I'm even kinda like the King. He's a jerk, but he's not so different from me."

I frowned, but nodded to signify reluctant agreement. I returned to my attempts to divulge my name— Rumpelstiltskin, of course, in the story. (My goal was obviously to reveal my name publicly, so the Queen could get off the hook for the hay-to-gold caper.) So I left St. Joe's Catholic Church—which David and I had decided was the structure most like a castle in Minneota—and entered the courtyard, where hundreds of people were mingling after the church services. "'My name is Rumpelstiltskin,' I yelled. 'My name is Rumpelstiltskin.'

"The people started throwing rocks at me. Discouraged, I returned to my cabin. To worry. I had not planned on this turn of events. I had not imagined that no one would be interested in my name—a name, after all, of some originality and even beauty."

"The Queen, too, was worried," said David. "What if she failed to guess the magician's name? She decided to tell me—King David—the truth, the whole story. She asked my advice.

"I had, by this time, come to love Sally, so I was quite distressed by her revelations. I had been tricked into marrying her! I might lose my child! Worst of all, my scientific experiments had been subverted by this trickery! I had proclaimed widely the first demonstrable success of alchemy; would it have to be repudiated? Was it a fraud? What an incredible loss of face!

"I calmed myself with the realization that, although my Queen was not an alchemist, someone was. Someone had changed the straw . . . , oops!, the hay into gold. This weird little man, that's who. He would save my reputation. And, better yet, he had presented me with another intriguing scientific problem: How to discover a man's name.

"I called in my astrologers and obtained their opinions—worthless, as usual! I have to do everything myself! I ordered the census takers to prepare a list of all the male names in the kingdom, arranged by frequency of occurrence. The next day the Queen read several long lists of names I had worked out. Rumpelstiltskin was not one of the names on my lists. Actually, it was on my lists, but it was so badly misspelled that the Queen mispronounced it and you, as desperate as you were, did not recognize it."

"But I had a plan," I interjected, "which I now put into action. I laughed at the Queen, trying my best to sound evil. (In fact, I sounded naughty.) I contorted my face in an attempt to look menacing (which made me appear drunk). I told the Queen that she would never guess my name, for it was known only by me and one other—'My master, Satan! Where do you think I got my powers to turn straw, I mean hay, into gold?' I cackled naughtily. I told Sally that I would return to my cabin in the forest and this night build a great fire to summon Beelzebub, my master, who lives in fire. I would tell him to prepare for a sacrifice, an infant girl, who would be burnt in his fire the following evening. I laughed a drunken laugh and left.

"As I had hoped, the Queen—disguised as a wench— followed me into the courtyard. As I started for home, I saw the great horse who had rescued me from the soldiers. The soldiers were beating the horse for his disloyalty. I ran to the soldier in charge and seized the whip from his hand. The others turned on me, their whips slashing my face.

"Sir Dingus, remembering what the Queen's guard had said about my evil powers, stopped his soldiers. Apologizing profusely, he offered me the great horse as a gift, which I accepted. The Queen observed these events and followed me to my home.

"At my cabin in the woods, I fed the horse and gave him water. On his wounds, and mine, I put a salve made from the sap of the balsam tree. Aware that the Queen was watching, I gathered wood and built a roaring fire. It was dark in the forest, and the orange flames leaped like evil fingers. I danced around the fire, shouting my name."

"May I finish?" David asked. "It seems pretty clear.

"The following day, when you arrived at the castle, the Queen was quiet. 'You knew I was in the bush,' she said. 'You deliberately let me know your name. Why?'

"'The Princess should be with her mother, who loves her.'

"The Queen did not understand, but she was convinced that you meant her no harm. She wanted to offer you something, but she had learned enough to know that such an offer would be offensive. So you left, returning to your cabin in the forest. Never again were you disturbed, for the Queen spread rumors about your evil powers. From time to time, you emerged from the forest to help someone in need. Always you asked for something of great value in return for your aid, and always you managed to let yourself be tricked out of your reward.

"Like the Queen, you had learned a valuable lesson."

Teacher Arrested for Sex Crimes

Daniel Swenson, history teacher at Minneota High School, was arrested today in Galveston, Texas. He was charged with carnal knowledge of a minor.

Swenson, 43, ran off with one of his students at the school in Minneota, a small town in southwestern Minnesota, leaving behind a wife and four small children. Swenson and the unnamed student had been lovers for quite some time, according to Roger Mohn, chief of police in Minneota. When the student became pregnant, the two decided to start a new life together. They would have succeeded, said Mohn, if the young girl had not sent cheerful postcards to her friends and family as they drove from Minnesota to Texas.

Swenson is also charged with auto theft, because he bought a late-model Ford from Sorenson Ford in Minneota; he had made only one payment before the star-crossed lovers made their escape. Ray Clijsters, a mechanic at Sorenson Ford, took a bus to Galveston to pick up the car. On the return trip, Clijsters got lost in Kansas City and returned to Minneota a month later. "I got lost in the red-light district," said Clijsters, who was referring to traffic lights (we hope).

6

Sweet Sally's Revenge

I tried to determine if there was feeling in my arm, in the lower part cut off by Sally's head. I wiggled my fingers. I was relieved to see that I could still move my fingers, but I felt nothing.

"Are you waving to someone? To me! You're waving goodbye!"

I had thought Sally was asleep, so her voice startled me, as if someone—my wife perhaps—had entered the bedroom and discovered us. What would I do? Not much, I thought. Wave goodbye. What else could I do? "Listen, Darling, this is not what it appears—"

"You should leave," I said to Sally, "if you know what's good for you."

Sally replied, as she always did: "If you think I'm going to leave you, Danny Swenson, then you've got another think coming!" Sometimes she just said, "Another think coming!" She loved the idea of "another think"—like another helping of mashed potatoes.

I nevertheless continued the routine we had developed, listing the reasons she should get the hell out of my life before it was too late. It was like a vaudeville routine, a scene from not-quite life, with overtones of comedy and undertones of tragedy. She should stop seeing me because I was married and had four children and she was our baby sitter and she was 16 years old. "So what?!" is the only possible reply to this list of incontrovertible truths, and after a dozen punch line replies, it still made me smile. Well, then I should divorce my wife and marry her, in proper fashion. This proclamation never failed to send Sally into gales of laughter.

"You'd be lucky if my father didn't empty his shotgun into you right on the spot," she would note. And then in a serious tone, "Besides, I don't want to get married. I'm only 16 years old. What do you think, I'm crazy?!"

"You just like to fool around," I would sometimes say. "Well, you listen to me! You're going to get into trouble!"

But Sally didn't just like to fool around. In fact, she hated "fooling around," which she took to mean "fun, but not important," a phrase that could be applied to her entire life, not just to sex. Sally wanted something more. She wanted love.

"Well, you have that. You certainly have that."

In this Midwestern, offhanded way, I told her of my great love for her. I ached to say it directly, but I never could. I read the story of Cyrano de Bergerac, imagined myself Cyrano (instead of Christian, whom I closely resembled), and dreamed of telling Sally of my love in poetry. When I read the words of Cyrano, I felt embarrassed, although I was alone. I wrote a poem of love of my own, in my own words, and I felt even more embarrassed. Once I read a few of Cyrano's words to Sally, disguising my purpose as one of reading great literature. I still felt embarrassed, and so did Sally. I never showed her my own poem.

But an offhand manner was sufficient. "If I have what I want, why should I leave?" asked Sally, toward the end of our routine. It was a silly conclusion, we both knew that; I was right in the first place. Trouble loomed, though we didn't know exactly the form it would take. But there was nothing to be done. Certainly we were not about to stop.

* * *

"Sitting Bull was a practical joker, did you know that?"

"No," said Sally reluctantly. She frowned. She feared another lecture. I liked to talk between the first lovemaking and the second. I had a fondness for politics and religion, a fondness Sally did not share. She also disliked the tone of my voice when I started off on one of my lectures—a schoolmaster's pitch and rhythm that threw her back into the classroom where we first met.

Sally once confessed that her mind wandered during my lectures, but of course I never noticed. She wondered if it was like this for other couples, with all this talk between sex. She thought not; I was a talker. Others just lay there, kissing and hugging, as they awaited the next opportunity. So Sally thought. She did not know that others hurried their sex, then lit up cigarettes, went to bathrooms, fell asleep—no kissing, no hugging, no talk, no between. She would have been horrified.

"When the railroads made their final connection between the eastern and the western lines, they asked Sitting Bull to speak. This was after the wars were over. Sitting Bull was living on a reservation. He had become a kind of celebrity. He even traveled for a while with a wild west show. Buffalo Bill's Wild West Show.

"The Army sent a young officer who could speak Sioux. He was supposed to help Sitting Bull with his speech. Together they worked up a few words of welcome. The idea was that Sitting Bull would deliver the speech in Sioux, then the officer would stand up and translate it into English.

"On the day of the speech, Sitting Bull gets up and says, `I hate all the white people.' The young soldier—the only white person who knew what Sitting Bull was saying—is stunned. Sitting Bull goes on: `You are all thieves and liars. You took our land and murdered our people.' On and on he went, one zinger after another. Once in a while he would pause, smile, and nod at the audience. They applauded wildly.

"Finally it was time for the soldier to stand up and translate Sitting Bull's remarks. He had a small piece of paper with the translation of what Sitting Bull was supposed to have said—a few words of welcome. It was too short to be the English version of the lengthy diatribe Sitting Bull actually delivered. The soldier threw in every stupid Indian cliché he could remember: `Those who live in the sky smile upon the work of their children,' that sort of thing. When he finished, the crowd erupted in a standing ovation. Sitting Bull stood up, smiled, and bowed."

"Did they ever find him out?" asked Sally.

"No. The whole affair was so successful, the railroad invited Sitting Bull to St. Paul for another ceremony."

"Did he go?"

"Of course."

Always it was the same. Each precious night was a repetition of the first, a routine worthy of a married couple except for the fiery passion we maintained. Immediately we began, falling hopelessly into each other's arms, desperate with desire, needing raw sex the way a parched animal needs water. The bed jumped around the room, threatening to wake my children, but in this as in it all we were helpless to resist.

The second time each night was quieter, more intelligent—an epic lovemaking. The first time was fierce, the second playful. The first time was hopeless, the second prayerful. The first time was a war, the second time was a dance, a ballet, a pas de deux of lovers. Sally sometimes fantasized that we were on stage, performing the act of love for a audience stunned by our brilliant virtuosity.

Between the first time and the second time, we talked.

Politics it was this time, worse than religion. I was droning on about some Republican I didn't like. Sally's mind began its wandering, alighting briefly on transient points of interest. A gray hair among the five or six long black hairs that circled my nipple. She pulled on the gray hair, straightened it with her tension, let it snap back. She touched the nipple and watched it rise, as if it had a life of its own, as if it were as bored as she with my pedantic drone. I seemed to take no notice of my nipple's other life, Sally thought. (In fact, I found Sally's fondling very erotic and very distracting! But I was a teacher. . . .) Sally and the nipple played together for a while, as I droned on. ". . . opinion poll. You know, like the Gallup Poll? Well, Henry Bergtold is the incumbent . . ."

The smell of sweat attracted Sally's fancy. Mine, hers, the commingling: mine was musky, hers was sweet, and together it had the aroma of some mythical creature without sex, or with both sexes, a hermaphrodite. It was a very pleasant smell, totally unlike the smell of sweat that came from fear. Sally thought about dogs sniffing each other, checking each other out: Are you afraid of me? Or are you ready for love? Sweat is good stuff, thought Sally. It glistens, too. And it feels slippery. Good stuff. People will do almost anything to keep it from appearing in their armpits. Wonder why it has a bad reputation, thought Sally; like me. Sally conjured up an image in which she would unexpectedly appear in people's armpits whenever they were hot or emotional. People would find a spray. . . .

"Well, don't you think that's funny?" I asked suddenly, breaking her reverie.

Sally thought to herself, "Now why does he do that?! Does he really think I'm listening?"

"What's funny, Sweetie?"

"You weren't listening?" I don't know why I say that; she never listens to my lectures, even in school. "What were you thinking about?"

"Sweat."

"Sweat?"

"I was thinking about what it would be like to be sweat, and come out in people's armpits during lovemaking."

I gave Sally a look half of disgust and half of distress. "I did this opinion poll for the Democrats. I called a hundred people in Minneota, asked if they planned to vote for Henry Bergtold or Peter Sorem; 9 said Bergtold, 5 said Sorem, and 86 declined to state."

"Declined to state?"

"Well, that's the box I checked for them. What they actually said was —"

"None of your goddamned business!"

"You got it! Funny, huh?"

"Yes. That is funny."

So I started in on why I thought Peter Sorem was a candidate far superior to Henry Bergtold. Sally's interest turned off like a plugged faucet. She wanted to savor the idea of the opinion poll. In a small town like Minneota, people knew pretty much everything there was to know about a person, but they defended their privacy like polecats. Politics and religion were two of the big No-Nos, although everyone knew exactly how everyone had voted and would vote and everyone knew exactly everyone's religious beliefs and the degree of religious commitment. But the principle was the thing: It's my business, it's none of your business. Sally wished that her love of me could be like this: her business, none of their business. Why did they make it their business? Moralistic SOBs, that's what they are. Think all sex out of marriage is evil. Think home-wrecking is a sin. "Well, OK, maybe home-wrecking is a sin," she said. "I believe that, but I'm not trying to wreck a home. This is love. Love is not a sin. God is love, for Christ's sake! Why don't they just mind their own business?!"

When her thoughts took this turn, as they inevitably did, a cool sense of danger washed over her, replacing the warm spirit of community. Community had its cold spirit, too, for people at the fringes. Her friends and neighbors had already begun to turn against her—to refuse the milk of human kindness, to starve her into submission. To get her to stop this foolishness with Danny Swenson. They would keep it up, too, until she caved in . . . or until she died. Her friends and neighbors, her community, her people: How could they do it? It was like discovering that your parents are about to kill you for the insurance money. She would suddenly feel very alone and afraid. Reflexively she would grasp my body and snuggle, assuming a fetal position. Sometimes she whimpered, and then I would notice her pain and respond to it.

"Come on. Come on. It's all right."

Sally told me the story of the incident at Coleman's farm. I was filled with rage. "David Sorenson," I said. "That little twerp!"

"You can't blame him. It was a good joke. Everybody likes a good joke. It was me, that's all. I blew it. I was so selfish. Oh, God! I was a coward."

"It was only a joke. It wasn't for real."

"Yeah? Tell me about it! Tommy wasn't really shot, there wasn't any danger. But I was real. I wasn't acting, I wasn't part of the joke. I made it damn clear that I would have let Tommy die to save myself. You can't say it doesn't count. They all saw it. Everybody treated me different after that."

"It's just your imagination."

"I asked David about it, you know? He was the only one I dared talk to. He said he felt terrible afterwards, because of me. They didn't expect anything like that."

"David agreed with you? He said you had done something bad?" I was still steaming.

"Well . . . yes, actually. I was glad he did. What's the sense of lying to me? But David said I took it harder than I should. The others just wanted to forget it. David said they all felt it could have happened to any one of them, in the right circumstances. Sometimes people are strong, sometimes they spook."

I thought about this remark for a while. I decided that it was about as comforting as possible, under the circumstances. In spite of my newly generated hatred for its author, I let it stand.

"David tried to cheer me up with some stories about himself," Sally continued. "Baseball stories. Once he made six errors on one play."

I couldn't imagine such an athletic collapse.

"Once his pants ripped sliding into a base and he stood up stark naked."

Sally's obvious affection for David was making me uneasy. But I laughed for effect.

"He told me a story, it was a complicated story, I didn't understand it, not really, it was about missing a fly ball because he was trying to step on a bee. He let the team down, that was the gist of it. He had to live with doing something stupid, he said. He said that was kinda like—in a small way—kinda like what I did at Coleman's farm."

"How did you feel about all this?"

"Ha! Well, to tell you the truth, it didn't help. It didn't make me feel any better. What it did was, it made me think about how boys learn about things like this, and girls don't. It made me mad, if you want to know the truth. Little boys playing games, but really it's not games, it's real life. How to act when you're standing naked on third base. Everybody makes errors in baseball, everybody does something stupid sooner or later. What do you do next? You make a comeback. You swallow your shame, and you make a comeback. Boys learn how to do that. Girls, we learn how to cook."

"You can't cook a lick!"

"I don't mean me, I mean girls in general! We learn how to sew, boys learn how to survive. It's not fair! I get to thinking that I would have done something different—at Coleman's farm, I mean—if I had played baseball and football. I coulda come back."

A to-the-bone insight about the role of sports in the social development of boys—brilliant! Whenever she came up with such insights, I was floored. Sally was pretty, full of fun, but ignorant. Knew nothing of important issues such as politics and religion. Had no culture. Wasn't intellectual at all—almost purely sensual. But then out of her mouth comes something like this, a brilliant observation about life and human nature. It happened often, yet it always amazed me. I began to wonder if she weren't from Mars. Or two different spirits lived in her body.

I loved both.

I decided to explore Sally's relationship with David. "Were you dating David?" I asked.

"Now and then. But David started dating Sandy Kringen pretty serious-like. I had to find someone new. You! See? It's all fate!" Playfully, Sally drilled her knuckles into the side of my chest. I jumped but persevered.

"Do you think David stopped dating you because of this joke?"

"No. He was after Sandy long before that. David and I became, maybe, better friends, better than before. Not dating, but real good friends. But the others . . . , the others started acting real strange."

"You sure? It could be your imagination."

"Well, Goose loved to tell the story. And she did, to anyone who would listen. She loved it; she thought it was a terrific joke. My part in the story got worse and worse. According to Goose, I was yelling `The hell with Tommy! The hell with Tommy! Let the son of a bitch die!' Stuff like that.

"And Trudy—Jesus Christ! Trudy felt good about her part, she was a hero. She tried to save Tommy. She thought her life was in danger, but still she tried to get back to Tommy. She started thinking she was better than me. She'd ignore me, she'd put down everything I had to say. I can handle that stuff from some people—I mean, I didn't think much of myself, not then—but from Trudy! Jesus Christ! She's such a clinker!"

I didn't respond, just hugged her tightly. Sally felt better, having gotten this off her chest.

* * *

Soon after the incident at Coleman's farm, Sally plotted her revenge. Demoralized as she was, her heart was not in it, but she felt instinctively that an attempt must be made. In a community like Minneota, a victim of a practical joke was required—"by law," Sally said—to play an escalating game of joke and counter joke. Sally's opportunity came soon enough.

On Saturday and Sunday, July 7 and 8, 1956, the town of Minneota celebrated its 75th birthday. Men grew bushy beards for the occasion, and women and girls dressed in the clothing of the 19th century. Events included carnival rides, a rodeo, a talent contest, rollie bollie, and a water fight between the Minneota fire department and that of a neighboring town. There was a parade—over 30,000 people saw it, according to the Minneota Messenger, crowding the streets of a town that normally counted 1200 citizens. Each evening a historical pageant was performed at the ball park, with a cast of 250 residents. David Sorenson was one of the participants.

As valedictorian of the class of 1956, David had been asked to deliver a few remarks to the assembled crowd, welcoming them to the pageant, preparing them for the chaos of actors, dancers, singers, and twirlers and bands and choirs to follow. It was not a task David was looking forward to, as shy as he was, as anxious as he was about public speaking. The fact that the speaker's platform was almost exactly over third base, where in a previous public performance he had made six errors on one play, did not escape his notice.

"Citizens and friends of Minneota, I welcome you," he started. "Welcome you, welcome you," came an echo he had not expected. He felt control slipping: a constriction in his upper chest and throat meant that he would soon become short of breath; a flush in his face meant his hands would become drenched in sweat, so that when he shook hands with the mayor later, the mayor would look at his hand with disgust and wipe it on his trousers, and the crowd would laugh; his right eye began its characteristic nervous twitch, and his right knee began to wobble. "On behalf," he said and gasped for breath, "of the people," gasp, "of Minneota," gasp, "past, present," gasp, "and future," gasp, "I welcome you!" He meant to add "to the pageant depicting our origins," but a concise style seemed appropriate to the circumstances. By emphasizing the word "you," he managed to make it sound as if he had completed a thought, and the festive crowd roared.

Sweat was leaking through his eyebrows, clouding his vision. He strained to read the words he had memorized in the afternoon. "As you know," he stammered, "the village of . . . Minneota . . . was incorporated . . . on the 21st . . . of January . . . 1881." How would they know that? he wondered, and fear rose up in him again. His mouth felt like a desert, and he imagined the faint clucking sounds made by his sticky tongue were being amplified throughout the ballpark. He clutched the microphone for support. Sweat trickled down the microphone stand, and a spectacular electrocution scene flashed in his mind.

The people in the stands thought David was speaking a little more slowly than usual—he was none too nimble-tongued at his best—but they weren't listening anyway. Thus, most were interrupted in conversations with old friends when the loudspeakers crackled, buzzed, and a very loud "BURP!" sounded through the park. "Oh, excuse me!" followed. Puzzled, the crowd looked up at the stage. They saw a young man with a frightened face clutching the microphone stand. Another BURP, then "Good beer! Really good beer!"

The young man was down on one knee, and Father O'Shea was by his side. Was he drunk? Even in the fading light of dusk, he looked a little green.

"How did you manage it?" I asked Sally, months later.

"Jon Coltvet helped me. We rigged up a tape recorder to cut in on the ballpark public address system. We made a tape of two burps and the other stuff and just played it while David was speaking."

"Did you get caught?"

"Well, that depends on what you mean by `caught.' We had it rigged so that we could pull off our mike and amplifier and leave only some cord for them to find. But nobody found anything. Nobody even considered the possibility that it wasn't David. They all thought David had burped. Even David."

"Even David?!"

"Yes! It was the strangest thing. He thought he had done it. He apologized and apologized to everybody."

"He thought he said `Good beer!' and all that stuff?!"

"He couldn't remember for sure what he said. He didn't think it was `good beer,' though. He thought maybe it was `good cheer' or something like that."

"That's incredible!" I said.

"Well, of course, it was tempting to let it lie, never tell the truth. But you can't do that. You have to take credit for your revenge."

"So you told David the truth."

"In the presence of his friends."

"It must have been a very satisfying experience."

Sally was quiet for a moment, remembering. "No. No, it wasn't fun at all. Everything worked like a charm, but all I remember is my friend hanging onto the microphone, tears running down his face, the crowd roaring with laughter."

Sally moved, irritably. "Who said," she asked, "revenge is sweet?"

"Revenge is never sweet," I said in my teacher's mode. "Revenge is a duty."

Tears formed in Sally's eyes, and since she was staring at the ceiling, they rolled down her temples into her curly red hair.

* * *

Oh Sally, sweet Sally! Your face in sleep, so serene. Untroubled. Your troubles are surface troubles. Down deep, everything's all right. If only you could believe it. If only you could sleep forever. Sleep, sweet Sally. Sleep forever.

Everything's all wrong, of course. It's me, I'm all wrong. My wife . . . my dear wife . . . my kids . . . What can I say? You have to understand. Understand what? That this is a great moment in the biological history of the human species. A moment of perfect love. Sure, sure, that's what they all say. It's important for the world to know, people should know that perfect love exists! That it's possible!

Well, Danny, of course I understand. Here is your freedom. I understand perfectly. Sally can stay in our guest room.

Sweet sixteen. How can you know so much? Where do you get your ideas? Are you a god? Are you a siren, in communication with the devil? What have I gotten myself into? Is it a moment of perfect love, or is it something more sinister?

Maybe it's a practical joke! I'm being set up for a fall. My wife and kids will come bursting through the door, David Sorenson and Jon Coltvet, all of them bursting through the door yelling, "Surprise! Surprise!" The joke's on you.

Maybe all love is a joke.

Maybe it's just sex.

I've never experienced sex like this, Sally. How can a sixteen-year-old teach me about sex? Where do you get your ideas? Sex and music are the same thing. What is that, some deep philosophical insight? Or some kind of brute animal awareness?

Did the great composers think about sex?

How could they not have?

The first movement is alert and playful. The second is calm. The third builds to a climax. We're on a brink. We pull back, and approach again. We hover on the brink, hovering lovers, humming like hummingbirds. Suddenly it's the end, the cannons of the Overture of 1812. The whole world explodes.

Where did you learn those moves?

You lied! You've made love to other men!

Not likely. I would have heard about it.

Where did you learn those moves?

Instinct.

How you shout! Aren't you embarrassed? The kids, you'll wake the kids!

I'm not shouting! You're shouting!

Are we both shouting?

I feel selfish. I feel that the sex is all for me, that this is the greatest experience of my life. It's all for me, Sally, and, yes, it is. You work to create my pleasure. But that creates your pleasure. I work to create your pleasure. But that creates my pleasure. I get confused. It doesn't matter. I've never felt less selfish.

It's a goddamned religious experience!

. . . and then the smile. I think it's the smile that I love the most. What a smile! A smile of love and tiredness, a smile of satisfaction and satiation, a smile of appreciation and exhaustion. Oh, my sweet Sally, I'd do anything to earn that smile.

Anything.

Well, I've been thinking again, and you know what happens when I start thinking, I get confused, and I need the help of my readers to set me straight on the matters that float, like butterflies, through my mind as I shave, or make popcorn, or just sit at my desk, when I should be working, and daydream. Like ear wax. I have often wondered why human beings come into the world with ear wax and exactly what is the real purpose of the substance. It doesn't seem to do any harm and I don't believe it does much good either but I do believe that everybody has it in their ears, although maybe some people have more than others, I've heard, because Doc Klein says some people are almost deaf because of the accumulation of the stuff, and it has to be flushed out. I was talking to Doc because of something else that I was thinking about, which was an article I read one day where it said that the lightning that comes with a storm is good for the crops because it causes a chemical reaction in the air and makes nitrogen which is like a fertilizer. I asked Doc if he thought this was so, Doc being the smartest, most educated man I know, I figured if anyone knew the answer, he would be the person. But Doc said, and he had a big smile on his face, "It's really the rain that does the good." Got me again, I guess!

Here's another thing I've been thinking about, in fact I've given it quite a bit of thought, and I think it's a perfect idea for one of those survey studies that one bureau or another in Washington is always doing, to no avail, since I've never read a one that arrived at any kind of a definite conclusion, so this one, according to my deep thinking, should be right up their alley. Here it is: Among all automobile drivers, whether left or right handed, which drivers make the most right hand turns and which make the least? The reply, most likely, would be the people who are right handed because that arm is the stronger of the two and also, most likely, has the better coordination.

And, also, it could be deduced that the sight of the right eye is stronger so naturally the right thing to do would be to turn in that direction. I haven't come up with any plausible reasons why some drivers are right-handed and some are left-handed, but the matter seems to me to be worthy of consideration. You want to know when I thought this up? The other morning as I was preparing my oatmeal porridge, I noticed I was stirring it clockwise, not counterclockwise, and I thought to myself, gee, I bet that's because I'm right-handed. I tried to stir the other way around, but that is not nearly so comfortable for me. I believe, though I have no reason for this belief, that a left-handed person would stir his soup or gruel in the counterclockwise manner. Then I thought, well, gee, this would be a good subject for some governmental agency to study and to survey but I don't believe that it really matters so long as the food being cooked turns out to be tasty and nourishing, and the same is true for cars being driven by right-handed or left-handed drivers, although there are more accidents on the highway than in the kitchen.

Well, the farmers are complaining again, this time about grasshoppers. Seems the little devils are everywhere, like boxelder bugs, except boxelder bugs don't do anyone any harm, and the grasshoppers eat everything in sight. Doc Klein tells me that the locusts of the Bible were really grasshoppers, and as we all know, a visit by swarms of locusts was considered a plague in those days. It wasn't so long ago that grasshoppers were a plague in this country, destroying whole crops, but now I guess science has them under control. Doc says they`re using fighter planes to spray the swarms of grasshoppers in the air. It works great, but Doc says there's some danger that people on the ground will inhale the spray and, well, be exterminated. If it's not one thing, it's another; that's the way the world goes these days.

7

If Not One Thing, Then Another

Well, I think history is pretty interesting, especially the Indian history in Minnesota. But the white man's history, the history of Minneota, is interesting, too, like the naming of the town. Very interesting. Too much water in the whiskey, a perfect name for us.

Maybe I'll be a historian instead of a scientist.

Anyway, Halvor Haakenson, the editor/publisher/owner/janitor of the Minneota Messenger, asked me to write a historical piece on the "locusts" in southern Minnesota. Good news, I'd say; another publication for David Sorenson. I'll have quite a resume by the time I graduate from college.

Maybe I'll be a writer.

But doesn't a writer have to be associated with some kind of content, like science or history? Not necessarily. I do have my novel. But the Swede says it's not very good.

Anyway, here's my historical piece on the locusts.

* * *

In 1855, the first white men came to Lyon County, in which, as you know, Minneota is located. One of the first settlers was James W. Lynd, a prominent fur trader who, in 1861, was elected to the state senate. A small town in Lyon County is named after him, as you know. Lynd later moved to the lower Sioux trading post near Redwood Falls and died there in 1862. He happened to be in Myrick's store the day the Dakota came to stuff Myrick's mouth with grass.

It was near Lynd—the town—that the grasshoppers were first sighted. It was the summer of 1873. That spring the farmers of Lyon County planted their first crop of any magnitude, mostly wheat, and by June it was clear that the promise of the magnificent dirt that covered southern Minnesota was, if anything, understated. The crop was going be bumper.

On the 17th of June, a group of friends was picnicking at Watson's Grove, near Lynd. The day was clear and bright, a beautiful day, so the sudden darkening was noticed immediately. There appeared in the sky a great cloud, like a sheet of dull silver. The cloud spun around in a circular pattern. "It seemed to be floating," said one of the picnickers. As the cloud came lower, they heard the sound; the cloud was alive—moving, buzzing, buzzing, buzzing. Alive. The cloud settled upon the earth not far away. The picnickers ran to their horses, who seemed jittery and worried.

Reports of the grasshopper cloud reached Minneota and other villages in Lyon County—"locusts," they were called. Many of the farmers did not believe the reports; they put them in the same category as the wild and inaccurate rumors, heard regularly every six months or so, that hostile

Sioux bands had returned to the area. A group was delegated to investigate.

The deputized farmers rode to Lynd without seeing any sign of a grasshopper invasion. When they reached the Redwood River, they went to the shallow, narrow part known as the Muzzy Flat—the place they usually crossed the river. At first they saw nothing amiss; it was the horses who balked. The farmers blinked and saw. The ground was undulating, said one farmer later. Extending from the river a hundred yards on either side, as far in both directions along the river as they could see—grasshoppers. The cloud was now a rug, covering everything. Grasshoppers everywhere. "At no place did I find less than a pile two inches thick with the creatures," said one farmer later, "and where they covered bushes, there might have been several feet of them."

So the invasion was confirmed. More grasshoppers arrived, and most of the farmers' crop was destroyed. It is in the nature of these insects to swarm together, so the destruction was somewhat patchy: one farm would be wiped out, the neighboring farm untouched. The state legislature set up a relief fund, but few farmers sent in applications, because it was feared that if people back east knew the extent of the destruction, they would think twice about coming out west to settle. The few desperate families who requested aid were denounced by the community. The local newspapers reported "fair crops" for the year.

In 1874, the eggs laid in the fall hatched in early May. The crop of grasshoppers was fully ten times as big as the 1873 population. Fields were stripped bare; roads, even railroads, were blocked by piles of the insects. In late June, the neonatal locusts rose from the earth, formed another living cloud, and swarmed away to the east. A week later, an even larger swarm from the west appeared in the southern Minnesota skies. A rumor of hostile Sioux spread, and several families packed their belongings and headed back east.

"The sound of them, oh, the sound!" wrote one pioneer woman in her diary. "When the silver cloud descends to earth at dusk, it's like the roaring wind. I hear them out there, eating our crops. I hear them! It's the sound of a hundred hogs turned loose in the fields. And they eat the clothing I hang on the line to dry!"

The locusts returned in 1875 and, in 1876, they ate most of the crops in 29 southern counties of Minnesota. Governor Pillsbury and the state legislature struggled to stem the tide. They set a bounty for grasshoppers—a dollar a bushel—and for grasshopper eggs—four bits a gallon. Pillsbury, a religious man, proclaimed a day of prayer: April 26, 1877. He asked the citizens of the state to set aside their religious differences for that one day and to pray with one voice that the land be freed from its plague. On April 27, a violent and unseasonal storm covered the southern half of the state with sleet and snow. Grasshoppers were never again a significant problem for the farmers of Minnesota.

So I was at the Swede's shack, reading from my novel-in-progress. The Swede had promised to hear it all, and criticize it, constructively. My novel was about the end of the world. "I'm not interested in the end of the world," said the Swede. "Only in the end of personal worlds, like death."

"But the idea! Doesn't the idea excite you?" I asked, plaintively.

The Swede shrugged, resigned to his fate. He alone, among all Minneotans, was about to hear a two-hour version of one of my ideas. What rotten luck! he probably said to himself, wallowing in self-pity, enjoying the wallowing, doing his duty as a listener to this young intellectual, very much like himself at this age, and thinking perhaps he was saving this young artist from the life of misfortune he himself had led. "David, you can't write novels about ideas. You'll never make a cent. You'll be frustrated and angry, and you'll turn to demon rum, like me. Like half the writers who ever lived. You'll turn into an artsy-fartsy alcoholic, like me."

"Why do you suppose so many novelists have been alcoholics?" I was diverted, I was on the track of another idea.

"Because they're so damn interested in ideas!" Many years later, I discovered that the Swede had written a novel, and maybe a thousand poems. A shocking discovery, because when he was alive, nobody knew this—not me, not even Sally. When I found the manuscripts, rummaging through his belongings after he died, the yellowed, dog-eared papers were in the process of being consumed by some unknown insect. There was a short, handwritten note of more recent vintage, in an envelope attached to the top of the old whiskey box that housed the decaying ideas. In his note, the Swede claimed to have identified the insects as boxelder bugs, and he claimed the bugs were critics, devouring poorly written sentences and leaving the good ones. And he said that he read from his novel, to himself and to his cat, once a year, on New Year's Eve, from 10 p.m. to 1 a.m. precisely. It was the only night of the year that the Swede did not take a drink and was completely sober.

"Why don't you write a novel about emotions, David? Why not the end of Sally Engstrom, instead of the end of the world?"

"I don't know why she killed herself."

"Well, find out. The only way to find out is to write the book."

My novel was terrible, as the Swede had feared, pure idea, lacking characterizations, color, and poetry. It described in numbing detail the formation and ultimately the collapse of a kind of stock exchange for gamblers, the Bet Exchange, like the Stock Exchange, in which the value of bets rose and fell as a function of their odds. The IDEA, as I explained again and again, having a multitude of characters say it in the same words, was that the bets were about the end of the world. "War" was one of the most popular bets, "Famine" was another. As international tensions increased, the odds on "War" being the cause of the end of civilized society in the Northern Hemisphere dropped. War bettors, who kept the odds assigned at the time of bet purchase, found their bets increasing in value and could sell them on the Bet Exchange, making huge profits.

Half of my novel was taken up explaining the mathematics of the idea. The other half was equally technical, equally soporific, explaining the actions of organized groups of bettors, who were trying to increase the value of their bets by making their particular catastrophe more likely. "Overpopulation" bettors, for example, lobbied congress for a baby bonus, and "Garbage" bettors hired scientists to invent a disposable car for rental agencies. Industrial production shifted from consumer goods to doomsday devices, although it was difficult to tell the difference.

The bettor organizations then discovered that it was more cost-effective, in ways that I laid out in unintelligible verbal formulas, to make other catastrophes less likely than it was to make their own more likely. Thus "War" bettors produced a nonpolluting car that increased the odds of "Pollution" bets and, simultaneously, decreased the odds of all remaining bets, including "War."

Soon an antidote to each and every world-ending calamity was discovered. Cheap and effective methods for cleaning air, water, and, yes, even lungs; international strategies that made wars ridiculous and costly; means of providing food, shelter, and clothing for everybody in the entire world.

Odds on all bets skyrocketed, their value all but disappearing—panic on the Bet Exchange. Capital dried up, and the economy could not adjust. It was the end of civilized society in the Northern Hemisphere.

* * *

"Well, how did you like it?" I asked, eagerly, breathlessly. When the Swede hesitated, I added quickly, "For a first draft. It's not finished, you understand. I plan to make revisions, and your criticisms —"

"Clever. It's very clever," said the Swede. "People betting on doomsday; it's ludicrous, but likely. Greed. High finance. Scientists prostituting themselves. Scientists seeing trees but not the forest. I like that part. My mother hated scientists, too."

It never occurred to me that the Swede had had a mother, and the idea made me nervous, for some reason. Why? I wondered to myself. But I responded with "I don't hate scientists."

"We used to have one of those crystal balls, you know the kind, there's a scene inside and you tip it over and it starts to snow inside. When I was about 15, I became convinced that the white particles inside were coconut. To prove it, I broke open the crystal ball. It wasn't coconut. I don't know what it was."

"I used to take things apart, too," I replied, "to see how they worked. My mother used to get really mad."

"My mother found out I had broken the crystal ball, and why. She said, 'That's what scientists are. They take something beautiful, and they've got to figure it out, and, in the process, they destroy it. And what they discover is not worth knowing.'"

I had once become interested in communication. Language, I had decided, was the source of the humans' dominance over other animals, the source of their intelligence. I read books on the origin of language—Freud said it came from grunts made during sex, an IDEA that I considered pure genius: anything that combined sex and science was, well, what more was there to life? I read books on linguistics, the arguments about nature versus nurture— are humans "speech birds" who learn to speak the same way songbirds learn their songs? And, so, human music: what was that, if not communication? if not sex? Sally had this idea, too, that sex and music were related, that great music described sex, and that that was the source of its attraction, its power. We had had many discussions.

I loved the story of Sequoyah, an illiterate Cherokee Indian, who invented a written language all by himself. Sequoyah was about 30 years old—the year was about 1800—when he became convinced that the secret of the white man's power lay in their "talking leaves" (pages of printed material). So Sequoyah, though he himself could not read English, set out to create a written form of the

Cherokee language. People laughed at his attempts, and not without reason. He first tried to create a symbol for each word, but he could never remember his own symbols. Then he had his great IDEA: he categorized the syllables that make up words in Cherokee, and he discovered that the number of syllables was quite small, at least when compared with the number of words. There were 86 syllables, by his count, and so to each Sequoyah assigned a symbol. The symbols were often English letters, some lower case, some capital. Some were English letters turned upside down— why not? Some were original artwork, original creations.

Sequoyah's tribe was upset with him, believing that he was neglecting his tribal duties to work on these mysterious markings, with little apparent purpose or product. Finally the community turned against him, and he was accused of witchcraft. A trial was set. Fortunately, Sequoyah had completed his task and he had taught the symbol system to his daughter. At his trial, he astounded his accusers by writing a letter to his daughter, conveying to her, in the written symbols he had created, any and all of the messages that his accusers could suggest. His accusers stood and cheered Sequoyah. This is why I loved the story of Sequoyah, perhaps more than any other story of science. "His accusers stood and cheered"! What could be greater reward, what could be greater satisfaction? A type of giant tree was named after Sequoyah: what greater tribute?

The Swede, too, he had a tree named after him: The Swede's Bedroom. When he lived in that big elm tree in my father's equipment lot, to keep my father from cutting it down. He outlasted my father, thank God, and the tree was spared.

I also learned sign language, the language of the deaf, in a rudimentary fashion, enough to know something of the way it was used to communicate; sign language, a language of hand forms, no voice required, was it not a miracle? And the poor cousin of sign language: blunt, stupid, but effective gestures. I was intrigued by gestures. I was especially interested in hand gestures. Hand gestures were used so often to communicate among students, one had to learn the basic ones, at least to differentiate the friendly from the hostile, like the wave (friendly) and the thumbs-up (friendly, positive) from the middle finger upraised (hostile) and the thumbs-down. It seemed to me that every hand and finger gesture had been used; each had some meaning. Jabbing all five fingers skyward meant "Treat your family!!", the pinky alone meant "Your 12-year old sister!!" Most of the meanings were hostile, aggressive. I was appalled. I wanted there to be more gestures of friendship, fewer of animosity.

I convinced Jon Coltvet of this need. The only finger presently unused, I said, was the fourth finger. We should define it, I told Jon. The fourth finger upraised should be defined as friendly, positive: I love you. That's what it should mean. Jon, who was going through a religious phase, thought this was a terrific idea. He agreed to practice it and to use it, the new gesture, in communication. He used it first on Sally. From down the block, he raised his fourth finger to the sky, in a gesture of friendship and love. Sally was stunned to see (what she thought was) Jon giving her "the finger" (a sexually hostile gesture). She returned the gesture, using her middle finger. Jon, from a distance, thought she was returning the fourth-finger gesture of love. He smiled, and he felt, suddenly, that the world had become a better place.

I read what was left of the Swede's novel as soon as I found it. It was much like my own, maybe worse; both crashed and died on the iceberg of ideas.

The Swede's novel had a scene in it, a scene in which the hero encounters a belligerent, strong, and ignorant adversary. It was the kind of scene in which, in a small town in the heartland of America, the adversaries would fight, pummeling one another with their fists. In the Swede's novel, the scene was intellectual: The physically weak, intellectually strong young man challenges his opponent to a different contest: "Let's say we have a list of questions, about general things, like history and biology. Each has ten questions. The one who answers fewer questions correctly, he gets a finger cut off. What do you say? The winner can cut off the finger himself. Get the whole thrill himself. Slice it right off, blood and flesh. It's the same as the other way, where the guy who's better in the strength department gets to inflict the damage. What do you say?"

The adversary agreed, an incredible response, I thought—one of the many problems with his novel. Nevertheless, the adversary agreed, and to make it less incredible, he cheated. He got to the guy who was making up the ten questions, threatened him with physical damage, and got the answers to the questions.

Question number 1: What is the hypothalamus, and what is its relation with the endocrine system?

The antagonistic lout was trying to remember the answer he had memorized: "The hypothalamus is a part of the `old brain' that is buried deep inside of the cerebral cortex. It controls, and is controlled by, the pituitary gland, the so-called master gland of the endocrine system, which uses hormones to influence bodily functions. Together the hypothalamus and the pituitary gland control many of the basic motivations, including hunger, thirst, sex, and aggression."

But the Swede's hero, who knew the lout had cheated, acted to distort the lout's memory: "Hypodermic. Hypodermic," said the Swede's hero, out loud. "Needles make pits, that's for sure. Hypodermic needles are pit makers, that's right. The hypodermic is related to the pit maker, but it stops disease, that's for sure. It ends disease. End o' disease, that's what a hypodermic is for, we know all that."

The lout wrote on his paper: "The hippodermic is a needle stuck deep inside of the brain, where it makes contact with a deep pit, and stops disease, but also sex."

The Swede's hero cut off the lout's finger.

Silly story, I thought. Even had the Swede's hero won the intellectual contest, the lout would not have accepted the judge's decision. No fingers would have been cut, unless the lout, in a rage, would have cut the hero's, and maybe it wouldn't have been his finger, either, maybe some other body part. Intellect depends on rules to win, strength has its own mechanisms. Intellect will win over strength only when intellect manages to play the strength against itself. Like when Dingus Anderson was sent to the wilderness, to avoid what he thought was an imminent attack by a physically superior adversary. The intellect won, because it created a powerful and frightening idea.

Maybe someday, I thought, I would revise the Swede's story, make him famous.

Maybe not, though. Pretty intellectual stuff. Not much emotion. Maybe throw it out. It is pretty contrived. All the intellectual stuff is contrived. Contrivance is the foundation of intellectual story telling.

Maybe I should just shift the focus to emotion. The blood and gore of a finger sliced off, sliced by a dull knife on a kitchen table with a plastic table cloth, the knife cutting the plastic, blood and tissue flowing through the cut to the oak table underneath, staining it. The fear (controlled by the hypothalamus), maybe focus on that. Tension building. Someone is going to lose a finger. Is the lout going to play by the rules? If he is losing? The lout tries to cheat; the lout never plays by the rules. The intellectual wins the contest, but loses his finger. Might makes right.

* * *

I droned on with my novel. The Swede told me later that he simply could not concentrate on my prose, it was too dull. Like a knife that could not cut a finger, it was too dull. The Swede's mind wandered. He wondered what he was doing here, listening to this dull prose: Is this some kind of role in life he had come to assume, to encourage young intellectuals who would never amount to anything? To encourage them to do things he himself had failed at? Maybe he should warn them instead. Might makes right, and you'd better not forget it! Ideas have no power, unless the purveyor is totally ruthless. And, even then, it's not the ideas, it's the power. The ideas are the surface justification for the ruthless use of power. Should he tell me this truth?

Maybe, he thought, he should tell me not to take life so seriously. If you take life seriously, you get depressed, and you take to drink, or you commit suicide. The only way to survive is to think of life as absurd; the French existentialists told us this, Camus and Sartre. Life is crazy, and to think so doesn't mean that you're crazy. Maybe he should tell me this.

What's important in life are the crazy things. There's another scene in the Swede's novel, a stupid, crazy scene: His hero is trying to watch television, but the antenna is pointed in the wrong direction. The Swede would have to describe the problem, as it existed in 1956, of few TV transmitters, maybe a total of three that someone in a small town like Minneota could pick up, maybe three stations that you could receive, each in a different direction, a problem that required for its solution a device on your roof, a motor that turned your antenna to the different directions, pointed your directional antenna to the proper station, only then could you get a good picture. Not a great picture, but a decent picture, one you could live with. Snow, but not too much snow, not so much you couldn't understand what was going on. You could tell it was Lawrence Welk and not a football game. Maybe that doesn't seem like much, but in 1956, it was impressive. People would come to your house, just to see. Yes, it is a musical program. That's incredible, that we can see that.

So the direction of the antenna was critical. The direction was controlled by the motor. In the cold Minnesota winters, the motor froze up, wouldn't work, wouldn't turn. You'd turn the dial to the right direction, but it didn't make the right sounds. Not the "clack, clack, clack . . ." that meant that it was turning from Minneapolis to Sioux Falls, just a "mmmumph, mmmumph, mmmumph . . ." that meant that it was froze up. The picture on the TV gave the same message; it stayed the same, or it got a little more snowy, because maybe the antenna turned just a hair, and of course then you couldn't get back to the old station, it was stuck between two stations, and you couldn't get either one. This happened almost all the time in winter.

Your antenna was stuck between two stations. You had nothing to watch.

So of course you had to climb up on the roof—and it's snowing, and the temperature is below zero, and there's a howling wind—and you're climbing up on the roof, really, with ladders, and slippery steps, and a roof like a sheet of ice, a two-story house, with a roof slanted at a precarious angle, designed to let snow fall off the roof onto the ground, likely to let you fall off the roof onto the ground, and icy, too, an impossible situation, dangerous, life-threatening. But if you want to see the show, you have to get up there. There is no other way.

It was a real scene! It happened often, and on many rooftops. Up onto the roof, scramble up to the rotor motor with a jug of hot water. Pour it on the motor. Jake on the roof, pouring hot water. OK to Karen, the teenaged daughter on the lawn, OK, try the rotor again. OK to Carol, inside, she turns to Sioux Falls, and it goes "Clack, clack, clack . . ." and the pointer moves, and all is right with the world.

Carol jumps up and down, waving to Karen, who starts jumping up and down and waving to Jake. The picture comes in clear. Well, maybe not clear, but you can hear the comedian's jokes and you can almost understand why the women's costumes are attractive.

I finished my novel, but the Swede had drunk too much, and fell asleep. I pushed on the solid gray door and let myself out. Walking back through the weeds and debris, back to civilization, I felt immature. I had "potential," as the Swede had said, but "achievement," whatever that was to be, seemed far in the future, along a path with many obstacles. If someone as talented as the Swede had stumbled—had failed, let's face it—how could I hope to succeed?

Indeed, what was success? (Placing the right bet on the destruction of civilized society!) And where lay success for me? In art, or in science? I felt pulled by each. In truth, I viewed art and science as the same. No, not that art should be logical or scientifically explainable, but that science is artful. A great theory, a significant empirical breakthrough—I knew these scientific events as intuitive creations of extraordinary beauty, like great paintings or great poems. I loved science, the way a musician loves a great symphony.

Emerging from the field that lay between the main road and the Swede's shack, I noticed that my jacket was covered with cockleburs. My mind ran to an article I had read in Science Digest, an article that described how scientists were using the principle of the cocklebur to create fasteners for dresses and trousers and other clothing. Velcro, it was called, or something like that. That's what scientists are, I thought; they take something totally worthless—analyze it, figure it out—and create something of extraordinary value. Extraordinary value, extraordinary beauty. How could someone not want to be a scientist?

The church? Heck, yes, I go to church. Faith Lutheran, that there's the name of it. And there's the Catholic church, too, over by Shorty Peetroons's, Saint Joe's we call it, it's real name is Saint Joseph's. That's it, pretty much, in Minneota; you're a Lutheran or you're a Catholic, and if you ain't one of those, you're pretty much out of luck. I mean for goin' to church.

Heck, the church, yes, the church is, well, it's the House of God and all that, but it's for to see your friends and neighbors, that kind of stuff. Pastor Greenfield is our preacher now, he's pretty good, but lots of people don't like him 'cause he took over from Pastor Bakken, who was here for a long time but then he went to Madison, and I think, well, goshdarn it!, people forget. I remember when Bakken first came, and nobody liked him then, 'cause they liked Pastor Johansen, who went senile on us. Greenfield ain't a bad preacher, though, I kinda like him. Sometimes he gets a little carried away, but then they all do, now and then.

The thing I always liked about the church was the standin' around after the service, outside if it wasn't rainin' or snowin'. That there's when you get to talk to your friends. It's a blamed funny thing, too, it is, the way you do this. A lotta people in the church don't even know this, I mean, like Lofty Sovik was really surprised to hear it when I told her, but she knew it was true, once I said it. See, people got their own spot out there in front of church, same as their own spot inside of the church, well, you know people always got their own spots, even in the parking lot, and everybody knows what they are, whose is whose, that kind of thing. People know that, even Lofty knew that. But they don't put the two and two together, and figure out where the spots are. Like Pete and Teddy Sorenson, who live in town, have a spot right in front of the steps, and all of them guys who live in town are right by them. The farmers, like me and all my buddies who live out here south of town, we got spots, too, and all our spots are on this here side, over here, on the right side of the steps. Those guys who live north of town, Kenny Dahlberg and his buddies, who live out by the dump and beyond, they's all over here, on the left side. Don't you see? You can tell where a person lives by the place he stands after the service is over. Most people don't know that, I'd say, they just knows that everybody got spots.

Well, all kinds of things go wrong, and geez! I just get a bang outta watchin' it, 'cause you know it's gonna happen. Like, pretty much all the close-in spaces are taken, see, and, well, the biggest problem is when you have guests or somethin', or worse yet, some strangers come to church, and want to be friendly after the services. There ain't no room for guests and strangers, so of course they gotta stand in someone else's spot, and that family gets pretty steamed up about no place to stand, and all us regular people are watchin' them to see what they are agonna do. Of course it's church here, it ain't like the baseball game or somethin', where if you take someone's spot, you might get a punch in the jaw. It's church, so they have to be nice. But they'll do little things, like start crowding the guests or strangers. Like last week, Spider Coltvet come out of church there, and he found someone standing in his space, well, it was really funny, 'cause they was guests of his! His family, a cousin or somethin' come out from Pennsylvania or someplace, but they was takin' up his space, and he just seemed to get mad, doesn't mean no matter it was his own kin or anything, he just stand right up next to them, crowdin' them, belly to belly, and you could see them gettin' uncomfortable and all, you can see the steam from his mouth goin' in their face, and maybe he steps on a shoe or somethin'. Well, it ain't long before Spider's cousins is movin' into Pete Sorenson's spot, and you can see Pete gettin' double mad, 'cause it ain't even his kin. And he's throwin' daggers with his eyes at Spider, but Spider, he don't care, so long as he's got his spot. Every man gotta protect his own spot, that's the way Spider thinks of it.

But guests and strangers ain't as bad as the other things, things that change things long-term. Like Tuffy Steensland, he had a mess of kids, and, of course, they all grow up and get bigger, stop playing in the yard, and start standin' in the family space. So the Steenslands need a bigger space, but heck!, like I said, all the space is used up. So one of the families outside of them, heck, we was one of them, and Sten Lillehaugen and his family, too, we all gets squeezed, and we may be havin' kids, too, and so we need more space when all of a sudden we got less! Goshdarn it! Sometimes it really gets funny, 'cause now you got two families belly to belly, and every darn Sunday! And nobody's going to give an inch! They're fighting for their space. In the Christian way, of course. Steppin' on shoes. And another big problem is trees. Funny thing about trees, they keep gettin' bigger and bigger, and we got a lot of those Christmas-type trees, evergreens, which are shaped kinda like a woman's skirt, biggest at the bottom. So these trees get bigger, at the bottom, and the family that has their space next to the tree finds their space getting smaller and smaller, 'cause the tree is takin' it. They start movin' over into somebody else's space, 'cause they figure they's good Christians, too, and it ain't their fault the tree is takin' their space.

The church is a funny place. I could tell you lots of stories, like, oh, there's so many funny things, like when Pastor Bakken, one time, he spilled the sacramental wine, all over the Swede, of all people. One time Spider Coltvet almost got in a fight with a bishop who came to visit, 'cause the bishop took Spider's parking spot.

One time some kids dropped a marble in the balcony and it rolled down, real slow, and dropped into the hairdo of Joy Oberstad, and they couldn't hardly find it for a week or so, and she didn't want to do her hair over, just 'cause a marble fell in there. Geez, it just makes me laugh to think about it. Geez, I sure do have a good time at church!

8

Communion with the Devil

My mother taught Sunday School, and my father was a deacon or something like that. The Sorensons were pillars of the church, as Pastor Bakken once called us. I don't think I was much support for the church—an institution about which I had grave doubts—but I had a very pronounced sense of ethics. I was intrigued by the idea of morality, the idea of doing right, the idea of doing good. Powerful ideas, wonderful ideas. My actual behavior, however, was about average on the morality dimension. "Lukewarm" was the term I used to describe it, a biblical term from Revelations, used to warn the followers of Christ that nothing less than fanatical devotion to moral principles would be acceptable; the "lukewarm," said the holy apparition to John, "I will spew from my mouth." I worried about this, about being a point or two shy of Jesus's standards of morality. But I couldn't seem to adjust my behavior accordingly. I imagined Jesus spitting me out of His mouth.

The place where I discussed ethics was Church. I spent quite a bit of time in Church: most of Sunday, often on Saturday, a night or two during the week, and Wednesday afternoons, when the schools "released" the students for an hour of religious instruction at their churches. As in all small Midwestern communities, the churches played a major role in the social life of Minneota. My church was Faith Lutheran. Most of the Norwegians belonged, and most of the Germans. The Belgians belonged to the Catholic Church across town. The Lutherans bought Ford cars and John Deere tractors and considered themselves to have a superior religion. The Catholics bought Chevrolets and Farmalls and considered themselves to have a superior religion. I was warned against dating Catholic girls, an activity that might lead to a "mixed marriage," but I did it anyway. My mother accused me of having lukewarm morality and left religious tracts on my bed.

My church was a member of an organization that was later to become the American Lutheran Church, which means that is was liberal Lutheran, not nearly as strict as the fundamentalistic organizations known as Wisconsin Synod and Missouri Synod. I once went to a Missouri Synod church, or tried to. I was stopped at the door by the pastor, who quizzed me on my religious beliefs.

"Do you believe the Bible to be the word of God?" asked the stern looking man in black robes.

"Well, sort of," I answered, shuffling my feet.

"Do you believe the Bible is literal truth?"

"Literal truth?"

"That everything in the Bible is literally true, exactly as written?"

"I believe the Bible is essentially true," I said boldly. I still hoped to get in without lying. A girl I was dating was a member of this congregation. A very pretty girl.

"Essentially true. Essentially true, is it? You think you're smart, young man. Let me tell you something, something in the way of life and death. You're fooling around with ideas that are life-and-death matters. You think you're smart, but you could be wrong. If you're wrong, you'll be in hell for eternity. I'd give that some thought, if I were you.

"Do you believe that Jesus rose from the dead and ascended directly into heaven?"

I had always considered this story comical, so I smiled, coughed, and said, "I think the story of Jesus rising and ascending is a colorful metaphor —" Words practiced in a speech class at St. Olaf, they flowed smoothly through my lips. I knew my case was lost, and I had decided to play the scientific Christian.

"Enough, please. I haven't the time now. If you really would like to discuss these issues, come around after the services. I would enjoy such a discussion, and I sincerely think you need it. You are in danger. But I cannot allow you in the church for services. Services are for believers."

So I didn't pass muster in the militant arm of the Lutheran forces. In my home church, however, a more liberal environment, I was accepted, even loved. Here I passed my catechism easily, regurgitating memorized answers to predetermined questions. What a strange way to learn! I favored Socratic methods, with doubt and questioning leading to reading and synthesis. Rote memorization is all right for the multiplication tables, I thought, but for religious issues? I did not see how it was possible to learn how to achieve eternal life by memorizing some words constructed by a committee of the church.

At Faith Lutheran, in Sunday School, at "release," and in catechism classes, I was accepted, but I was known as a troublemaker. For my questions, not for my antics. "Why did God the Father have to put His Son on earth? Why did Jesus have to die? Seems rather bloodthirsty to me."

Once I, along with my friend and classmate Tommy Lillehaugen, formulated the theory that Jesus was not divine and never claimed to be. The message of Jesus, according to me and Tommy, was that we are all sons and daughters of God, Jesus no more than Tommy and me. To prove our theory, we found a Bible with everything Jesus ever said printed in red. We examined every single such passage, and of course we found none that contradicted our theory.

Mrs. Gilsrud, our Sunday School teacher, listened to our presentation in stony silence. "Aren't you boys Christians?' That was her response. No questions, no criticism, simply direct attack on us blasphemers. I felt superior as she marched us down to the office of the reverend Peter J. Bakken, pastor of the congregation. Pastor Bakken will be interested in our theory, I thought; we will have a dialogue.

The knock on my door, the sheepish look on their faces. David again, and Tommy, too, this time. These kids! Heresy and blasphemy. And this from the best of the lot! It's the prophecies of Revelations. They're coming true. It won't be long now. Thank God.

I wonder what it is this time. Mary wasn't really a virgin, or it's scientifically impossible for Moses to part the Red Sea. Nobody lives 600 years. If it's not one thing, it's another. How I hate these conversations with David.

I wish I could get back to writing my sermon, I only have an hour. It's still rough, but I think it's going to be one of my best!

Of course, I couldn't let the boys know how distasteful these discussions were. So I said, "Very interesting theory, boys. I'm glad to see you taking such an active interest in the Bible, and in the historical Jesus. We'll have to discuss this at length sometime. But not now, I'm afraid. I have to prepare for this morning's worship. You understand, I'm sure. But we'll talk soon. I'm very interested. It may surprise you to learn that this is not the first time I've had to debunk this theory; it comes up commonly. I think I can show you another interpretation of Jesus's remarks. You must be aware that many great minds, over the centuries, have studied the message of Jesus. What we preach is the distilled wisdom of these great intellects. If the theory of two young boys is different from the interpretation of thousands and thousands of great minds, well, that might give you pause. Don`t you think so, David?"

"Yes, sir," David said, in that defeated voice of his. "I suppose." David no doubt felt that they were making a contribution to Christian philosophy, not attacking the divinity of Jesus. He had envisioned me as supportive, and he was disappointed with me. Of course, I knew how to get to him by now, how to shut him off. All I had to do was suggest that his theory had been proposed before, not once but many times. His idea was not original. It destroyed him.

I could see him wilt when I said it. His mind began to wander; he lost interest in the discussion (as I had hoped). He was staring at my vestments, the white robe in particular. For some reason, he was fascinated by the robe. "It has the look of silk," he once told me, "but of the practical variety, like parachutes, and with the same kind of smell, fresh and stale at the same time." I told him that many people had commented on it in that way.

"It would help if we were shown where we were wrong and where the great minds were right," said Tommy defiantly. "We shouldn't accept something just because someone says so."

"You're absolutely right, Tommy," I said, with an outward smile and an inward frown. "You should wait to be convinced. And I'll do that, I promise you. I'll convince you. Later."

I got up from my chair, as if to end the discussion, but I turned swiftly and added, "You must realize that when all the intellectual arguing is over, you find you don't know everything, and you can't know everything. You have to make a `leap of faith.' Sometimes you have to accept a truth without evidence."

David was embarrassed, as I knew he would be; he hated statements like that. "I don't know if I could do that," he said. "A scientist doesn't do that sort of thing." I felt a wave of boredom sweep over me. How many times had I reenacted this primordial scene, the young skeptic, the older, wiser guru? The science angle again. A straw man, easy to refute. I chuckled. "OK, maybe the evidence of the truth of our faith is not scientific, not as you know it." The waves of boredom grew more intense; it was like repeating the catechism. "But scientific evidence is not the only kind of evidence, David. There are some things you know with your heart, not with your mind."

"Are these things I know with my heart incompatible with what I know with my mind?" David's interest rose again, with a good epistemological issue. This was the discussion he had hoped for.

But I had no similar interests; I wanted them to leave. "No, sir," I said. "But the truth of the heart covers areas where your science of the mind fears to tread. Matters of faith. Matters of value." A mistake, I thought, as soon as I said it.

"Well, I believe you can have a science of values," said David, as I expected.

"I can see that you boys are here because you think a lot about spiritual matters. I think that's great. As you can see, some people get upset when you ask questions about

things that are sacred to them. Not me, no sir. I'm the same
kind of guy. I love this sort of talk. And any other time, I'd
talk for hours. But, spare me please. I have to work on my
sermon. We'll talk later, OK? I'd like that very much. I think
I can introduce you to someone, the spiritual Jesus. Our
Savior. He'll enter your heart and provide you with evidence
that will knock you for a loop, David. You, too, Tommy."

"I hope so," said David.

"But what do you mean . . . ," Tommy started.

"Later, Tommy. Not now, but soon." I smiled my
no-nonsense smile, and it was over.

We never had another discussion about Jesus.

When I came home after my abortion, I was
determined to get my life in order. I turned, of course, to
the Church. The prospect of seeing Pastor Bakken terrified
me, and I expected the worst. Why should the Church
accept me after what I had done? Danny was in jail, Danny's
wife was under a doctor's care, and most people considered
abortion to be a form of murder. My abortionist—a kind
and gentle man, an excellent doctor, a man who believed
that that there were no cut-and-dried moral issues, not even
abortion, but who personally found abortion repugnant, a
man who spent the better part of a day trying to talk me out
of the abortion, who charged me nothing for the operation,
who kept me in his home for three days after . . . he too was
now in jail, thanks to my father, who tracked him down and
had him arrested.

There's nothing to do for it except seek forgiveness. Yet
I had this nagging feeling, as I walked to the parsonage,
that I had done nothing wrong. I reviewed the events in my

mind. The "affair" with Danny. OK, yes, that was wrong. He was married, not to me. But I couldn't, couldn't think of it that way. It wasn't wrong. It was the one-in-a-million kind of love that should be given priority over a mundane commitment Danny had made to another woman, long before he knew me and before he knew what love could be. It was a mistake to get pregnant, that was wrong. We had been very careful, always using rubbers at first and then later having me fitted with a diaphragm. The device failed; should we be blamed for that? What did people expect, that such a love should not be consummated?

Then, finally, the abortion, the intentional murder of my unborn child. Yes, even I thought of it that way, as "intentional murder." I felt terrible, I felt guilty. But I was scared. I was petrified. I tried to imagine playing with my beautiful little daughter, loving her, watching her grow, but the image always dissolved into one of a lonely life, in a rundown shack, nothing to eat (I couldn't cook anyway), a dirty little girl crying without intermission. I had no husband, no prospect of one. I had no job, no house, nothing to provide the child with a reasonable chance in life. My abortionist-doctor had asked, why not have the baby and offer it up for adoption? It would be a joy in someone's life. Not in yours, but in someone's. "How do I live for these nine months?" I had asked in reply.

"With your parents, who deep-down love you."

"My parents have kicked me out of the house," I replied.

"Well, then stay with me and my family," said the doctor.

I started to cry. I have to say, I was tempted—I'm only human—but I just couldn't do it. I felt I had to erase my mistake; it was my only chance. The doctor reluctantly complied.

So. I'm on my way to see Pastor Bakken, to seek forgiveness for actions for which I feel no remorse. Pastor Bakken, though liberal compared to Missouri Synod Lutherans, considers all of my behaviors sinful in the extreme. Is there any chance at all that this meeting will turn out well?

I touch my index finger to the doorbell, and the first few notes of a familiar hymn are heard from the living room. "Rock of ages, cleft for me . . ." runs through my mind. To this day, I don't know what "cleft" means; it's a word I associate with babies with birth defects. "Let me hide myself in Thee" follows in my mind, though not on the doorbell. I can understand that desire.

I suppose I frowned when I opened the door and saw my night visitor. "Sally Engstrom. My, my!" It's all I can think of to say.

"I need to talk. Can I come in?"

I hesitate a beat too long, a delay that makes my words sound hollow. "Certainly, Sally." Another beat. "Of course."

I wish she had told me she was coming. And why did she have to come on a Saturday night? I thought I was going to have the entire evening to write my sermon. And I'm certain that this will be one of my best ever.

I step aside, and Sally enters. Through the archway to the dining room, Sally sees my wife and eldest daughter at work on a jigsaw puzzle. Mother and daughter look up to see who has arrived. Recognition forces their eyes to open wider, and my daughter's jaw drops, opening her mouth, making her look mentally retarded. It probably makes Sally wonder if her baby will be healthy.

"Let's go into the study, Sally. We can talk privately."

"Yes, that's it. A private talk. That's what I want," replies Sally. Her courage seems to be draining like blood from a serious wound.

Balaam, my beloved old black lab, comes up behind Sally as she turns toward the study. He shoves his nose between her legs and nuzzles her crotch. Sally is startled; I'm embarrassed; the dog's tail flaps wildly in eager friendliness. "Balaam!" I shout. "Bad dog!"

Sally smiles, and Balaam graciously accepts a few pets. The three of us enter the study. Balaam curls up by the fireplace and farts loudly, a trumpet heralding the opening of the plenary conference.

I fold my hands and try to look compassionate. "What can I do for you, Sally?"

"I want to make a new start in life," Sally says.

"I should think so."

"I'm ashamed that I've caused so much pain for so many people."

"I should think so." It's all I can think of to say. I imagine I sound like an idiot.

"I'm asking you to forgive me, and to help me make a new start." This seemed to be the last of the memorized material, as Sally flushed and fell silent.

"I'm so pleased to hear you saying this, Sally." I rise from my seat behind my desk and start pacing around the room. "God will have to do the forgiving, of course, but I would be very happy, very very happy, to help you mend your ways." And I am indeed pleased; this is what pastoring is all about—shepherding the flock. "Where shall we begin? Your baby, I think. You are pregnant, aren't you, Sally?"

"Well . . . , no, sir. Not any more."

"Oh, my goodness! A miscarriage! That's something, that's really something! You'd be surprised how many illegitimate pregnancies end in a miscarriage. I'm certain it has something to do with guilt."

"I had an abortion, Reverend Bakken."

I stop too abruptly and stumble forward a half step, a Laurel-and-Hardy move I know has compromised my authority. Instead of looking at Sally, I stare at the cross on the mantel. I don't speak, nor does Sally. The only sound in the room is Balaam's erratic snoring.

Finally I rub my forehead and say, "Sally, how could you?" It is more a cry of anguish than a reprimand.

Sally has prepared a speech on this topic, and now it runs its course. "Reverend Bakken, what's done is done. It's all in the past now—the bad ideas, the stupid things I did, the terrible things that happened, everything. I don't want to talk about the past; there's nothing I can do about it. I made some mistakes. Okay. Now I want to make a new start." Her voice weakens as she adds, "Can't you help me do that?"

"Sally, abortion is murder, in the eyes of the Lord. I can't overlook murder."

Balaam starts to twitch and moan, as if in pursuit of the ideal rabbit. Sally and I watch, transfixed. Neither of us wants to continue our discussion. Neither of us knows what to say next.

"Danny!" I suddenly exclaim. "Danny made you get an abortion! That's it, isn't it?!"

Sally is silent.

"Why, the whole thing is his fault, isn't it?! Dear God! What evil this man has wrought! He seduces an innocent child, gets her pregnant, tries to run away with her, forces her to have an abortion. . . . And to think that he was a deacon of our church! Of my church!" I'm pacing furiously around the room. I'm raving. "Do you know what this means, Sally?"

"No," a tiny voice squeaks, "what?"

"It's all my fault!" I'm screaming. "It's all my fault! I'm supposed to be the prophet, I'm supposed to watch for sin, I'm supposed to stop it before it goes too far. Me! I'm the shepherd of my flock! I should have known, I should have stopped him!" I slam my fist down on my desk, rattling a metal ashtray. Balaam leaps up and barks loudly.

"Yes, Balaam! Like Balaam's ass, you speak, don't you? There's an angel of the Lord, sword drawn, in the path of sinners! From now on —" I stop ranting suddenly and look at Sally. "But I'm too late to help you, aren't I? I'm so sorry. Can you forgive me?"

Sally sits stunned, seemingly unable to speak. Balaam, still excited, leaps up onto my back, pushing me forward into Sally's chair. I, Sally, and the chair fall into a heap by the double doors to the study, which suddenly open. It's my daughter.

"Are you all right, Daddy?" There is fear in her eyes.

Sally was reinstated as a full-fledged member of Faith Lutheran, portrayed to the board of deacons (now one member short because of Danny's incarceration) as a worthy reclamation project, and delivered into the hands of Margaret Gilsrud for proper handling. Mrs. Gilsrud, Peggy to her many friends, was a cheerful, nurturing sort of person who spent the greater part of her life seeking opportunities to display kindness to others. She accepted her commission with Sally with some reluctance, given the heinous and unkind nature of her sins, but Peggy was not one to dwell on the past. Nor was Sally, these days. Peggy Gilsrud, a saint about to celebrate her fiftieth birthday, found herself becoming fast friends with Sally Engstrom, a sinner still shy of her twentieth.

Sally's appearance in church that first Sunday caused something of an uproar—an agitated, quiet uproar composed of sharp whispers, rollings of church programs, crossings and uncrossings of legs swathed in shiny gabardine or nylon, coughs and clearings of throats, a soft whistle from the back left, a faint "Oh!" from the front right. Peggy, who had picked Sally up for church, marched her right down the center aisle and sat with her in Peggy's spot—third pew left—and even let Sally have her seat on the aisle, where the light appeared to form a halo around Pastor Bakken's head when he delivered his sermon. Peggy thought twice about relinquishing the seat that gave her so much comfort and spiritual reassurance, especially today when she had not yet come to know Sally. But the alternative was to put Sally between her and her husband, a deacon who was already upset by the whole affair and who, with a nasty and unpredictable temper, might create an unpleasant scene. Perhaps the sight of Reverend Bakken's halo would be just the medicine this poor young girl needs.

As a matter of fact, Sally did notice the halo of light and did take it as a favorable omen. The day went well, better than Sally had hoped, much better than she had feared. The attention she attracted at first shifted during the early parts of the service to the balcony, where some boys in the farthest pew were playing instead of worshiping and dropped a marble, which rolled slowly down the inclined balcony on the bare-wood steps, step by step, rollll . . . kerplunk, rollll . . . kerplunk, until it fell from the balcony onto the parishioners below, who were awaiting the marble with the kind of petrified tension that people in London must have felt when they heard German buzz bombs, waiting for them to drop from the sky. The marble landed with a dull thud in the beehive hairdo of Joy Oberstad, where it remained for the duration of the service. The neighboring worshipers were racked by silent laughter; only Albert Gulbrandson, a merry farmer, failed to keep his laughter in check, and every five or ten minutes thereafter his high-pitched giggle skimmed through the church, reminding Sally of the cry of the loon, her favorite bird.

Albert's giggle combined with Pastor Bakken's sermon to produce some unusual effects. Pastor Bakken's sermon, he had announced at the outset, was not the one listed in the program: "Is Sin an Action or an Attitude?" Instead it was a somewhat disorganized but obviously fervent speech on the topic, "Balaam's Ass and Our Response to It." Albert, of course, was laughing at the marble in Joy Oberstad's hair; his giggles were unrelated to Pastor Bakken's words. Nevertheless, even random pairings often seem to make sense, especially when a word like "ass" is being bandied about. When Bakken opened by asking, "How many of you are familiar with the story of Balaam's ass?", Albert was thinking about the marble and giggled.

Bakken told the story of a man named Balaam who was asked by the Moabites to curse the wandering Israelites who had appeared on the border. Balaam, a God-fearing man, rode his ass to meet the Israelites, to curse them, and thus kindled the anger of the Lord. An angel of the Lord stood three times in the path of Balaam, sword drawn, ready to slay him. Balaam could not see the angel, but the ass could. Three times the ass turned away from the road, saving Balaam's life. Each time Balaam beat his ass in anger (and each time Albert giggled). Finally the ass spoke, complaining about the treatment it was receiving. Then the Lord opened Balaam's eyes and he saw the armed angel. He realized that the ass had saved his life. Bakken read from the Bible, "`. . . and he bowed down his head, and fell flat on his face."

Bakken at this point looked up, pausing for a moment to prepare his audience for the stinging conclusion. Suddenly Albert convulsed in a diarrhea of giggles. A group of adolescent boys in the back right broke into uninhibited laughter. For a second or two, the laughter infected the entire crowd, producing an outburst followed by decreasing haws and titters and familiar sounds that can only be described as people trying to swallow their mirth.

Bakken's face turned beet-red with anger. He, of course, had no idea why his congregation was laughing; his concentration on his sermon was so intense that he had been unaware of the marble. He paused, then seemed to collect himself, apparently deciding to ignore the laughter and make his point.

"The Bible is full of prophets, men of God, who take a stand against sin. These men seek out sin, and they root out sin. They find a sinner, and they say, `Brother, you have sinned. You are sinning!' Like Balaam's ass, they say, `If you don't stop going down this path, you will feel the wrath of the Lord!'"

The next words on Bakken's hastily handwritten pages were, "I will be your Balaam's ass!" Suddenly it came to him that all this unexplained laughter was due to the word "ass." Disgust rose up within him. What a juvenile reaction, he thought. He decided to challenge his congregation. "We must all be asses for the Lord!" he cried aloud.

Silence.

Good, he thought. Say anything with authority and it commands respect. His anger receded, and he pronounced the benediction. The sermon was over. A little disorganized, he thought, but passionate. Passion is better than order, he thought.

When Pastor Bakken told Sally and me about his thoughts during his sermon, I thought it was complete nonsense. Of course, a lot of people believe that passion is preferable to order, but not David Sorenson. I believed the opposite was true: better order than passion. Order was good, passions were bad. Passions, particularly anger and lust, had brought me many times to the brink of sin, if not thrown me over it, whereas order . . . well, order was the basis for Science. In my not uncomplicated philosophy of life, order was the unifying principle, explaining ethics, aesthetics, epistemology, and metaphysics. An ethical life is a principled (ordered) life, beauty is a characteristic of a pleasing design (order), knowledge is the product of the scientific search for regularities (order). And God is order, or at least the intelligent hand behind it all. "God is love," Mrs. Gilsrud had often asserted; "No, God is order," I had always replied. Mrs. Gilsrud worried about my soul.

My ideas were worse than she imagined. Not only did I believe that God is order, I explicitly denied the proposition that God is love. "Love," in my ordering of the universe, was an interruption of the natural order, an intervention that caused events to proceed in a way they would not have normally done. God's love, in my reading of the Bible, disrupted the natural order, creating miracles such as the parting of the Red Sea, the healing of the sick, and the raising of the dead. These acts of love were disturbing to me; they frightened me. It was like a game in which one was supposed to play by the rules, and then the referee would grant a dispensation to one player he was fond of. It wasn't fair. And, worse yet, it was unpredictable. I didn't believe any of it. I developed my philosophy of the Bible's miracles as "colorful metaphors."

Twice, however, I experienced God's love directly, and my faith in order was tested. In one, at Bible Camp, where I spent two weeks each summer of my teen years, I and the other campers had gone early to vespers, the evening worship in the small log-cabin chapel. We had done so because of the rain, a soft and sticky rain that came at the end of a hot and sticky day. Midway through vespers, the rain turned from a drizzle to a torrent, and the lights went out, leaving only a dozen altar candles to provide an anxious glow. A great wind began to howl. The camp counselors got up and tried to close the wooden shutters on the windows, but the shutters popped from their hands, pulled by a mysterious force.

Then I heard a sound that reminded me of a train in the distance, and I knew immediately what it was: tornado! I had learned early, perhaps as an infant, to fear the cues to an approaching tornado: a hush, a rush, and the sound of a distant train. It was part of the training for children in middle America. The old chapel began to creak and groan. Or was it me that groaned?

We're goners, I thought. The chapel was the worst place to be, on a small hill in one of the few unforested areas. The tornado will seek us out; like winter sledders, tornadoes love a hill, love to ride it up, bounce over the top, and float back to earth, spinning and happy with a great leap. The tornado will surely take the unforested path, the line of least resistance; every natural disaster, from lightning to floods, chooses a route that expends the least amount of its energy. We're goners.

But the tornado rumbled by, missing the chapel by maybe a hundred yards. I felt God's love. I sang with a great spirit, "Nearer my God to thee!," and I believed it. I discovered the next day that the tree against which I had been leaning just before the call to vespers had been pulled from the ground, its giant roots exposed. Had it not started to rain, I would have been standing there when the tornado hit. I decided that God had spared me for some purpose.

The second inspirational experience occurred during a meeting of the Luther League, a group of young Lutherans. Pastor Bakken asked me to take the collection that night, to pass among the others with a collection plate into which they put nickels and dimes to offset the minor expenses of the League. I agreed readily to any task that did not involve public speaking. About halfway through the meeting, however, I happened to look down at my corduroy pants and saw that my fly was open. I placed a song book discreetly on my lap and yanked the zipper. The zipper seemed to be caught on a thread. I yanked harder, and the zipper came up, but too easily. I had a sinking feeling. I raised the song book and saw that the zipper had popped out of its track on one side. The zipper was at the top of his fly, but my fly was still open. In five minutes, I would be asked to pass the collection plate—with my fly open.

I considered my options. I could refuse to pass the plate: that would require an explanation, and I could think of none. I could make gagging noises and run from the room: possible, but tricky, since standing up would expose my open fly. Any other alternatives? (I never considered telling the truth.) I decided to pray. Stranger prayers than this have been answered, I thought. Moses was in a bind, too, when the Red Sea parted. And I had just read about the locusts that invaded Minnesota in the late 1800s and were eliminated by a statewide day of prayer. So I composed a silent prayer: "Dear God, please get me out of this one. I know it seems like a small thing to you, but it's a big thing to me. Please, please, please, please—"

Pastor Bakken broke into this silent chant. "David, would you take the offering?"

But Tommy Lillehaugen, the president of the Luther League, took the plate from Pastor Bakken. Tommy made a little speech about the rising debts of the League ($9.79 now) and asked the Leaguers to kick in a little extra this evening. He passed among them. I dropped a five-dollar bill into the plate. Tommy looked up, more in astonishment than gratitude. My face had a smarmy look.

Even I was impressed by this miracle, that God would have time in this worrisome world to think about my open fly. "Even I," I say, because I really expected God to be involved in everything, in matters trivial as well as profound. My favorite Biblical passages had to do with this point— passages in Matthew and Luke, for example, that insist that God knows the life histories of individual sparrows, and that all the hairs on a person's head are numbered and recorded in one of God's files. God's involvement with trivialities fit with my philosophy of life, with its emphasis on order; if God is order, then God is present in the details of events. It wasn't so much that I thought God would be ignorant of my malfunctioning fly, it was that I didn't think God would bother Himself with a matter that . . . well, was so nearly sexual.

* * *

Sigrid Huseth, president of the Ladies Aid, was fuming. She admired Pastor Bakken greatly, maybe a little too much. His sermon today, a little disorganized perhaps but full of energy and heat, had stirred her deeply, and she was eager to take up the sword of the Lord against the sinners. She was fuming because she, like Bakken, had assumed the congregation was laughing at the word "ass."

Sigrid was leading her women in the coffee-and-doughnuts after the service when Peggy Gilsrud entered the dining area with Sally Engstrom. Indignation swept over her, then anger. Her second wave of anger, this one was particularly intense, almost pleasurable; it had no doubt built on the fuming anger of before. Sigrid was not the sort who would analyze the sources of her emotions, but she recognized the intensity, and it gave her great satisfaction. Her eyes narrowed to slits, and she watched Peggy and Sally take coffee and snacks and move to a corner. Peggy's husband joined them, Peggy's husband Don, a deacon of the church. A deacon of the church!

"Kinda turns your stomach, doesn't it?!"

Sigrid jumped, startled, but didn't bother turning her gaze to the fat young woman addressing her. "Marianne, it certainly does. You wouldn't think she'd have the nerve to show her face around here, after all she's done."

"She went and got an abortion, did you hear that?" Marianne Brynestad tried to yank her girdle down from where it had ridden during the services, but it was a hard pull today; it couldn't be done casually. She would have to visit the ladies' room soon.

"Yes, I certainly did, Marianne," said Sigrid, her eyes riveted on the small group in the corner.

"Why do you 'spose the Gilsruds are having anything to do with her?" It was an honest question, for Marianne really didn't know and wanted to.

"I don't know, Marianne. You know Peggy. If there ever was a Pollyanna, she's it."

Marianne nodded vigorously, though she didn't know what a Pollyanna was. It was enough to know that she didn't want to be one.

"Perhaps it's time to take up the sword of the Lord and cut off a few heads," said Sigrid. The head of John the Baptist appeared in her imagination and she shook it off, since it was the wrong vision. "I mean figuratively," she said, realizing that she was speaking to a woman who more than once had forced soapy water into the mouths of children who, others said, ought to have their blasphemous mouths washed out. Unfortunately Marianne thought "figuratively" meant "literally." Marianne continued throwing daggers with her eyes.

Across the room, David joined the enemy camp. Now a freshman at St. Olaf College, he had hitchhiked home for the weekend. He was glad to see Sally, and he told her so. Sally thought, well maybe there's some hope; so far the day had not gone half bad.

David recalled the day he and Tommy Lillehaugen had developed the theory of Jesus the man. He apologized to Peggy Gilsrud (who laughed and said something like "Boys will be boys"). David said that he had proposed the same theory in a religion class at St. Olaf and that the theory had been demolished by a "brilliant theologian." "At least it made me read the Bible a lot! So it wasn't all bad!" Peggy smiled, and Don smiled, and Sally smiled, too.

A cozy little band of sinners and heretics, thought Sigrid across the room. She had had run-ins with David before, with his wild ideas and his stubborn debating style. Once he had discovered an old Jewish folktale about a woman named Lilith, who was supposedly Adam's first wife, before Eve. Can you imagine? A Jewish folktale, besides. David had claimed that Jewish mothers used to sing to their babies,

"Lilith, abi," which in Hebrew meant "Lilith, stay away" or "Lilith, go away" or something like that. From this came the word "lullaby," according to David.

But Sigrid had handled him just fine. Do you think God would have let a divorced man into the Garden of Eden? David had had no reply to that.

Across the room, the little band of heretics and sinners was convulsed with laughter. "A marble fell into Joy Oberstad's hair?" laughed Don. "My goodness! It'll be a month before they find it!"

Albert Gulbrandson, standing nearby, overheard them and started to giggle again. He joined the merry band and gave them an eyewitness account: "We was sittin' there, singin' the hymn there, and I heard this noise. What the heck is that? I says, and I look at Wilma, and she looks at me, and I think, Oh, boy! Somethin' is rollin' down the balcony, and goldarnit if we ain't sittin' just about, well, I figures it's goin' to drop right about on us. We all was listenin', and I was tryin' to count the steps, and darned if I didn't go and lose the count, but I knew that the blamed thing, whatever it was, was agonna come down on us there pretty darn soon, so I throws up the hymn book over our heads like a darn umbreller. No sooner I done that and this here marble comes fallin' from the balcony and what happened? The blamed thing lands kerplunk in her hair, what's her name. Joy Oberstad I think it is. Well, Holy Smokes! It don't come out! It's in there for keeps, the way it looks. So I starts to laugh. And laugh. Shoot, you heard me, I couldn't hold it in. Still! Still it makes me laugh." Albert giggled, as did the others. "I betcha that marble is still in there."

Albert laughed heartily. What a warm and friendly man, thought Sally. A face like an open fireplace.

Wilma Gulbrandson, Albert's wife, came up looking distressed, as if her refrigerator had gone off and all the food were spoiling. "Come along, Albert. It's time to go." Mrs. Gulbrandson forced herself to look at the Gilsruds, and nod. But she steadfastly avoided looking at Sally or David. "All right, Ma," said Albert cheerily. "Well, I guess I see you guys later, then," he said to the others.

Wilma yanked his arm so hard he nearly stumbled. Albert's smile faded, and he looked at this wife, puzzled, afraid like a child that he had done something wrong without his knowing it. She dragged him off toward the door.

David looked around the room. He noticed that, as the crowd thinned out, an empty zone was forming around the Gilsruds, Sally, and him, and he felt isolated, as if he were on an island, far from the mainland shores. An island under siege, besides. People were avoiding Sally, that was clear. Was it because she made them feel uncomfortable, or was it more active, something like hate? Christian hate, a terrible concept. David caught the eye of Sigrid Huseth across the room. Jesus! There's the hate! David could not hold Sigrid's gaze, and looked away. He shivered uncontrollably, which Sigrid noticed with a smile.

Peggy Gilsrud took Sally over to talk to Pastor Bakken. David found himself alone with Don Gilsrud, whom David likened to a cigar-store Indian: solid, reliable, silent, a personality made of wood. But before David could slip away, Don grabbed his arm and spoke with animation. "Bakken made her. She wouldn't have done it if he hadn't asked her to. Pleaded with her. He was desperate, as you can imagine."

"What are you talking about?" asked David, anticipating an unpleasant exchange of views on Sally.

"Peggy. I'm talking about Peggy. Peggy would never associate with Sally if Pastor Bakken hadn't insisted. She's got too much of a kind heart, can't ever say no." Don was nervous. He was speaking rapidly, without the usual Midwestern drawl, and he kept rubbing his forehead as he spoke. "We certainly don't approve, you know that."

"Sally's made some mistakes, but it looks to me like she wants to get back on the straight and narrow," said David. "Mrs. Gilsrud is a very Christian person, very forgiving. I'd say what she's doing reflects well on her. I don't know if you can have too much of a kind heart. Most people don't have any. Look at Sigrid Huseth over there —"

Don looked over at Sigrid. He too shivered and looked away. "I think Sigrid feels like most of us feel. It's a little late for Sally to mend her ways."

David wiped a sweaty palm on his trousers. "Jesus forgave the man on the cross next to him. Better late than never."

"The man on the cross was a thief, David. Sally killed her unborn child."

"There's only one unforgivable sin, Mr. Gilsrud. And abortion's not it." David liked his response. A relevant Christian fact. Surely the puny intellect of his rival in debate would have difficulty matching his point. Perhaps he had won, with a single salvo.

"Are you defending her, David? I realize she was a friend of yours, but, Dear God!, she's a murderer, David!"

David could not think of a response. He felt the debate slipping, but he wasn't sure how he had lost hold of it, so soon.

"She chose pleasure over responsibility, David, and when it came time to pay the piper, she killed her infant child."

"It wasn't born yet," said David weakly.

"You'd best give this some thought," Don said. "You can't choose friendship over morality." With this, he walked away, leaving David with his thoughts.

David's thoughts were racing. He had done poorly in the exchange with Don, had lost the debate. How had this happened? He was not concerned with Sally at all, only with his own inability to defeat a cigar-store Indian in an intellectual argument. Don had shifted from the intellectual issues to something else, something personal, and he had lost poise. He had become inarticulate. He had wanted to shout obscenities at Don, he wanted to say that Don was a heartless, unforgiving, unchristian son of a bitch who had sex with sheep. Somehow Don had said that sort of thing to him, but Don had the skill to say it in a civil manner. He didn't have that skill. He wondered if he should try to develop it. It seemed to win more arguments than logic did.

His thoughts turned to the concept of the unforgivable sin. Apart from the concept of original sin, which David had finally dismissed as "unfair and ineffective," no idea in religion so captivated him as the notion that there existed a sin that God would not forgive. "Blasphemy against the Holy Ghost"—that was it, the unforgivable sin. David used to sit in church, with some uneasiness, muttering to himself, "The Holy Ghost is a turd." Nothing happened. But David still wondered. Perhaps, in that instant, he had cut himself off from all prospects of Heaven. Like Sally, he thought now. "The Holy Ghost has sex with sheep," he muttered to himself. Nothing happened.

People, like God, have a concept of an unpardonable sin. Don Gilsrud obviously had such a concept. Neither Don's nor God's, however, could David pin down in his mind. God's unforgivable sin seemed to have something to do with rejection, Don's seemed to have something to do with sex. The unintelligible sin, thought David, is more like it.

* * *

For supper that evening my mother heated up some leftover liver-dumpling soup. I was still thinking furiously, trying to order the pattern of events of the day, of recent weeks. I slathered butter on a Nabisco cracker and pushed at a dumpling, watching the butter melt and form greasy little islands in the soup.

"What do you think of this Gilsrud kid, David?" asked my father suddenly. Don and Peggy's son was the quarterback of the high school football team this year, and the team was so far undefeated.

"I think he has sex with sheep," I said.

"David!" screamed my mother. "What a thing to say!"

"I'm sorry. I think I've had enough of the Gilsruds for one day."

My mother agreed with this statement. "Yes, you'd think Peggy would have more sense. Imagine parading that tramp around like she was her daughter or something. Sitting with her, right up front."

"It wasn't her idea, Mom. Pastor Bakken made her do it."

"Well, then, you'd think Pastor Bakken would have more sense."

"It's his job, Mom. He's in the forgiveness business."

"Forgiveness is for those who show remorse and ask for it. Sally, it looks like to me, is still in communion with the devil."

I didn't reply, so my father seized his opportunity to turn the conversation back to football. "Well, I've been in communion with the coach, and he says . . ."

I tuned him out. Communion with the devil, communion with the coach, blasphemy against the Holy Ghost, a theory that Jesus is not divine, and a marble in Joy Oberstad's hair. My soup was cooling, and the buttery grease on the surface began to look like wax.

Stanley DeBays

Stanley DeBays is dead. He died yesterday in Our Lady of the Sorrow's Nursing Home in Redwood Falls, where he had lived since 1960, rising to the position of Chief of Police before his retirement in 1990. Some say he was fired, which is quite possible because we know he once knocked the mayor out during a council argument. Just as well, though, for Stanley went senile on us a few years later. And then he got cancer, and that's what killed him.

Stanley DeBays was born in Minneota on June 9, 1934, to Paul and Priscilla DeBays. Stanley was a soldier for a while at the end of the Korean War, returning to Minneota to drive a truck for . . . someone, I can't remember who. Probably Oberg's Hatcheries. In 1960, Stanley took a job as police officer in Redwood Falls, which surprised us because, in Minneota, he was a wild kid. He surprised us again by doing a bang-up job as police officer; by all accounts, he was the best Chief of Police in the history of Redwood Falls. He knew all the tricks of the young hoodlums and thwarted all their plans. Good for Stanley!

Stanley was married three times, the first to Mary Braun of this community, and the last to Beulah Anderson of Redwood Falls. In spite of all this marital activity, Stanley had no children. That we know of. Services will be held at the Norwegian Lutheran Church in Redwood Falls on Saturday, April 22. Stanley's wife, Beulah, died two years ago, so Stanley's only survivor is his mother, Priscilla, who lives on in the Minneota Rest Home. She lost her mind about five years ago. In times like this, that's a blessing. Believe you me.

9

Gratuitous Sex
and Violence

As I read the obituary in the Messenger, a wave of relief
swept over me, quite unexpectedly. Debil, the name by
which we all knew Stanley DeBays, had been my tormentor
during the first twenty years of my life, a constant thorn
in my side, the evil presence in my nightmares, the bully
whose cackling laugh I still hear at times as he sees me, a
pencil-thin teenager with thick glasses, and hurls his most
terrifying epithet—"Sissy!" It is synonymous with "Queer!"
He's sitting in a black Studebaker tipped to the driver's side
by the weight of the driver, Debil. He has a pack of like-
minded friends who sit with him in the car and cackle in
unison with their leader. I am walking in front of the car,
walking to my father's hardware store, mercifully close,
only ten more steps . . . But I can't seem to get my legs to
move, they have frozen for some reason. I entertain the
idea of lifting my leg with my hands, placing it forward,
but I know if I do, Debil wins, so I don't. I smile at Debil,
a smile full of fear and shame, a sickly smile that I know
looks just like the smile of a homosexual. I think perhaps
Debil is right, perhaps I am queer. My right leg crumbles
as I shift weight to it and I stumble, preventing a fall only
by a hand on Debil's left fender. "Get your fucking hand

off my car!" says Debil, cackling. Distracted, I lose control of my bladder, and a warm sensation covers the front of my corduroys. Luckily, it's cold, and my coat covers the stain, or so I hope. I fall to my knees and walk that way, on my knees, to the hardware store. I climb the steps on my knees, which I find extremely difficult, and I'm nearly knocked to the ground when Albert De Flandre comes barging out. Albert looks at me on my knees; he shakes his head but doesn't say anything. As Albert holds the door, I scuttle past, into the store, where feeling returns to my legs, and I stand up straight, surprised to discover that I have not peed in my pants. "Surprised" is not the right word; more like "proud." I have survived.

Two years later, I read a second obituary: Priscilla DeBays, Debil's mother, is dead at 95. Another wave of relief rolls over me: She cannot again spawn a devil-son like Debil.

Isn't that silly?!

When I was young, I hated fiction (except, of course, science fiction) because it made me extremely uneasy to read the kinds of stories that were popular then, in which someone evil made life miserable for the story's hero, was a constant threat until vanquished in the last pages. Like Fagin in Dickens's Oliver Twist - no, better, like Bill Sikes. When I was young, I did not see the source of these fears, but now I do. Debil was my Bill Sikes, Debil was my constant threat. And now he's dead. And his mother, dried-up womb and all, is dead, too. There will never be another Debil in my life.

Debil, in my life, was the personification of evil. Evil, I decided, is someone who wants to do you harm, cause you pain. I still believe so, I think it's a very good definition. So "good" is defined at the same time. Good is someone who wants only your happiness, free of pain.

Perhaps Debil did me a favor: I learned what evil was, at a young age. And by teaching me about good, Debil made it possible for me to love. Love, virtue, and happiness became the same to me.

How could I fear a man who did all this for me? Is fear necessary to learn the great lessons of life? I hate to think so.

The world breaks everyone, but some are stronger at the broken places. So said Hemingway. It's true for me: The bullies in my life made me stronger, gave me the edge when facing later evils, gave me the power to stand up to evil, for myself. Bullies are like dragons encountered on the hero's journey, to be devoured so the hero may rise, Phoenix-like, from the ashes.

I wish Sally had been able to devour her dragons. Instead, they devoured her.

✳ ✳ ✳

Bright, clear, unseasonably warm but crisp, like the crackling leaves all around, leaves with the earth's colors—brown, orange, yellow, red. A bad day for hunting pheasants, thought David; they'll stay on the ground, they won't flush. But with a day so beautiful, who needs game? A hike through the tall grass, the ripe corn, and the fields of thistles and cockleburs, it's enough, with a sun like this. It's not a day to inspire killing.

Sally had a headache, a splitting one, a hangover from the night before. Looking out the window of her rented room, she saw not the Indian Summer that David saw, but bright light, painful and angry. A day like this will bring them out, Sally thought, out of their cozy little houses, off their cozy little farms, promenading up and down, stopping to chat, smiling without interruption, enjoying the weather. Well, they won't flush me; I'll lie low.

Sally flopped onto the creaky old single bed with the roll-bar at its head. She watched a spider in a corner—Rosemary was the spider's name. Rosemary was busily repairing her web for a new day's trapping. The sheer industriousness of it made Sally's head pound, so she closed her eyes and watched little spots and tubes float on the inside of her eyelids. Who had it been last night? Oh, yes, Billy Anseele. In the bathhouse at Dead Coon Lake. Cheap beer. Red Fox, something like that. Cheap booze always gives me headaches.

Is there an end to this?

I met Catherine Engstrom in 1888. She was one of the Indian lovers, one of those who thought me a hero, a god, really. I told her that Sitting Bull was only a man, a man who had been beaten, a leader of a people who had been crushed; I was a failure, and my people were suffering, cold and starving on barren reservations. She was about thirty years old, with a son, about 15, I'd guess. In 1890, she moved into my cabin and shared my bed. They called her "Sitting Bull's White Squaw." I was grateful for her comfort, and my wives didn't mind. She tried to start a school for us, but McLaughlin of course refused.

I was twice her age, and my body had been mutilated and wounded, so I wasn't much of a lover. She would pour oil on my body and rub the pain away. She was nice to me and always talked about my "good qualities." I was grateful for her comfort. She was a painter, though not very good, and she painted my portrait.

In the time of the harvest, I asked her to leave. We had a terrible disagreement about the Ghost Dance, which she, like all the white people, feared. She said she thought it was nonsense, a stupid religion that promised salvation for the Indians (and the cleansing of the land of white settlers) without having to do anything. I said it's all we have, it's our only hope. And, I asked, is it so different from the Christian's day of judgment? She said it would get the white soldiers riled up. They would come after me and kill me. They wouldn't dare, I replied. So I took her to Cannonball, where she and her son, Christie, got on a down river steamer. I never saw her again. I loved her.

I heard later that Christie stepped on a rusty nail. He died of lockjaw on the steamer. Catherine had lost me and now her son. I heard that she was devastated. She went home to some place in Minnesota, so I heard, although I don't know where, exactly. I heard that she was "with child" when she left me—my child. I hope Sitting Bull Engstrom is a comfort to her.

McLaughlin is putting pressure on me to stop the Ghost Dance. The soldiers have already driven the dancers from the Pine Ridge and Rosebud agencies, and my spies say they are headed for Standing Rock, they are after me. McLaughlin may have to arrest me to save my life. Or perhaps he will shoot me himself.

But I will die at the hands of a Lakota. I know because the meadowlark has prophesied it, and the meadowlark is never wrong.

＊ ＊ ＊

A pretty black and red bug crawled slowly up the wall of Sally's small room. A boxelder bug. Sally's eyes opened partially as she squirmed to relieve the pain, and she spied the bug. Her eyes closed again, and she felt memory pulling her into the past . . .

It was a day like today, an Indian-Summer kind of day. David and I were going to study the lowly boxelder bug— "scientifically," David said. For once and for all, we were going to answer the burning question, What do boxelder bugs do? No one knew. They didn't seem to do anything but congregate on the side of boxelder trees and, occasionally, in other spots, where they didn't seem to do anything but look pretty and, occasionally, move short distances with no obvious goal in mind.

And why are they popular? asked David. People don't seem to dislike boxelder bugs, the way they do other insects. Some find their sheer numbers oppressive, especially in the fall, when cold weather impels them to find small cracks in the foundations of people's homes and march by the hundreds into people's toasters and coffee pots and radios and other warm things. But most people are willing to admit a certain fondness for the bug. The beauty was one reason; a mess of them on the side of a tree was a brightly colored flag of black velvet and red silk. And boxelder bugs don't bite or buzz, David pointed out; they're perceived as harmless. "Useless," I countered, pushing my scientist to precision. It was something David liked in me.

Useless. No one knew why God placed them on this earth, no one knew their purpose in life. No one knew what they did all day long, not even that! Well, that is a question we can tackle, David said. This day of my memory, this day of unseasonal warmth, David and I set out to find an answer.

"You choose our subject," said David.

"The bug to follow, you mean. OK, this guy." I pointed to a fine specimen that had parted from the company of a thousand others and was proceeding at a hurried pace down the sidewalk in front of the Icelandic Lutheran Church.

David began writing in his notebook. "Let's see . . . time is 2:30 . . . better make that 14:30 . . . subject: male bug, approximately 1/2 inch . . . "

"How do you know it's a male?"

"It's big. Males are bigger than females. Look at us." David laid his hand on top of my head, as if he were measuring my height. He felt my hair, part of my body, and his hand . . . twitched. I noticed. And I remembered.

"Not with bugs! Remember that film in Biology on Black Widows? She was this huge, sexy monster, and he was this scrawny little thing, scared out of his wits."

"Absolutely right!" David scratched out a line in his notebook and began writing something new. "Subject: slightly larger than average of others nearby; sex indeterminate. Hereafter referred to as 'it.'" He paused and then added, "I wonder if the size means it's older than the other bugs. I wonder if that's safe to say."

"Yes. It's an elder bug."

David gave me a shove and I tumbled into the grass and leaves of the church lawn.

"Ooh! Ooh! My back! My back!"

David ran to my side. My grimace of pain turned into a diabolical grin, as I pulled him down on the grass beside me. Like a cat I leaped astride him and tried to pin his arms down. He was too strong. He threw me off and assumed the same position on top of me. I struggled for a minute or two. We were both laughing. David's face was close to mine. We were breathing hard. I glanced at my sweatered breasts, saw them pressed against David's chest. I hoped that David would kiss me. He had a funny look on his face, as though he might. I stopped struggling, stopped laughing, and tried to convey a message of love with my eyes.

"Sorry," David muttered. "I didn't mean to hurt you."

Great! I try for a look of passion, and I get a look of pain. "I'm fine, OK?" I brushed myself off. "We probably lost our bug, thanks to you." If I couldn't have my kiss, I'd make him suffer.

David ran to the sidewalk, then smiled. "He's . . . it's still here. Hasn't moved very far." I peered at the sidewalk. David peered, too. For the next hour, we were destined to do a lot of peering.

I kept up a constant chatter.

"Why do people have sex, David?"

David looked at me with puzzled eyes, uncertain of how to respond. "I mean, scientifically. Why are there two sexes, and not just one? Or three?" I'm sure David had thought about this, since most of his "scientific" questions had to do with sex. Nevertheless, he shuddered when I asked, as if he were cold, or afraid of something. "Genetic diversity, I think," he answered. "That's why there're two, anyway. Genetic diversity is good for the species. For the individual, too. Otherwise you get monsters, like with incest. If you had sex with yourself, if you were both mother and father, that'd be the ultimate incest. Sex between close relatives makes monsters, and there's no closer relative than yourself. So sex with yourself makes monsters, which isn't good. The reason is genetic diversity." David was babbling. I thought about asking how genetic diversity worked, but I hesitated because of the babbling and shuddering. Something odd was going on inside David. "Now, why aren't there three?" he continued. "I don't know. I never thought about it. But, gee, it's an interesting question. In lots of animals, the male services more than one female. Pheasants. Chickens. Cattle, bulls and cows." I was smiling a big smile that I knew made David uneasy. He was afraid that I found him ridiculous. "With two males and one female, there'd be jealousy, lots of fights, I think." He looked as if he wished he hadn't said that. He looked forlorn. "Maybe it's genetic diversity again. When it's one and one, there's more people involved than when it's three or more. I mean, overall. If one guy has many girls, lots of guys have none, or if one girl has many guys, some have none. More people, more genetic diversity. I'll bet that's it."

David breathed a sigh, relieved to be at the end of his monologue, no doubt, especially one that wasn't going well. He spoke the words "genetic diversity" over and over, as if practicing. Probably rehearsing his Nobel Prize speech.

"Genetic diversity, huh? I'll bet nobody thinks about genetic diversity while they're making love." I kept my smile. It seemed to be spilling over the edges of my face.

"Of course not! That's what pleasure is for. God gave us pleasure to make us do the things that are necessary."

"I'm glad He didn't use pain. I suppose He could have."

"Or like an itch you had to scratch or go crazy. Cats are like that."

"Maybe that's why we worship God. He's so good to us."

David said he had never discussed these questions with anyone other than his best friend, Tommy Lillehaugen; certainly not with a girl. He was impressed with me and said so.

"You think I'm like you because I try to understand things, is that it?" I was mocking him.

"Right!"

"And therefore I too am a wonderful person."

"Right!"

I gave David a shove, and he wheeled sharply into the grass, nearly toppling. I gave him a second shove, upsetting his precarious balance, and he fell. I leaped upon him.

"You're such a creep, David. I'm not like you at all," I said. I kissed him hard.

"I mean, you have a mind," David said, gasping.

"Yes. You're right about that." I kissed him hard again and then let him go.

David and I followed the boxelder bug for about an hour. David made several notes in his notebook, noting for example that the subject slowed down and often stopped in sunny spots. Whenever it encountered something that appeared edible, it stopped. Whether it sniffed, or chewed, or did anything whatsoever other than stop, David couldn't say. I was convinced the bug was "dining."

"How do you know it's eating?" asked David: a scientific question.

"It seems to suck on the stuff, don't you think? It puts its mouth right down there on the leaf. Nothing seems to disappear, though. Maybe it gives it a good lick."

"Maybe a good lick is how a boxelder bug eats," suggested David. He said he felt "really good about us." We were a team, we were working out a theory together. I think the really good feeling was more like sexual arousal.

I smiled, both on the day this occurred and on the day this was remembered.

David decided to try a few experiments. He turned the bug around, "to find out if the direction it's going in is important to it," he explained. It wasn't. The bug marched merrily off in its new direction, oblivious to change.

I picked up a flat twig and laid it in the bug's path. "The obstacle test," I said, impressing David once more.

The boxelder bug walked up to the twig, gave it a good lick, then turned around and marched off in the opposite direction.

"Incredible!" exclaimed David, and I laughed out loud.

"Here's my scientific conclusion," I announced. "The boxelder bug wanders around until it finds some food, and then it eats, or until it finds some warmth, then it stops for a while. It's not headed anywhere in particular."

"That's very good!" said David, writing furiously in his notebook.

"Boxelder bugs are just like human beings," I said. "Except they're prettier, and they're not so tense." I laughed, and David managed a half-frightened smile. The sun shone brightly, and a gust of wind picked up brightly-colored leaves, propelling them like airborne sailboats over the sidewalk where David and I and our boxelder bug stood motionless, enjoying the unseasonal warmth.

✳ ✳ ✳

The past cleared out of my memory and I returned to my dismal little room with a bug on the wall. The day is similar, I thought, but how other things have changed. A scene from the more recent past—last night—flooded my mind. My head began to throb, but the scene would not go away.

Billy Anseele, the one the others called Pimp, was trying to get me drunk.

"How're you doing?" Billy asked, speaking in loud, slow, rounded forms. "Want another?" He waved a bottle of beer. He wasn't drunk himself, but he was trying to portray the kind of behavior he expected of me: warm, fun-loving, slightly out of control.

"No, I'm fine," I said. "Billy, what are we doing here? It's colder than hell in here. I sure hope you're not going to make a pass at me. You'd freeze your fucking buns off!"

I laughed raucously. I took a swig of watery beer. Each sip seemed to sober me more, sharpening my senses. The last thing I wanted. . . .

Billy sat quietly, trying to think of a reply to my last remarks. Twenty five years old, he still had bad acne. His forehead was covered with tiny pimples, like the measles. Down each side of his nose and on his chin, beneath his lower lip, larger infections grew, as if he had been sniffing poison ivy. He preferred darkness to lighted rooms, for darkness covered his blemishes.

That had been one reason he had brought me here. Another was that it had been a fairly warm night, and he had thought he could get me drunk and screw me right here, in the deserted bathhouse at Dead Coon Lake. The plan was not working. "They call you Pimp because of your pimples?" I asked. "Yeah, I suppose so. Cruel bastards!" I was used to talking to myself. Billy was not much for conversation.

"Are you waiting for me to get drunk?" I asked. "Because if you are, you're going to have a hell of a long wait. This horse piss you brought is having no effect at all, except it'll probably make me sick before too long. Besides, I can drink you under the table anytime." Which was true, I could indeed. Alcohol had very little effect on me, especially when I wanted desperately to deaden the pain, when I wanted desperately to lose consciousness. Many's the night lately, my date plied me with liquor, matching me drink for drink, until he, not me, slumped to the table, out cold. Some nights I had a hell of a time getting home.

Billy sat there in the bathhouse looking frightened and confused.

"Look, Billy, if you want to make out, why don't we get in your car? There's a blanket in the back seat, I saw it. And we could turn on the heater for a while, to warm up."

Billy only looked more frightened. Finally he spoke in an embarrassed voice. "Sally, I like you. I really do. I think you're a real fine girl. I don't know why . . . , I don't understand why the guys .... I'm sorry. I mean, I'm sorry you're cold. It was a dumb idea to come out here. I thought it would be warm tonight. It was warm today, so I thought . . ."

I was a little startled by this outpouring; Billy never said more than a few words at a time.

"Why do the guys call you a slut?" Billy clearly wanted to ask this question, but now, with the words out of his mouth, he looked sick. His eyes started rolling around in their sockets. I thought he was going to throw up. I, however, laughed. I was pleased with the question, pleased that Billy had asked it. He's not such a bad guy.

"Well, Billy, my friend, the main reason is, I am a slut." I laughed again. "You know the story as well as I do. I seduced poor Danny Swenson, the church deacon. Then it was open season on Sally Engstrom, every man for himself. Want a little loving? Just pick up Sally. Give her a good time and a little booze, and you will probably get lucky. That's a slut, ain't it, Billy? If that ain't a slut, I don't know what is!"

"You don't care if they call you a slut?"

"No. Why should I?"

"Don't you think it's a bad thing to be a slut?"

"Let me ask you something, Billy. Suppose a girl came to you and asked you to go to bed with her. Would you do it?"

"Are you crazy? Hell yes, I'd do it."

"And then another girl comes along and asks you to go to bed with her. Would you do it?"

"Yes sir! I surely would."

"Why?"

"Why what?"

"Why would you go to bed with them?"

"To get sex. Sex is fun! Are you crazy?"

"Well, I think the same, that's all. Would it bother you if the girls called you a big stud?"

"Hell no! I'd like that!"

"So why should I care if the guys call me a big slut?"

"But . . . But, for a girl, it hurts her reputation."

"Well, fuck my reputation!" I threw my half-filled beer bottle across the small dressing room. It hit the cement-block wall, shattering; pieces of glass flew around the room; a small puddle of beer fizzled on the bench.

Billy sat motionless, staring uncontrollably at the fizzling puddle. I walked over to where he sat, took another beer, and sat down next to him.

"That's the same thing Sigrid Huseth and Marianne Brynestad told me," I said. "They said they had taken it upon themselves to inform me of how the women of the church felt about me. They said my reputation was ruined."

Billy and I sat quietly for a few minutes.

"Debil DeBays said the same thing. He said I had no reputation to protect, so why try?"

"You could build it up again, if you were careful. Maybe it'd take ten years, but you could do it."

"Yeah, but what's the cost? They want too much. They want me to lie down in front of the Cross and say, 'I'm a whore, I'm a murderer, I did wrong, and I'm sorry.'"

"That's too much?"

"Billy, you're such a creep!" I gave him a playful push.

* * *

I pulled a large cocklebur off my sleeve and continued my search for the noble pheasant. David Sorenson, the intrepid hunter. I loved the smell of the weeds, a dry, dusty warm smell, full of exotic flavors, especially on a warm day like today. I was walking along the banks of the Yellow Medicine River north of town. My dog, Dipstick, a ratty-looking cocker spaniel, was gaily snuffling among the reeds and cattails near the river, still exhilarated from the rabbit chase of a few minutes ago. Dipstick knew that I wanted him to look for pheasants; he'd had plenty of dead birds thrust in his face. He knew, too, that I didn't want him to chase rabbits; why else those angry and frantic shouts? But he seemed impervious to training in this regard, as if he believed that dogs had the right to chase rabbits, whenever encountered. He seemed to believe that his reputation among neighborhood dogs would suffer if he let a rabbit go unchased.

Right now, his snuffling had intensified. He was picking up patches of a strong scent. Bird snuffling, it looked like. Probably a mess of pheasants. Close. Get ready. Getting ready did not stop my thinking, of course. My mind was playing with the contradiction between my respect for the birds and my hunting of them. All the hunters I knew had the same ambivalent attitude, only it wasn't ambivalent for them. They thought it was natural to respect your prey.

The male pheasant is a truly beautiful bird, with colors galore and a white-ringed neck. A substantial bird, a good meal, not like those partridge that occasionally found themselves in my path, screaming and fluttering like excited children in a haunted house. The pheasant files with slow and powerful strokes, almost as if it were rowing away, not like ducks, who come in like kamikaze pilots. I knew some hunters who respected ducks, but I was not among them.

But pheasants! Proud, majestic birds, a worthy prey, an adversary. In the off-season, I worked for their welfare. Hunters were the only people I knew who were interested in conservation, which to me meant the preservation of the pheasant. Though I was merely a junior member of the Conservation League (whose members were all hunters, except for the Swede), I helped with the fund drive to buy uncultivated farm land, which the League kept wild for pheasants and other animals. Each year in the spring, I and other members got pheasant chicks from the state and let them go in fields and ditches around Minneota. In the winter when the snows were heavy, I and the others set out corn for the pheasants to eat.

In the off-season, relationships were friendly. I often sat by the road after I spread the corn for the pheasants. The birds came out to eat, unafraid—"grateful" is how I saw them.

When the hunting season began in the fall, all that changed. The pheasants became vigilant, running at the first sign of hunter or even car. Running is a very good defense against hunters, who might be able to outrun a bird on a level road but not over a plowed field or through heavy brush. And most hunters will not shoot a bird on the ground; it's considered "unsportsmanlike." So if the bird doesn't panic and take to the air, he is reasonably safe.

Of course, with a dog along, the pheasant loses the option of running. Dipstick had caught birds on the ground, those that stayed down too long. With a dog hunting him, a pheasant had to fly.

Outside of sex, I couldn't imagine a more thrilling experience than flushing a pheasant. Unexpectedly, one or more of these giant birds would explode out of the brush, usually within a couple of yards. The beating wings made a distinctive sound, something like a fan belt slipping, an anxious whirring, which merged with the keening cry, the vocal lamentation. With each downward beat, the body of the pheasant rose, and as the wings relaxed, the body fell, giving the flight its peculiar bounce.

What interested me most about hunting pheasants was the shooting. It seemed so automatic. The shotgun came to my shoulder while I pushed off the safety; I sighted and pulled the trigger. The entire event—the takeoff and the shot—happened so quickly that I could not improve my shooting by following admonitions to aim more carefully or to squeeze (not jerk) the trigger. What amazed me was that I shot at roosters but never at hens. Admittedly there is a world of difference in color alone between the brightly-colored cocks and the drably-camouflaged hens, but color didn't enter my consciousness until after the shot. Once in a while, I pulled the trigger and a bird fell from the sky, and I realized that the victim had no color. I had shot a hen (which was illegal and, even more to my distaste, threatened next year's pheasant population). But when I found the dead bird, invariably (no exceptions) it turned out to be a young rooster, so immature that its body colors had not yet appeared. How did I manage this incredible feat? Was it something in the way males fly, or cry? I had no idea; it was another fascinating scientific mystery.

When the bird went down, Dipstick found it and kept it from running, if it was still alive. I, elated, ran to the scene, picked up the bird, and swung it in a tight circle, wringing its beautiful white-ringed neck. I had nothing but admiration for my worthy prey.

* * *

When I heard that David and Sandy Kringen were getting married, it didn't surprise me, it didn't sadden me, it had no impact. I was surprised that David would marry so young, in his first year at college, and Sandy, just about to graduate from high school. Probably Sandy's pregnant, I thought with some irony. A happy pregnancy, not like mine, with a happy ending, not like mine.

By chance I went to David's bachelor party, the night before his wedding. I was waiting that night outside of the Municipal Liquor Store, hoping to spot someone who would buy me some beer. Jon Coltvet was there, too, waiting as I was, hoping to get some booze for David's party. A beggar's lineup. Why didn't Jon get the booze from the Swede? I asked. The Swede would come to the party, Jon said, but he wouldn't buy liquor for kids. He had his principles.

Luck was with us, as Wilson Howard staggered up in a cheery mood. He got me two six-packs and, as requested, he delivered with incredulous murmurings a quart of lime vodka to Jon. "Tommy Lillehaugen thought it sounded nice. He saw an ad," explained Jon with unexpected embarrassment.

"You'll throw up for sure," Wilson predicted, "and you won't like what you see."

Jon convinced me that David would want me at his bachelor's party, and he was right. David was very pleased to see me. While the others drank the lime vodka—except the Swede, of course—David and I sat in a corner with my beer. (Jon and Tommy and Curtis Braun all threw up later, and they didn't like what they saw.) David confirmed that Sandy was pregnant. He didn't want to marry her, but he didn't see an alternative. He thought the marriage was a terrible mistake, for both of them, and he felt that all his plans for a career "as a scientist" were now out the window. Sandy's plans, if she had any, were out the same window; she would get a job in Northfield, where David was going to college. She would have to quit school, because the high school didn't allow pregnant girls in the hallways, not even married ones. David thought he would soon have to quit college, too—after the baby came. All is lost, he said. As he drank, he became more and more morose.

About midway through the evening, Tommy Lillehaugen (about midway to his sickness) announced it was time for the "fun." Tommy had it in his mind that a bachelor's party should be raunchy, with dirty movies and naked women. Without such resources, he did the best he could. He passed around a little device that looked like a miniature telescope. Inside, one saw a photograph of a naked woman. Then he passed around something that looked like a small comic book. If one flipped the pages properly, one could actually see a woman taking off her clothes. Jon Coltvet was particularly good at this. Then Tommy announced that everyone (except David) had to tell the dirtiest joke he knew, or she knew, in my case. I told an old joke I had heard from Billy Anseele about two men who could see up the skirt of a woman sitting several rows back at a baseball game. It was by far the dirtiest joke of the evening.

As the party drifted into sleazy inebriation, David and I resumed our earnest conversation. David seemed to have a need to talk, and I was happy to listen. David talked about his life in very abstract terms, comparing himself unfavorably with me. He was trapped; I was free. I was strong; he was weak. He was selfish and lazy; I was loving and industrious. I did not dispute him but watched his eyes carefully. They were glazed, partly from drink and partly from tears, but they were intense, burning. David had taken my hand and was holding it, stroking it as he talked, and occasionally he stroked my face, too. He said he loved me. I believed him.

Soft music on the radio: David and I danced. I felt his warmth as we danced, glued together like two jigsawed pieces, scarcely moving, hugging to music. How well our bodies fit. I had never felt quite so physically intimate, not even with Danny. David kept talking, mostly about his miserable future, sometimes about what a fine example of God's art I was, but it had become a background hum. No one was listening, not even David.

A few other kids turned up later for the party, including a cousin of Sandy Kringen's. They didn't stay long; it wasn't a welcoming scene, with Tommy and the other drunks reading passages from Ecclesiastes, and David and I undulating vertically by the fireplace. I felt a twinge of some unidentified emotion when I saw Sandy's cousin, but it was smothered by the warm, gooey feeling that David had created for us.

With sounds of violent retching coming from the bathroom, David and I left the party. We walked slowly toward my apartment, David silent now, his arm around my shoulder. We walked up the outside stairs to the second floor of the old house where I lived now, to my door. David stayed one step down, which put his face about level with mine. "I love you," he said.

"Yes, I know," I replied. "You always have."

Tears were running down his face, and probably I was crying too. David moved his head slowly toward mine until our lips barely touched. My lips tingled, and my knees buckled. Suddenly David pulled back, turned around, and walked quickly down the stairs, never looking back. It was the last time I saw him.

* * *

I was leaning against one of those big columns that ran through the middle of the Big Store, cleaning my fingernails. Business was slow, as usual. So I didn't have much to do, so I saw Sally come in. Ohmygod!, I thought, here comes trouble. Sigrid Huseth and me had told Sally a thing or two at church—Sigrid said we were being asses for the Lord. We told Sally that she was a whore, she was a murderer, she was no good, and she never would be. Everybody had her pegged, she wouldn't be able to pull any more stunts around Minneota. She was not welcome anywhere, especially not in church, where people are supposed to be good people, not whores.

Sally didn't talk back, but neither did she come back to church.

Maybe she came to the Big Store for revenge. We'll see about that! Marianne Brynestad against Sally Engstrom. We know who'll win that battle!

Me, I hope.

I scratched my thigh (my girdle always picked the worst times to itch!), and I looked around the store, to see who I could count on if Sally should start hitting me. I saw that everybody—the other four clerks and also Lofty Sovik, the cashier—was staring at Sally, and there was three or four customers doing the same. I felt good, like I was part of an Army. Sally couldn't take us all on.

I went right up to Sally and said, "Can I be of service to you?" Very polite like, but squint-eyed and said with a growlly voice, to let her know what's what.

"I need some pants, some underpants," said Sally.

I couldn't resist a chance like that. So I said, "Sure thing, Honey. What's the matter, yours all get ripped?" Well, maybe that was a little mean, so I took some of it back: "Or something?" My girdle started to itch like crazy.

Sally did not reply and appeared to be looking for something on the floor. I looked for it, too, but I didn't see anything. Sally's head jerked up and she said, "No, Sweetheart. It's just that . . . , well, you know."

"I know?"

Sally leaned real close, but she whispered loudly. "After a while, all those juices build up in the crotch."

"Juices?" I felt sick.

"I don't mind it, you understand. Fond memories, you know. But it gets stiff as a board. It's like wearing panties made of wood."

I started to scratch my leg; I couldn't help it. I wanted to go home. My head started to jerk, I don't know why.

"You know what it's like, don't you, Marianne? You get a little now and then."

I wasn't sure what Sally was talking about, but it sure was making me uncomfortable. I couldn't think of anything to say. I tried to say something, but all I did was squeak.

"I knew it! You and me, Marianne. We're just two peas in a pod."

I thought about this. I wondered what it meant. It was like one of Jesus's parables—an important message, but why don't they just say it straight. "We're both laborers in the vineyard," I said, hoping it was somehow related to peas in a pod.

Sally pounded me on the back, nearly driving me into the display case.

I saw Lofty Sovik signal Joy Oberstad. Lofty could see everything from her perch, way up high, and I guess she saw that I wasn't doing too well. Joy came running over.

"Any problems, Marianne?" asked Joy. Sally asked Joy if the marble was still in her hair. Can you imagine anyone being so rude? Of course, Joy's hairdo was pretty funny. It looked like concrete painted blond, not a hair out of place even in the strongest wind, and sometimes dust or leaves got caught in her hair, like it was glued.

"Marianne and I were just having some girl talk," said Sally. "Right, Marianne?" Sally slapped me again on the back, just as I was about to answer. Spit flew out of my mouth and landed on Joy's blouse. I forgot what I was going to say.

"Sally wants some underpants," I said quickly. "Hers are all full of juice."

"Marianne! What a thing to say!" Joy turned to Sally: "What size, Sally?"

"Five."

"Any particular color? White? Pink? We have a couple of blue fives."

"Pink," said Sally, quiet as a mouse.

I watched Joy handle her, and I thought, gee, I wish I could do that. I was just standing there, scratching.

"How many, Sally?"

"Three, I think."

"Very good." Joy took out three pairs of pink panties and wrapped them in tissue, then put them in a bag. She wrote a number on a sales slip. Sally handed her a dollar bill. Joy put the bill and the sales slip in the wooden cup and hung it on the wire. She yanked the handle and sent the cup flying up to Lofty Sovik. Lofty took the dollar and put thirteen cents and the sales slip back into the cup. She fired The Slingshot (that's what I call it) back to Joy.

I love the way the cup whines when it goes along the wire. I love The Slingshot, all the wires all over the store, cups flying back and forth. So much more fun than cash registers all around.

This time, however, I wasn't thinking about The Slingshot, I was thinking about Sally. And how Joy could handle her, and I couldn't. I think maybe I shouldn't have said that thing about her panties being ripped.

The Slingshot arrived with a sharp click, and I was thinking about something else, so it surprised me and made me jump.

"Here's your change, Sally. Thank you for shopping with us." Joy was so good at this. Like she handed the bag and the change to Sally in a way that to get them, Sally had to take a step toward the door.

"Thanks," said Sally, starting for the door. She walked slowly. I think she was waiting for Joy to leave. When she saw me alone, she came back.

"Knitting needles! I forgot knitting needles! In case I get pregnant again!"

I tried to make myself smaller, which for me is not easy. I had no idea what she was talking about. And my girdle was killing me.

"Well, maybe tomorrow," said Sally. "I'll come back tomorrow." And Sally left the Big Store.

The community is saddened indeed by the recent event of the past week, in which we lost one of our own, a beautiful young girl, taken in the prime of life. Surely we'll all miss her. Sally lived right down the road from me, and I knew her pretty well, and I know she had some difficulties at the end, but most of her life, I thought she was a pretty good kid. She was always friendly, and she often came over when I was weeding the rhubarb patch or the rutabaga or something, and she'd chat with me about, well, almost anything. She was interested in everything. She liked animals, I remember that, and she was very angry with me for trying to kill the gophers that were undermining my garden, and she liked spiders, too, and tried to salvage them from my savage but inept attempts to rid my house and garden of the insect, although I have to admit that the spider is an essentially beneficial bug. I just don't like finding spiders in my bathtub! Spiders have their place and I have mine, and doggone it! I wish they'd show a little more respect. Sally told me to call her if I found a spider in my bathtub, and she would come over and take it outside, to a new home. But I was, of course, in my birthday suit when about to step into the bathtub, so I could hardly take her up on her offer. But she had a love of living things that I admired. She used to say that a living thing was worth all the gold and jewels of the king's treasury, which I think was a reference to a fairy tale I cannot remember.

Did you know that rutabaga by another name is the Swedish turnip? In Europe, I'm told, they call it The Swede. I like rutabaga, but most people don't. David Sorenson tells me—he's big with the scientific facts like this—that 75% of all rutabagas are eaten by Republicans, and the other 25% rot in the field. I don't know where he gets numbers like that. Does he go into homes and watch people eat? But he may be right, since I am of the Republican persuasion. Maybe it's a joke of his.

I was talking about Sally. It just seems to me so tragic, everything that happened. This was not a bad kid, at least not when she was growing up, and it seems to me that, somehow, the community is partly to blame for what happened. I mean, you know me, I'm always trying to champion the virtues of living in a small town like Minneota, where everybody knows everybody, and we all support one another. Well, what happened to Sally? Maybe she made some mistakes, maybe she made some bad mistakes, but couldn't we have done something? Couldn't we have helped her, somehow? I didn't know much about what was happening—I still don't, if you want the truth—but so what? She was a friend in need, why didn't it work out that I could have helped her, as surely I would have, had she asked, or had I known that she needed help. Or something. Why didn't our community work like it's supposed to?! It just makes me mad!

I'm sorry; I'm rambling on, and I don't usually do that, at least not in print. It's just that I'm so sad, I'm feeling so bad, I feel like I've lost a friend. Sally is gone now, and I feel that I myself failed her.

10

The Dancing Ghost

I made my way slowly, dragging the 16-gauge shotgun behind me. I half hoped it would hit a rock and discharge, blowing me away without the need for courage to pull the trigger. I held the barrel with two hands, to make sure the gun was pointed directly at my back, just in case. The safety was on, so there was little chance of an accident, but one can hope. A last daydream.

The butt of the shotgun scraped and bounced along the lawn as I walked through the backyard toward the woodshed. The Engstrom backyard was large, centered by a huge cottonwood tree, sleek, impressive, with a prominent branch that took off at a right angle from the trunk and served to hold all the climbing ropes and swings that entertained the Engstrom children over the years. I looked at the old tire hanging on a rope, the latest Engstrom swing, rarely used now; I was the youngest. I thought of it as my swing. I thought of it as a friend, and now, seeing it so still on this breezeless summer's eve, my heart fluttered. My goodness, Sally, the swing seemed to say, you aren't going to kill yourself, are you? Whoever will love me, if you die? Come, tell me what's the matter, as you've done so many times before. Together we can fix it.

I turned my head away. I looked at the woodshed, which had nothing to say to me. I never considered the woodshed part of the backyard, though it clearly was. A plain and simple structure, white except where flecks of paint had peeled off to reveal gray wood beneath, it looked like a small garage, with two large "barn" doors that allowed my father to back in the pickup full of wood for the winter's fireplace and the wood stove in the extra room. Of course, as in all woodsheds, there was more junk than wood: rusty tricycles, an old box spring mattress housing a family of mice, an old ladderback chair housing a family of spiders, odd-sized drapery rods, a broken lamp, scraps of metal and wood. So much junk, in fact, that it spread to the outside, where chipped flower pots and broken rakes lay among the mounds of weeds hiding God-knows-what. The debris kept the lawn from being mowed in a ring about 15 feet around the shed, which set it off from the well-kept backyard, which is one reason I didn't think of it as part of the yard.

Another reason is, my father used to take me out to the woodshed for spankings and an occasional beating. The woodshed was also where I had my first cigarette. The woodshed was where Jon Coltvet undid my bra and made first male contact with my breasts. The woodshed was where I hid my clothes and toothbrush when I finally decided to run away with Danny Swenson. None of these memories was pleasant; they filled my mind with thoughts of pain, uncertainty, and desperation, and now, as I was about to enter the woodshed to end my life, it just seemed more of the same. My life would end as it had been lived, with pain, uncertainty, and desperation.

"Oh, come on! It hasn't been allll bad! You've had some good times." The words seemed to form in my mind, as part of my inner dialogue, so it wasn't the words that attracted my attention. It was the movement of the swing on the old cottonwood tree. I was not conscious of recognizing the voice, but I knew it was the Swede.

"A shotgun, oh dear me! A shotgun is very messy, sweet Sally. They'll be picking parts of your skull out of the ceiling for years to come. If you become famous, they'll come over and pick out the splinters and sell them. I could make a fortune!" The Swede was very drunk. "You are going to stick it in your mouth, aren't you? You aren't going to try to blast your heart out, are you? Because Dickie Esboldt tried that. Very messy, totally unreliable. He lived for three months. Take my advice. Stick it in your mouth."

"Why would I be famous?" I asked, moving slowly back toward the swing. I was pleased to see the Swede. No one else had showed up for my suicide.

"Famous? You're already famous! You ran away with a married man. You had an abortion! My god! You're the first abortion in Minneota, the first! Firsts are always famous. And now you're going to add to your legend. You're going to kill yourself! Great stuff, Sally. Someday David will write a book about you, and you'll be even more famous."

"I really screwed it, didn't I? My life, I mean. I really screwed up." I sat down in the grass next to the swing. The thought flashed through my mind that the grass would stain my skirt.

"Who can say? Who can say? I suppose. You managed to turn the community against you, that's pretty impressive. Doesn't happen often. The community usually protects a person, shuts out outsiders, helps its own . . . But you, you they turned against. Why? That's a gooood question." The Swede swung in a wobbly rhythm, repeating "Gooood . . . question" in synchrony with his swing.

"I never did anything to them."

"Oh, oh, oh! That's a lie! You threatened them, you scared them. You scared them so much they did something they don't like to do—attack one of their own. You threatened their morals! You threatened the family!"

"I—" I meant to defend myself, but . . . "Oh, what's the use?"

"You think you were justified because you were after love! You think you were misunderstood!" The Swede burst into malicious laughter; he kicked out his feet, and the old tire swung wildly, turning as it was thrust out. "You think people didn't know you were in love!"

I had no reply to this; I did think that love was a good enough reason for what I did, and I was stunned to hear that others did not share my belief. I really believed that they would accept my reasons, my love, once they knew the truth. They wouldn't hate me. I thought they didn't know I was in love, so therefore they considered the affair frivolous, promiscuous, disrespectful of love relationships, and therefore damnable. A small kernel of doubt began to form in my mind. Why am I killing myself? If I'm wrong about what they think, maybe I'm wrong about this, too. Maybe there's a way out.

"Love doesn't count?" I asked weakly.

"Are you crazy? Love is what they're afraid of! Love was your mistake! You don't realize that?"

"Realize what?"

"Realize that the town knew you were in love with Danny. I think you do. I think you're pissed because the town won't accept your love. I think you're going to kill yourself because you don't think you can live without love."

"Love gone astray," I said, wistfully.

"Love made paramount. Love over family, love over babies, love over sex."

"I guess."

"I feel the same way," said the Swede. "I think you're right. I'm in the same boat. I admire what you're doing. I'd kill myself, too, if I had the guts. I don't, so I try to kill myself without my knowing about it. With booze."

The Swede fell clumsily out of the swing. He grabbed his elbow in silent pain, lying in the dirt below the swing, where years and years of Engstrom children had kicked out the grass with their gleeful feet. He steadied the spinning swing with one hand and pulled himself up with the other. Suddenly he leaped up, straddling the rope on the top of the tire. With one hand on the rope, he let his body lean precariously off toward the spot where I sat. Leering melodramatically, the Swede said, "Don't cry, fair maiden. I'll spin your straw into gold."

"A living thing is worth all the gold . . ." It all seemed so hopeless. Finally I said, "Swede, I don't understand why you want to die. Maybe you haven't lived up to what you thought you should, but the people like you. They don't shut you out. In a funny way, they respect you."

"They have a place for me in the community. I'm eccentric, I'm an alcoholic, I'm a good handyman. They don't respect me; they tolerate me. You, my sweet Sally, could do the same. You could become the town whore."

The Swede said this with a lopsided grin that somehow struck my funny bone, and I giggled. "Geez, that's a thought, isn't it? Sally Engstrom, the town whore. I could live with you, Swede, and you could read erotic poetry out loud as I pumped the frustrations out of the village fathers. Lately that's what I've been doing, you know, except I don't charge for it."

The Swede's grin faded. "Forget it, sweet Sally. You couldn't do it. You'd kill yourself first." The Swede puzzled over his remarks for a moment and then concluded: "Which is exactly what you are going to do."

"You recommend I continue with my present plans?"

"That would be my judgment, yes."

I laughed. "I'm glad I had one good friend, Swede. I'm glad for you."

"Well, I'm sorry," said the Swede. "You need love to survive."

"Tell me the truth, Swede. Do you think it's a good idea for me to commit suicide?"

"Yes. I don't see that you have any choice."

Buffalo Bill gave Sitting Bull a couple of presents for being a part of his Wild West Show, a huge white sombrero and a trick horse who, at the signal of a gunshot, would sit down and raise one foreleg, as if waving or saluting. Sitting Bull prized the horse greatly; it became his favorite, and it was still his favorite five years later when Red Tomahawk shot him through the head, ending the Sioux era.

When Sitting Bull surrendered in 1881, he was sent to the desolate Standing Rock Reservation, about 250 miles northwest of Minneota on what is now the border between North and South Dakota. In the last years of his life, Sitting Bull became involved in perhaps the strangest phenomenon in the history of the relationship between Indians and the U.S. Government: the Ghost Dance. The story began in Utah, on the very first day of 1889.

There, then, the sky darkened, as the sun was eclipsed by the moon. An ambitious Paiute medicine man by the name of Wovoka fell into a trance, and when he awoke, he told of the vision he had been shown. Jesus was going to return to the earth, but as an Indian. He was upset with the white men—the Wasichus—because they had turned against Him, had killed Him on the Cross. When He returned, He would bring with Him all the dead Indians and all the dead buffalo. The Wasichus would disappear, and the land would belong once more to the Indians and their noble prey. All this would come to pass two years hence, in the time of new grass. Indians who were alive now need do nothing to bring this about, nothing but to believe and to dance the Ghost Dance.

Black Elk, a Dakota holy man, had been having a recurring vision, of men and women in a giant circle dancing around a dying tree painted red, forming the sacred hoop around the holy tree, painted red themselves, with eagle feathers, trying to restore life to the holy tree, trying to restore life to the holy nation. Your vision is the Ghost Dance, he was told, and so Black Elk went to see the dance that was sweeping through the reservations like wildfire. He was astonished to see his vision being enacted by the dancers, to the very last detail.

Black Elk took up the dance with the others, and he taught the dancers how to pray to the Great Spirit to give life to the tree. And so they sang:

"Who do you think he is that comes?
It is one who seeks his mother!"

It was the song of the dead. It was what the dead would sing as they entered the other world, looking for their dead relatives. The dancers were thus able to find their dead relatives while dancing. Good Thunder went to a buffalo-skin teepee and found his dead son and his dead wife; they had a long talk. Dancing and singing, crying and laughing, praying then seeing, dreaming, the dancers danced for hours, sometimes for days, calling upon the red Jesus to save them.

Dancing, Black Elk suddenly felt himself on a swing, gliding forward and back in longer and longer swoops. Then he fell clumsily from the swing and began to fly, alongside a spotted eagle that was making the shrill cry that is his. He flew to a beautiful land where many Indians were camped in a great circle, with drying racks full of meat, fat and happy horses feeding on the long green grass, animals of all kinds on the green hills, singing hunters returning, the people happy. Black Elk flew to the center of the great hoop, where he saw the holy tree all green and full of flowers. Two men appeared wearing holy shirts. They told Black Elk to bring back the holy shirts, which would protect the Indians from the Wasichus' bullets.

"The Indians were good at visions," I said to Sally. "They used a lot of drugs. They smoked Jimson weed and they ate mushrooms, just to have a hallucination. Their dances were hypnotic. And they'd dance until they'd have a vision, just from fatigue."

"Talk about a pipe dream, though. The Ghost Dancers must have been incredibly desperate to believe that vision."

"Well, I don't know," I said, while busily filling my pipe. "Is it really so different from the vision Christians have about the second coming of Christ? It is the Christian vision, complete with Jesus."

"How many of the Indians did the Ghost Dance? Was it a big thing?"

"You betcha! Many, many. Most. Most of those who heard about it." I lit the pipe, took a drag, and passed it to Sally.

"What is it?"

"It's a peace pipe."

"What's in it? It looks like weeds."

"Rope."

"Rope?"

"Rope."

Sitting Bull became the chief disciple of the Ghost Dance at Standing Rock, which made him potent among the Teton Dakota once again. Some said that he was not a believer, that he was putting on the robe of a new religion for power's sake. But the people followed him, as they always had.

Sitting Bull told the people that nondancers would not be buried with the Wasichus, but they would be compelled to live on small farms, supporting themselves, while the dancers would form a community as of old, with land held in common and game and produce shared in the old Indian ways.

Sitting Bull invited Kicking Bear to Standing Rock. Kicking Bear had made a pilgrimage to Wovoka, to hear his story and to learn his dance, and had become a devotee, a sort of priest for the religion, a sort of doctor for the medicine. He taught Sitting Bull and the other Dakota. The white agency officials and their Indian henchmen had begun to fear the Ghost Dance, not understanding it, and therefore the chief agency official decided to have Kicking Bear thrown off his reservation. He sent a force of about a dozen Indian police. The officers returned, duty undone, in what the chief official recorded as "a dazed condition"; they were afraid of Kicking Bear's medicine. Soon the Dakota were dancing so often that no work was being done, and no children showed up for school. Agency officials watched in disbelief as circles of Indians danced from dawn far into the night. The large circles were never-ending processions of desperate Indians, moaning for a lost past. It was eerie, awe-full, and the officials became crazed with fear. They tried to break up the dances, but the dancers donned their Ghost Shirts, the holy shirts of Black Elk's vision, with magic symbols that made them impervious to the white man's bullets. And they danced on. And the Indian police would not stop them.

Finally it was decided that Sitting Bull would have to be arrested. Lieutenant Henry Bull Head led a force of about forty Indian police. Sitting Bull said he would go with them quietly, but outside his cabin a group of Ghost Dancers gathered. The police and the dancers argued. A shot was fired, Lieutenant Bull Head was wounded. As Bull Head fell, Sergeant Red Tomahawk shot and killed Sitting Bull.

At that instant, Sitting Bull's horse tried to do his trick, confused by the multiple gunshots. He stumbled backwards, trying to sit down, and succeeded only in rearing up on his hind legs. He waved his foreleg in salute. To all assembled, police and dancers alike, he seemed to be performing the Dance of the Ghosts.

The moment passed. The horse ran off, and fierce fighting broke out between the police and the dancers. Several dancers fell, their holy shirts notwithstanding, their holy shirts stained blood red. The survivors fled to the forest. They were joined by others who had heard of Sitting Bull's death. They were afraid. They knew their only hope was to make their way to the Pine Ridge reservation, the home of Red Cloud, the last of the great Dakota chiefs. Big Foot was the leader of this group of pilgrims. He led 350 Dakotas to a camp on the way to Pine Ridge, a camp on the banks of Wounded Knee Creek. A detachment of the U.S. Cavalry was sent to arrest Big Foot and to escort the rest to Pine Ridge. The soldiers caught up with the Indians at Wounded Knee, setting up their cannons on the hills above the small river valley.

The soldiers demanded that the Indians surrender their weapons. They did, except for Black Coyote, who tried to hide his Winchester rifle. The soldiers discovered it. Black Coyote held the rifle high over his head, as if fording a deep river, as if keeping it from curious children. "Please!" he cried in Sioux. "It's all I have left." The soldiers had no idea of what he was shouting about. They ordered him to put the rifle down. But Black Coyote was deaf and did not hear the order. The soldiers opened fire. With the cannons on the hill and the Dakota in the valley, it was like shooting fish in a barrel.

Nearly 300 of the defenseless Indians were murdered.

* * *

I tried to teach Sally the Ghost Dance. She moved solemnly around the swing, trying to imitate my movements.

"Here's the key part, a little lunge. Do you get it?" I hollered back at her.

Suddenly Sally exploded in laughter and fell, laughing, to the grass. "Oh, my god! This is crazy! I'm supposed to be killing myself!"

This struck me as quite funny, too, as I fell, laughing, beside her.

"And what am I doing? I'm dancing a stupid Ghost Dance with a drunken Swede!"

"I'm not Swedish!" I said.

"You're not Swedish?! Why do they call you the Swede?"

"That's my name!"

"That's your name? Well, of course. I know that. Did you think I didn't know that?"

"Yes, I knew you knew that."

"Well, why did you answer that way then?"

"Because it was the answer to the question."

"Question? What question?"

"Why do they call you the Swede?"

Sally erupted into yelps of uncontrollable laughter.

"Who gave you the name?"

"The Norwegians."

Sally convulsed with laughter, and so did I.

The laughter subsided gradually, a soft slide peppered with occasional outbursts, like the end of popcorn popping. Finally I said, "I was hoping you would dance enough to have a vision."

"A hallucination?"

"Well, OK, that's what you white folk call it."

"Why, for heaven's sake?"

"I wanted you to see a future. I wanted you to see a new life, all your problems solved, everything set right."

"Oh, dear sweet Swede!"

"No luck, huh?"

"Some people don't fit, Swede. False visions don't help. Holy shirts don't stop real bullets."

"I had to try, you know. There's always some uncertainty."

"I appreciate it. I'll remember it."

I got up. I walked to the swing and stopped. Suddenly I kicked the tire. "Damn!" I said. Then I walked away.

* * *

I sat alone on the grass for a long while. I looked at the sky, dark, full of bright stars. I picked out my favorite constellations: the dippers, Orion's belt. A light flashed, and I thought, a shooting star! A star to mark the day of my death!

But it wasn't a shooting star, it was a firefly, and soon more appeared, flitting and flickering around the giant cottonwood. I watched them. I admired them, as I did the stars. Where I'm going, there's only darkness. So I admired, in the time I had left, light.

I felt a need for a ritual review of my life, a last act. But here, on the lawn, was not the place. For this a temple was appropriate: the woodshed. It was time to go to the woodshed.

I pulled myself up and looked around for my shotgun. I didn't spot it immediately, and the thought (a hope?) passed through my mind that the Swede had taken it with him. But I found the shotgun, and I carried it to the woodshed. I took a key from my pocket, a distinctive key with symmetrical sides. I inserted it into a distinctive padlock, with rings like a white steel tire, and I twisted it. The padlock popped open. I entered the woodshed. Something—a large spider or a small mouse—scurried toward the far end of the woodshed. The old ladder-backed chair was in place, as I had positioned it that afternoon. I pulled shut the doors and sat down, waiting for my eyes to adjust to the darkness. Smells of dust and mold and oil-soaked rags were all that I was sensible of, and for some reason this night they seemed particularly pungent. Gradually I was able to make out forms in the dark: a favorite sled, an old lamp I used to have in my room. It was deathly quiet.

Where did I go wrong? The Swede was right, it was long before the whole affair with Danny, long before. The abortion was the final straw, but they were after me long before that. They would have nailed me just the same.

Maybe it wasn't any one thing, maybe it was just me. I got myself into the scrapes, didn't I? The incident at Coleman's farm, how about that? A practical joke, that's all it was, but it, well, it kinda hurt more than it should have, it kinda broke my spirit. I was reasonably normal before that. Or was I? God, I don't know. I was always interested in sex. Romance and sex. I used to think that was normal, but I guess not. My girlfriends said they never thought much about it. I thought about it all the time. Like boys do. I was more like a boy.

Well, it's not fair. Why should boys get to think about it, and I can't? They get to do it! And I can't.

Maybe if I had been able to get something normal going with David, maybe I could have . . . Oh, but what the hell! There was something wrong there, too. I was too . . . He was too . . . Yeah, maybe it was David. Maybe it was David's fault all along. I wanted him, he knew that. He loved me, he told me that once. So why didn't we make it? If we had been sweethearts—Geez! What a thought! Sweethearts! "David and Sally are sweethearts, you know." "Yes, isn't it grand? I'm so happy for them both." Maybe everything would have been different. I wouldn't have needed to spend all my time daydreaming about fantasy lovers, I could have done something creative, write poetry about boxelder bugs, help pregnant teenagers, something. David, well, he'd be better off, wouldn't he? Better than now, with a fat wife and a dumb kid, trying to stay in school.

So why didn't it happen?

David said it was too much to put on him. The whole picture depended too much on him—him, the considerate lover; him, the faithful husband; him, steady and soothing. No, no, I said, it's not like that. Yes, he said, it's what he felt, and therefore it was the truth. The truth for him. He felt too weak to be that kind of person for me. He didn't want to be stable, he wanted to be crazy. He didn't want to be anybody's sweetheart, he didn't want the responsibility.

I guess I can understand that.

Dad used to tell me the same thing. "You're on your own, kid," he'd say. "Don't count on anyone else."

"How about you, Pop? Can't I count on you?"

"Hell, no, Babe! Especially not me!"

I began to cry, and cursed myself. Oh, damn! I so wanted this to be a straightforward suicide. I mean, the time for crying is over, it's long gone. When you reach the time for your suicide, the time for crying is over. But my sobs continued, a disgusting whimpering that filled me with shame and made me even sadder than before.

It is sad, though. I never seemed to achieve any of my desires in life.

I must have had unrealistic goals.

A scene appeared in my mind's eye, and I sat back to watch it. It was a familiar scene, it had a homey feeling. Might as well let it play one last time. The young me in my bed in the family's rented cabin on Lake Darling, near Alexandria. Cozy Corner. The cabin even had a name. How old was I? Twelve? Thirteen? Something like that. I in my bed, my parents in the living room, with friends. Friends they saw every summer. People who used to live in Minneota, but who moved away, to Alexandria. People who knew me when I was a little tot.

They didn't know that I could hear, or perhaps they didn't care. Well, come to think of it, I had to cup my ears to hear, and even then I missed a bit. They were discussing Marilyn, my older sister.

"My word, but Marilyn's really turning out nicely!" This from Harry, the red-faced man who used to teach with my mother.

"Yes, she certainly is!" This from Lucille, his wife, hair-sprayed head, girdled waist, thick ankles. "Marilyn is so pretty. And so mature. My goodness! It's just like talking to a grown up. She's so sensible!"

"Yes, she certainly is! I mean, really pretty! Some young man is going to be very lucky! Yes sir! There are times when I wish I was 20 years younger; I'd take a whack at her myself!"

"Harry! What a thing to say!" Lucille giggles, a pinched ripple of laughter that sounds like a bird being strangled.

"You know what I mean. I'm just trying to pay her a compliment. She's a darned pretty girl. Seems a waste to let her go to some pimply-faced kid."

"When she could have a real man like you!" Lucille giggles again.

"You know what I mean."

My mother breaks in. "Well, thank you. We're quite pleased with Marilyn."

There is a long pause, then my mother speaks again. "We're quite pleased with Sally, too."

Another long pause, until Lucille breaks the silence. "Sally sure likes candy!"

Everyone laughs.

"Yes, my god!" says Harry. "I couldn't believe it! She ate two Babe Ruths after lunch! Two! Can you imagine?"

"I'd get sick as a dog, if I did that!" says Lucille, enthusiastically.

"I said to her, 'You sure love those candy bars!' You wanna know what she said? She said, 'Sweets to the sweet!'"

Everyone laughs.

"I asked her, 'Why do you eat so much candy?' She said, 'Because it tastes good.'"

Everyone laughs. Harry laughs so hard, the laughs turn to coughs. The scene dissolves as Lucille nags Harry about smoking too much.

* * *

Sally felt the cold steel of the gun barrel. It is cold, she thought. I wonder why steel feels cold. I always thought that was just poetic exaggeration used by mystery writers.

It's a scientific question. She and David could find an answer. If they had the time . . .

She looked at the shotgun in the dim light. Apart from the cold, the barrel had a sensuous feel. Why is it so highly polished? There were two shells in the shotgun, one in the firing chamber and the other in the pump chamber. Why are there two shells? Because I put them there. But why did I put two shells in the gun? To make sure? In case I missed with the first, I could just say, "Oops!," pump in the second shell and fire away again. The thought struck her as humorous, and she smiled.

How am I going to do this? Where should I aim? My stomach? Messy, and I might survive it. Aim for the heart? Well, where the hell is my heart? Right side? Left side? I can never remember. I don't like it. It would mean shooting myself in the tit. The head, that's the only answer. Certain death. But where in the head? Through an eye, directly to the brain? I don't think I could handle that, looking down the barrel. In the mouth. Yes, that's what the Swede said, and he's right; in the mouth, it's really the only possibility.

Sally put the barrel into her mouth, the shotgun upside down between her knees. The barrel tasted faintly of oil. Her mouth tingled, and she kept the steel away from her teeth; she knew that contact would send a sharp pain through her fillings. Her tongue lay on a BB-shaped gun sight near the end of the barrel. "Well, God," she said out loud, "please forgive me." She reached down for the trigger, but discovered that she couldn't reach it. "God damn! Son of a bitch!"

She looked around the shed and saw a broken yardstick, now about two feet long. She unloaded the shotgun to see if she could trigger it with the stick. Yes, no problem. She put a single shell back into the gun, and she put the gun back into her mouth. She positioned the broken yardstick against the trigger. She closed her eyes. Why? she wondered. An old Army poem came into her mind, where had she learned it? This is my rifle, this is my gun. This is for fighting, this is for fun. Soldiers weren't supposed to call their rifles "guns." They were supposed to call their penises "guns." Sally felt the gun sight with her tongue. Uncontrollably she began to lick the barrel. Then the world exploded.

Taking His Cue from Mao, the Boxelder Bug's Life Is a Long and Persistent March

by Bill Holm

I

The boxelder bug,
Quick frozen in a matchbox
For a science project,
Thawed six months later.
The housewife sees
The skinny legs drop
To the kitchen table:
Continue their long march.

II

While I teach a class,
A boxelder bug
Falls out of my hair.
A young girl lights him
With a match.
He flickers, then lies still.
We light cigarettes from the same match
As the bug, singed and confused,
Lifts his foot
Over the edge of the ashtray:
Continues his long march.

III
Sick of them,
She called the fumigators,
Who poisoned the house.
After she buried the cat
And burned the food,
She put a towel over her nose,
Went back in,
Just in time to see
The bug crawl jovially
Through the arsenic:
Continuing his long march.

IV
Last night, I thought I felt
Her tongue inside my ear,
Whispering sentences
I'd longed to hear for years.
I woke and reached out
To find the boxelder bug:
Continuing his long and persistent march.

11

A Long and Persistent March

Well, it was my 25-years high school reunion that drew me back. But it was also the 3rd, 4th, and 5th of July—yes, the FOURTH OF JULY, more fireworks! And it was Minneota's centennial! One hundred years of stories. Everyone came home. Everyone. If there was someone you really wanted to see, from the past, I mean, then this was the time. The High School said it was a reunion for all-years, so everyone came. Everyone.

How many times had I been back? This was the second time, the first was when Dad died.

I rented a car in Minneapolis and drove to Montevideo (Mon ta vid' ee oh!) where I picked up my best friend and classmate, Tom Lillehaugen. We stopped at Camp Release, just outside Montevideo, where the Dakota gave up the fight against the Whites. This was where they surrendered. Well, this is where the first act ended, then it started up again in South Dakota, and in the third act Sitting Bull scored the only Indian victory at Little Big Horn. Camp Release was just a grove of trees, with a highway marker that noted it as a "historic site." The state of Minnesota had erected a monolith, about 50 feet tall, commemorating the event. I noticed the date: 1894. Over 30 years after the surrender—I thought that was a bit odd. A small plaque told of the savagery of the Indians, the bravery of the Whites.

"Did you know Sally Engstrom was part Sioux . . . I mean, part Dakota?" I asked Tom. "She was the great granddaughter of Sitting Bull."

Tom said he had heard that, but he didn't believe it. I told him of the affair between Catherine Engstrom, Sally's great grandmother, and Sitting Bull. "It's in the history books," I told Tom. "It's true."

We drove in from the northeast. Funny, the closer I got to Minneota, the more comfortable I became. Like the road signs, riddled with bullet holes—they seemed so familiar. We were coming home!

I spent a lot of time in the next three days thinking about community. A small town like Minneota is a tight-knit community in which everyone knows pretty much everything about everyone else, at least while they're living there. For the most part, a tight-knit community is a good thing: supportive, caring, loving. If the community turns against you, however, the tight knit becomes a cage where you're imprisoned, never to escape. The only escape is suicide.

How can such a good thing like a supportive community become such an evil thing? What do you have to do to get excommunicated? What is their unforgivable sin? What had Sally done that was so bad?

She wanted to turn straw into gold. She took the gold offered her, while the people of Minneota were content with their straw, with their watered-down whiskey. "Life is a series of temptations," Sigrid Huseth once informed me "To get into heaven, you have to resist these temptations, as Jesus did. As Sally didn't."

"So Sally sinned a little. Couldn't you forgive her?"

"What she did was not forgivable. She destroyed a family; she murdered her unborn child. She was unrepentant. She thought she had a right."

* * *

Tom and I stopped at the Korner Kafe for a bite to eat. The menu was a Xerox of a typewritten note with two items on it, neither with a price attached. The two items were "comm." and "sand." I asked the waitress what they meant and she said, "Commercial, of course!"—rather loudly, I thought. "And sandwich. What'd ya think it meant? Gravel?" She and several others in the restaurant laughed loudly. Bravely, I offered up my next question: "What's a commercial?" "Hot roast beef sand." "What's the sandwich?" "Beef. What'd you think? Pork?" The audience responded with another burst of raucous laughter.

While we were eating, a woman entered the cafe looking for someone. The waitress knocked on the door of the ladies restroom and eight or nine women in party hats emerged. Laughing and shouting "Surprise! Surprise!," the women settled at a long table, while one taped a large handmade poster on the wall. The poster said, "Happy Birthday, Jenny Lee!" The waitress brought a small cake with a few candles. The birthday girl, as the others called her, blew out the candles to great applause. One of the women snuck over to the poster and altered it with a marking pen to read "Happy 40th Birthday, Jenny Lee!" Three of the women nearly fell out of their chairs, they were laughing so hard. Jenny Lee ran to the poster, blushing crimson, and the covered the 40 with her hand. She refused to return to the table until they blotted out the number with the marking pen.

Later, after dropping Tom at his parents' farm, I drove out to the Faith Lutheran Cemetery, to visit Dad's grave. I don't know why we have this compulsion to pay our respects to the piece of dirt that houses a loved one who has, as Dad used to say, "bought the farm." But I do, and so do most people. The cemetery was crowded, which surprised me. There were fresh flowers on many graves. The centennial had brought the people back to Minneota, and they came out here to honor their dead. I was just standing there, enjoying myself actually, hot summer day, nice breeze, the most delicious smells of weeds and adventure. I noticed that they had forgotten to put the date of death on my Dad's tombstone. "Born July 26, 1895. Died," that's all it said. I was strangely pleased to see this.

I walked over to see Sally's grave, and found the Swede's beside it. The Swede had died 15 years ago—cirrhosis, no doubt. Both the Swede and Sally had the smallest possible grave markers. On the Swede's, it just said, "The Swede," nothing more. The Swede must have been a member of Faith Lutheran, otherwise they wouldn't bury him here. I didn't think the Swede had any time for churches. Maybe he was hedging his bets, just in case there really was a God.

The centennial celebration was a wonderful event. The people of Minneota dressed in old-fashioned costumes; the women looked particularly lovely. The men, overweight, bearded by decree, were not particularly lovely, but they had a kind of Amish look that fit. It felt like stepping back in time, maybe a hundred years, as if you had discovered Brigadoon, and there was a strange pull on me, to stay there, as if this magic would last beyond the celebration. You've come home, so stay home. That was the message.

I ran into several classmates and had wonderful, magical mini-reunions in advance of the reunion dinner the following night. Jon Coltvet, for example, reminded me of our philosophical discussions in high school. Jon had asserted that if angels were invisible, as they obviously were, since we couldn't see any, then they had no need for clothes. I remembered that the thought of angels walking around naked excited me immensely, even though I didn't believe in angels.

The comfort that I felt increased with each conversation, with each event. I decided to analyze this feeling of comfort. Where did it come from? Was I alone in my experience of it?

I asked a few of my classmates these questions. Strangely, they all had the same experience, although they described it differently: "I feel safe," they said. Why? Because reuniting with old friends leads to feelings of safety. Why? "Same old David! Can't take anything on faith," they said, shaking their heads, smiling.

But my classmates were right; the reunions were magical, almost sacred. It was magic like stage magic, which depends on trust; we could relax and conjure images because we knew we were loved and respected. The secure comfort of the reunion made all sounds harmonious.

And from what did the feelings of security and comfort derive? Those feelings must have something to do with the length of time we've known one another, but what? I felt safe, too, so I looked inside myself for answers. It has something to do with "worlds," I said to myself. I've lived my whole life in the same world as my classmates. Norman Rockwell drew pictures of this world. We were children when World War II was declared over, and we whined when the adults took our toy guns away. We knew polio as a fear and democracy as a hope. Of the McCarthys, we loved Gene, but we felt uneasy about Joe. Businesses were honest and had a sense of decency—not Donald Trump but Horatio Alger was our hero. Life was good in the fifties, but boring as hell.

We believed in God, Jesus, and the Holy Ghost, although we weren't clear on the duties of the ghost. We (men and women) thought women should be placed on a pedestal and adored. We knew that Catholics drove Chevrolets and Lutherans drove Fords. Sports was about fair play, being generous in victory and humble in defeat.

I'm not saying that our world was better than any other. Our world had many dangerous fault lines, especially the official view of blacks and women. Our world was run by rich white men, men we trusted.

The sixties, therefore, caught us by surprise. Somebody made a decision to extend the notion of fair play to blacks and women. The generation following ours created two great groups, the activists and the hippies, whose disparate paths converged in opposition to the war in Vietnam. For a long time, I and my classmates were incapable of understanding opposition to a war: "What are you telling me? That I've got a say in the matter?" And, "If I can't trust our leaders, then our political system is in bad shape," thinking that statement precluded opposition to a war. Not thinking of it as a prophecy.

An explosion of drugs in the sixties. I and my classmates were surprised to learn that booze and cigarettes were drugs, dangerous drugs at that. But we preferred them to the new drugs, marijuana and the others, which we knew turned ordinary people into ax murderers. We liked contraceptive pills, which we didn't consider to be a drug, because it permitted casual sex, which we enjoyed although we were never very good at it.

We came gradually to the conclusion that businesses are inherently corrupt.

We stopped the war, or so we thought. We nailed Nixon, who shot at us at Kent State. A new day was dawning.

Then came the seventies—the "me" decade—and self interest became (and remains) the nation's chief value. How the hell did that happen?

So, ups and downs, epiphanies and startling revelations, good times and bad. It was the best of times, it was the worst of times . . . I and my classmates lived in that world together for over 40 years. If you've shared all those experiences, if you've experienced the same unique world, you're going to develop similar beliefs and values. You're going to feel safe in the company of these people.

* * *

The weather was hot but sunny, perfect for the celebration. Many felt that God had given the town this weather, as a gift.

I explained to those who remembered me what my life was like now. I told them about my job. They didn't understand how I could have had two wives already, and none at present. I argued with those who claimed that everyone in California was a drug-crazed hedonist. I found these conversations unpleasant and tried to avoid them.

I took a long walk along the Yellow Medicine Creek. At certain spots, memories of pheasants penetrated my consciousness like puffs of smoke. I remembered a walk I once took there with Sally.

A young man in town announced that he was writing an anthology of poems about boxelder bugs. I sought him out, encouraged him, and told him about the research that Sally and I had done on the bugs.

On the evening of July 3, Tom and I went to the Historical Pageant at the high school gym. The Pageant began with some high school girls in scanty costumes, who did a sort-of-dance routine. At the end of the routine, the girls formed a row and passed huge cards along, over their heads, all the while jumping and kicking in a standard rhythm. The cards spelled MINNEOTA in school colors.

In one portion of the Pageant, two young boys portrayed Nils Jaeger and Doc Seals in 1881, in a scene that depicted the naming of the village.

In the rousing conclusion, the Centennial Choir sang a song especially written for the occasion. Sung to the tune of "Oklahoma," the first line was, "Minneota, in the southwest portion of the state." The audience was invited to join in, and did so with great gusto.

The next day featured the parade. My mother was in the parade, disguised as a giant Iris driving a small tractor. Behind the several horses in the parade, young boys with brooms, shovels, and garbage cans on wheels followed. They were listed in the parade program as Pooper Scoopers.

In the evening, the Class of 1956 met for the Reunion Dinner. I told my classmates that I loved them and I thanked them for their friendship.

Several female classmates were shocked to learn that I had been madly in love with them in high school. They were angry. "Why didn't you tell me?!" "How could you not know?," I replied. "You'd come into the room, and I'd blush, I'd stammer, I almost passed out, I'd run to the bathroom. If that's not love, then I don't know what is!"

The next morning, a Sunday, Tom and I drove around town in search of memories. We stopped at Faith Lutheran

Church, deserted because the community was having "ecumenical" services in the ballpark. In the parking lot we encountered a dead squirrel covered with flies. I have never seen dead squirrels except in parking lots, and the only parking lots I knew for the first twenty years of my life were for churches. I associated dead squirrels with church, and I've never seen one without thinking of hymns, robes, and incantations.

Tom had come to the church to find a half dollar that he had buried in the church lawn 25 years earlier. He had felt the need to bury money, in case of an emergency. Tom and I, two 43-year-old men, dug up nine square feet of the church lawn, but we didn't find the half dollar.

We walked to the edge of a small creek behind the church and tried to make noises by blowing on slips of grass and dandelion stems. The creek was barely a trickle in the bottom of the creek bed. Tom remembered a time when, after several days of rain, the creek was wild and raging. He had written a note and placed it in a Coke bottle with a cork in it. The note said, "My name is Tommy Lillehaugen. I live in Minneota, Minnesota. If you find this, please write me a letter." He threw it into the wild and raging stream and watched it float away. Two weeks later he received a letter from Shorty Peetroons, who lived half a block from the church.

Before I left for Minneapolis and home in San Francisco, I walked once more through town. I came to the Big Store, no longer a department store. There were piles and piles of mattresses inside. In the soft red bricks of which the store had been built, initials of kids and lovers were carved like sculptured graffiti. Beside one of the large display windows, filled now with relics of Minneota's past, I found what I was looking for: a heart with initials, DS +

SE. I thought about boxelder bugs and practical jokes and what might have been. It wasn't so much that my spirit was too weak, it was that Sally's was too strong. She wanted her dreams to come true. She wanted her love to be taken seriously. No community could tolerate what she had in mind.

Jim Geiwitz

JIM GEIWITZ was born and raised in Minneota, a small town in Minnesota. The population, in the 1950s, was about 1200 souls, and today it's about the same. Everyone knows everyone's business; that's the way it is in small towns. It's a good life, not always, but usually. Jim left Minneota to attend one of the many fine small colleges in the Midwest, St. Olaf (the same college that the Great Gatsby attended). He went on to a series of careers, including university professor, research scientist, industrial-hemp farmer, freelance writer, online-newspaper editor, book reviewer, political spin doctor, and consultant to businesses on how to deal with the unpredictability of nonlinear (chaotic) systems. He has lived in many large cities, including San Francisco, Santa Barbara, Pittsburgh, and Victoria (BC, Canada), but his heart remains in the Town of Watered-Down Whiskey.

* BOXELDER BUG DAYS

SEPT 7-10

ELCOME to

MINNEOTA

OP 1200 2

Becky
had
twins !!

Sol Books
Upper Midwest Writers Series

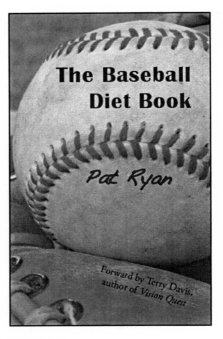

The Baseball Diet Book
Pat Ryan
ISBN 978-0-9818279-4-0

Pat Ryan won't offer tips on dieting in his collection of
short stories, but *The Baseball Diet Book* will appease
readers' appetites for small-town America's favorite
pastime—baseball. From Idaho to Minnesota, Mexico to
Panama, Ryan embrace those odd, both humorous and
serious, moments in life and portrays a reality not many
of us know. Each story stretches readers' imaginations
into extra innings, until they are lost in the timeless of the
game itself.

Bodywearers
Connie Colwell Miller
ISBN 978-0-9793081-1-6

Whether Miller writes of a
red-tailed hawk hunting for
mice or a lover's underwear
crumpled up on the bedroom
floor, her voice is filled with
a revealing breath of candor,
drawing our attention to the
small details in nature and of
the body, often showing us
beauty where we may not have
experienced it before.

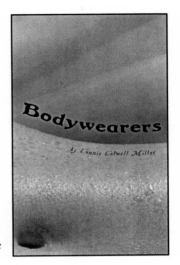

My Father's Gloves
David Speiring
ISBN 978-0-9793081-6-1

My Father's Gloves touches on
that most-conflicted of family
bonds, the one between fathers
and sons. With a hauntingly
painful voice, Spiering explores
the burdensome yoke of a
father's expectations, and the
struggles a son must face as he
grows into manhood.

Sol Books
Prose Series

The Prostitutes of Post Office Street
Frank F. Carden
ISBN 978-0-9793081-2-3

The Prostitutes Post Office Street drops readers into the
red-light district of Galveston, where crooked cops and
down-on-their-luck prostitutes dwell. Yet, in this seedy
part of town, Carden paints a picture of hope as his
characters seek to rise above the pain of broken hearts
and misplaced passions.

Well Deserved
Michael Loyd Gray
ISBN 978-0-9793081-7-8

From the small-time dealer to the returning Vietnam vet,
the townie grocery clerk and the new sheriff, the folks of
Argus know what they want out of life, but the paths to
their desires are conflicted. *Well Deserved* chronicles the
struggles of these four people as they come to the stark r
ealization that their paths are not solitary, but entwined,
and their very lives hinge on one shared moment.

Sol Books
Poetry Series

Mama Joy
Eileen Silver-Lillywhite
ISBN 978-0-9818279-2-6

These poems, searing with love and loss, narrate a
woman's life, from childhood and adolescence to
adulthood. In *Mama Joy*, Eileen Silver-Lillywhite's
poems are lush, elegiac, graceful. She captures a woman
who carries the lovely burdens of love, the tragedies that
almost crush her, and the ineffable surprises that wake
us all.

Gigs
John Davis
ISBN 978-0-9818279-0-2

Blues in D minor, big bellies over factory belts, and Elvis Presley license plates—*Gigs* shows us the gentle beauty of ordinary life. Davis's language breathes, without labor. His metaphors fit tight. And the rhythm of each word keeps pace with our innermost beats. Every poem hammers a rightly strung cord.

Pacific
Scott R. Welvaert
ISBN 978-0-9793081-0-9

Star-crossed lovers set out to fulfill their dying wish: see the Pacific Ocean. They begin in Minnesota, where they meet at an AIDS clinic, and *Pacific* chronicles their journey through the Black Hills, past Devil's Tower, and to Cannon Beach. Before reaching their final destination, they must first accept their fates.

Coming Soon . . .

The next addition to our prose series:
  The Wash
  Clyde Derrick

Like the torrential flash floods that plague the
town of Vista Linda, California, The Wash
sweeps you up, drags you beneath its currents
and desperately tries to drown you in the silt
below. Clyde Derrick's excruciatingly intimate
prose follows a boy contending with his mother's
disappearance in the flood, a catatonic father,
a racist brother, murderous ancestors and a
grandmother's mistaken profession in a brothel.
The Wash weaves a powerful family tapestry that
proves even the strongest of us survive the turmoil
as changed, and perhaps wiser, people.

CPSIA information can be obtained at www.ICGtesting.com
Printed in the USA
BVOW041953120812

297703BV00001B/1/P